SEA
WITCH
RISING

Also by Sarah Henning

Sea Witch

SEA WITCH RISING

SARAH HENNING

KATHERINE TEGEN BOOKS
An Imprint of HarperCollins Publishers

Katherine Tegen Books is an imprint of HarperCollins Publishers.

Sea Witch Rising

ISBN 978-0-06-293147-4

Typography by Carla Weise
19 20 21 22 23   PC/LSCH   10 9 8 7 6 5 4 3 2 1
❖
First Edition

To my sister Meagan—
I miss you every day.

And to Justin—
the car chase happened. Kinda.

Come away, come away—
O'er the waters wild.
Our earth-born child
Died this day, died this day.

Come away, come away—
The tempest loud
Weaves the shroud
For him who did betray.

Come away, come away—
Beneath the wave
Lieth the grave
Of him we slay, him we slay.

—A sailor's shanty known as "The Mermaid's Vengeance"

PROLOGUE

"You will have your voice for only a few more moments, my dear. Use the time wisely."

The girl swallows again and then takes a heavy breath.

"I first saw Niklas on the day I turned fifteen. It could be called love at first sight—but I'd seen his face before. In a statue I've had in my castle garden since I turned ten. Those red flowers I brought you, they grow—"

"Yes, the Øldenburgs love their statues," I say, sounding again very much like Hansa. "There is yet to be love in this story. Only coincidence and horticulture."

The girl licks her lips and recasts. "I stayed beside the boat all night, watching this boy. Then, after midnight, a great storm came, waves crashing down so hard, the ship toppled onto its side. The sailors were in the water, but I didn't see the boy." Here, her voice hitches. *"I dove down until I found him. His limbs were failing him, and his eyes were closed. I pulled him* up to the surface and held his head above water. We stayed like that the whole night. And when the sun returned and the ocean calmed, I kissed his forehead and swam him to land."

Reflexively, my tentacle tightens around her waist as I'm reminded of Annemette, even though I've read enough to know this story by heart. A storm, a shipwreck, a savior.

"And?" I ask.

"I placed him beside a great building. I stayed to watch, hiding among some rocks, covered in sea foam. Soon, a beautiful girl found him and sounded the alarm. I knew then that he would live. He awoke, and was smiling at the girl."

"No smile for you?"

"No." The determination returns to her voice. "But I wanted that smile—I want it now. I want him to know that I saved him. That I love him. And I want him to love me."

Ah. She's lied to me.

"But you said he already does."

The girl looks away, caught. Finally, she continues. "For the past year, I've watched him. And I know if I could just be human, he would love me. He thinks he's in love with the girl from the beach, but I saved him. I saved Niklas."

Like Anna, this girl believes she deserves something and she's willing to risk her life and all she knows for it. But this girl doesn't crave revenge.

She wants a happily ever after.

And for that, I cannot blame her. Even after all these

years, I still wish for my own.

"It is very stupid of you," I say finally, "but you shall have your way."

—From the final pages of *Sea Witch*

1

Evie

THE SHARPEST OF THINGS KEEPS ITS EDGE EVEN IN THE dullest of settings.

And so, my coral knife shines through the shadows I call home. Rendered ghost white with magic, the serrated blade sharp is enough to cleave a single hair in two.

Beautiful. Deadly. Perfect.

I only hope it's enough for when they arrive.

Because in the hours since the little mermaid left the sea for land, chasing her true love, I felt it. A tug. A thread pulled clear and released.

I felt it in my bones, rotting through the marrow, septic in my lungs, gut, and heart, and yet, this jolt of pain was bound to come. It needed to come. The sea's monopoly is not sustainable.

In the time that I've lived below the surface, the

magical balance has shifted, the power slowly tipping from land to sea, until the majority of the land's magic had sunk to the depths of the sea king's domain, destined to obey an unnatural master. Now the imbalance is so glaring it's all I can see beyond the lair that is my cage, beyond my forest of polypi, the fissures in the earth bubbling with turfmoor, and the violent whirlpools spinning sirens in the deep. Past the eerie blue radiance of the sea king's castle and its grounds, magic teems, heavy, overflowing.

After the little mermaid left, I began to think how impossible it is that the magic on land has all but died away, though it's simple, really. There were so few of us witches. Hunted, killed, banished. We were eliminated one by one for centuries, until the land was nearly drained of its magic and those who knew how to control it. From Maren Spliid and her death at the hands of the witch-hunter king, all the way through the years to me, each of us cast into the afterlife. But I did not die, not in every way, and so my magic is still my own, a mix of land and sea.

I remember my time above, and the thaw inside me crystallizes, clear and blue. I was a witch turned underground by fear—I didn't even know how to use my strength. It was how Tante Hansa tried to keep me safe. Hiding away my power, repressing it. As if it were something that could be shuttered away in a cupboard from prying eyes. Out of sight, out of mind.

But now, my eyes are open.

The balance of magic has always been precarious. Built on exchange, all of it. Not just the spells, the whole system. And the ebb and flow of power is skewed toward those who seek to own it. Yet as the little mermaid set foot on land, taking her powers with her, the scale tipped back toward the land just a sliver. The land's shockwave of relief sent a jolt of fire through my bones, but my brief pain is of no concern. I do not need this magic to live.

There is another who has much to fear.

I tuck the knife away, safe in my cave, and pull out my spell books, presents from Tante Hansa, one in each tentacle, plus two in each hand. I settle into the pewter sands and thumb through them. Tante Hansa always told me that magic will forever seek equilibrium. Now that the door has finally been opened, perhaps I can hasten the land's gain.

That's when the polypus closest to my cave clears its throat, and the voice I took from the little mermaid cuts into my insulated world. "Weren't your efforts to curb the Tørhed enough of a disaster? You want to try again?"

I startle a little—so used to fifty years of silence. Anna. She can surely feel the imbalance too. Though I gave her the little mermaid's voice, we've yet to talk much about what she did, why she did it, and why I did what I had to, to save Nik. But now is not the time to start.

"This is different," I say. My spell of abundance to end the sea's Tørhed and bring life to our fisherman's nets created an imbalance that angered Urda. My desire here is just the opposite. "I have to try."

"Fine," Anna goes on. "But you won't find what you want in those books."

I turn a page of my spell book in defiance.

Almost as an exclamation, there's the distant sound of an explosion, big enough to push the whirlpools off axis, turfmoor burping, sea floor quaking into the water and then drifting into a new arrangement. My polypi forest— like Anna, bodies discarded and moored by magic—twists and hisses, waving in the disturbance.

Yet another sea mine—a bomb hidden in the water, eager to blow a hole in the right ship and make bones of targeted men.

There's a war raging on the surface. Over land and sea, and even in the air, humans under many flags have banded together to kill one another. There is no magic involved, of course. If there were more than a meager amount of magic left on land, perhaps this war might not be waged. Still, the search for power—magical or not—will always be. Once the mines and the bullets stop, lines will be redrawn, and a different type of power will shift. Another imbalance.

Anna starts a tart reply. "Evie, you—"

"*Létta.*" Stop, I command. Because something's not right.

Then, as if in answer to the sudden silence, a great voice booms into my lair, echoing hard enough to rattle my teeth and bend the branches of my bone-thick polypi forest.

"It can't be—the great sea witch talks to herself?"

I freeze as he comes into view, power and magic dripping off him in a terrible wake.

The sea king.

His hair is the color of snow in the thick of winter, eyes crystal blue, skin glowing with almost too much life, flush and vibrant. Atop his head is a crown of pearls fitted to a cluster of eel skulls, jaws pried open in wide V shapes, their teeth on edge. I have never seen his crown in person before, but it is the very semblance of life and death, and power. A reminder of what can be taken—the fruits of one's labor, sucked out, even when one bares fangs.

The sea king smiles, and it is as brilliant and deadly as one would expect. "It must get so lonely, stuck in the shadows by yourself."

He would know. It's not my magic or memories that keep me here, it's the king's. So afraid of what I can do, though he floats before me, amplified in a way that isn't natural, even for magical creatures.

He has a penchant for the nectar of the rare ríkifjor flower—a drug that both harnesses magic and intensifies it. But surveying him now, it's almost as if the ríkifjor has fused to his blood, bone, and skin. That imbalance I feel, it leans hard into this man, who has absorbed as much magic as his body can hold and then doubled it through the constant, steady ingestion of ríkifjor.

Looking at him can only be compared to staring directly into the sun.

He *is* power.

But if he's here for the first time in fifty years, there is something his power cannot hand him.

"At times, Your Highness, this cove has felt like a prison," I say, and his smile curls up. "But just because I cannot leave doesn't mean I don't receive visitors."

The sea king's posture stiffens. Yes, this is why he's here. This powerful man has lost something important to him. His daughter is gone, and perhaps more importantly, so is her magic, which shares a direct tie to his. As I suspected, the thread pulled from me must have been so much worse for him. "Reverse the spell and bring her back. Now," he commands.

I smile, reclining on my tentacles like a queen. I cock a brow. "Do you even know which one is gone?" He notoriously treats his daughters like pawns in a game, using their beauty and their talents when convenient.

"Insulting me will bring no good to you," he says, but my smile doesn't waver except to grow with satisfaction when he says her name. "Alia belongs in the sea. Return her."

"Your Highness, you should know better than anyone that even you can't control a strong-headed woman," I say, and I know he's thinking of his first queen, Mette, the human he saved but then couldn't keep, her heart cracking as she longed both for him and for the life she was meant to lead. "Alia must be free to make her own choices and live her own life—experience love and freedom. But instead, you trap her, and all your people, under your thumb with false promises of protection from humans. Not since Annemette—"

"*Never* speak that name to me again," he growls, his fury sputtering between us. She's the one who left him, betraying him, his family, and the secrets of the mermaids. I hope Anna is really listening to him now.

As his nostrils flare, I look him dead in the eyes. "Like *Annemette*, Alia has four days to make the boy love her and live, or fail and die. Either way, you'll never see her again."

"I can destroy you!"

I bare my teeth. "Ah, but you haven't. Even with all the power you steal, you still need me." My voice gains strength with each word. He's desperate. He can't retrieve Alia on his own. There is an element of my magic he will never master. "I can bring Alia back, but I will need something from you in return. I have my price."

The sea king's lips drop open. I have him backed into a corner, and he knows it. My ask is simple, and only he can do it. He can't give me my life back, my lost time, or Nik—may he rest in the tide—but he can unchain me from my lair. The words are on my tongue, ready, when something nasty ticks across his handsome features.

"You have your price, Witch, but you forget your place."

His teeth click together, and the blue of his eyes goes cold. It's then that the wet, hard certainty of my mistake reveals itself to me. This man won't kill me, but for the abundance of magic that he is, heavy and unwieldy, he can hurt me so badly, I will wish I were dead.

The power within him—amplified, multiplied, looted from land and sea—expands, bursts outward, like a living bomb. A sea mine of magic, aimed straight at me.

"*Morna, herfiligr kvennalið!*"

Waste away, wretched woman!

The words hit my ears with a force of magic I've never felt, slamming into me with the power of the sun falling out of the sky and barreling toward the earth, bringing enough light to dissolve all of us the instant before impact.

And then my world, already so dark, fades to complete, flat black.

2

Runa

I SHOULD'VE KNOWN I WOULD LOSE HER THIS WAY.

To him.

The boy. That stupid boy. With his stupid dark hair and sparkling eyes and regal blood.

The one she saved in the height of summer, during a ferocious storm when she'd been stalking him yet again. Living in the wake of his ship, hoping for a glimpse of him with his brothers, with their cheekbones and songs and dogs. As if they'd been created from her heart's desires and plunked onto the earth, just close enough for her to want, just far enough—different enough—to escape her.

Always fascinated with humans, Alia.

Always fascinated with what she shouldn't have. Riding the edge of what was acceptable down below—testing our father's kingly patience and personal leniency. Rescuing that boy and then all but bragging about it by lugging into her garden that stupid statue that went down with him.

I was there when she first saw him above. Her eyes shone with immediate curiosity. We'd turned fifteen at the same time—twins so alike and yet more like two sides of the same coin. We had gone to the surface together, but the fascination with the world above was hers alone.

Once she learned his name, it wouldn't leave her lips. Niklas.

Now she's gone to him, I'm sure of it.

It's been a day since I've seen her, the longest we've ever been apart. I have no choice but to believe I've lost her to *him*, because the alternative—that she's dead or dying somewhere and my heart has yet to realize it—is too painful.

Not that it feels fantastic knowing that my twin left me, our family, our world for a *boy*.

A stupid human prince of a boy who doesn't even know her name.

"Oh, Alia. How could you do this to yourself?" I mumble into the morning tide, mermaid tail swishing hard, fists balled tightly at my sides, nails digging crescents into my palms. "How could you do it to *us*?"

The magic to become human has been banned forever by our father's own hand. He invented it himself, after he brought home his first queen, but the last time it was done, it nearly brought our people to ruin. Four days, one knife, and the truth about life beneath the sea spilling from the lips of one of our own, nearly exposing and endangering us, if Annemette had lived.

So, here I am, closer to land now than I've ever been, swimming in the shadows of a new morning, staring at the place I know in my gut Alia will be.

Øldenburg Castle.

Home of stupid Niklas and his stupid laughing smile and stupid dimples.

The castle is just as Alia said it would be. High on the hill and old enough to have Viking bones in its crypt. It's the biggest thing in sight, dwarfing the mountains at its back simply by a purposeful trick of perspective. The town below it is a warren of stone houses, shops, and the like. Bricks line the streets, slick under the weak light of a rising morning sun as the people of Havnestad run out for their errands.

I sink back below the surface. The waters will be safer near the castle—buoys keep ships from docking too close, so none will mar my path, even with the bustle of the morning. Plus, there are mines out here, bombs meant for ships in the humans' great war. I doubt they know or care how these hurt us below.

I set a course straight for the castle, my path clear though I've never swum it before, but still I know it. Late at night, Alia would whisper tales into my ear while our sisters slept. Tales of watching the grand summer parties from beneath a marble balcony, something new added onto the old castle in recent years.

Morning isn't the time for parties, but this balcony may be the only way I can see into the castle from the water. Beyond the buoys, I swim into a narrow channel, sheer rock faces on each side, protecting the Øldenburgs from visitors they'd rather avoid. And there, right as I enter the opening of a cove, the balcony's footings appear like skeleton bones, jutting up from the sea floor. They sweep out over the water and back down below the surface with the fluid motion of a dolphin's jump.

Above the balcony that sits atop those arches, the castle teeters from a cliff face. It juts out like the haughty chin of its founding king, eyes down on all that it owns, including the waters at its shores.

"The sea's not yours, greedy bastards," I say under my breath. My father could build a castle just as big as this one from the bones of Øldenburgs and their ilk who've fought the sea and lost over the centuries.

Gulls sweep the surface as a soft breeze caresses the tide, autumn sweet as it descends on 1914. Music tinkles out from the castle's wide-open doors and windows. Hope rises in my gut—no, it's not time for parties, but where there's music, there are people.

I hoist myself up just enough that I can see beyond the balcony and through three sets of grand doors that bring the outside in. Men in tea jackets, hair swept back as if it's shiny and wet though perfectly dry, crowd around something within. Ladies are there too, but most run around in stiff blue dresses with white aprons. Servants—I'd recognize the scurry and dutifulness anywhere.

I can see why Alia loved this balcony so—it provides cover that kept her from being spotted, while also allowing for an easy view of the happenings above. I watch for a minute, unsure what to do next except take it all in.

But then a servant moves aside, clearing breakfast plates, and—there. A glimpse of what's beyond.

A girl dancing in a dress of shimmering gold.

Alia.

Long blond hair trailing as she moves in time with the music, a glorious smile upon her face. She's always been graceful, yes, but it's difficult to be anything else in the water, our very atmosphere encouraging swirls, twists, spirals.

My lips drop open as I watch what she can do on two feet. A heavy feeling stirs deep within my bones that I could never move this way on little propped feet, not now, not with another lifetime of practice.

We are twins, but not identical in the least.

Yet, there she is. Moving like the water itself. It's magnetic. Everyone is watching her with the same intensity as I am, but where joy sparks in their eyes, mine soak in bittersweet relief.

My sister is alive. But she might not be for much longer.

I know the bargain. Everyone does, even if Father banned it.

The magic works for four days. Four days to earn a prince's love or spill Øldenburg blood to survive. Without either, she becomes foam in the tide.

One day is already gone.

I'm too fearful to whisper it here, this close, but a refrain sticks in my mind.

Oh, Alia, what have you done?

3

Runa

THE SONG ENDS AND APPLAUSE TITTERS THROUGH THE
room, along with calls for more. Alia curtsies, and when
she does, I see him in the corner, pointing his dimples at
her, dangerous as they are.

Niklas.

"Again, if you will, my dear," he says, and I hate that
he's already using terms of endearment. She has a name,
Niklas—use it. "Please, for our guests."

Alia obliges as a song strikes up yet again.

The relief of seeing her here and alive ebbs, and the
panic comes in double—triple—what it was before. I try
to shove it down, lock it deep within me. I have to get her
attention. I have to talk to her. Is the magic she used the
same as when Annemette made her choice? What did she
sacrifice to come here? Or better yet, *who*? No, no, I cannot

—15

believe my dear sister would harm anyone, even to achieve her greatest desire. Annemette was driven by revenge, my sister by love—or so she thinks.

Alia begins dancing again, and the crowd settles back into watching her—all but two boys, who manage to break away and walk onto the balcony. At first, I think I can stay still and unseen, but then they keep walking, all the way over into the corner right above where I've stationed myself.

Of course.

Careful not to let my tail make too much of a splash, I pull my body as far under the latticed balcony as possible, winding my fingers around the arcing pole that holds it up, taking care that my hands don't show.

One boy is tall, one is short, and both will be a huge problem if they happen to see me. But it seems to me as if they don't want to be seen themselves—their voices are low, gestures short.

"How many now?" the tall one asks, a handsome smile turning up at the corners of flushed cheeks.

"The numbers are fresh to me as of last evening," says the short boy, his hawkish features bending hard with each whisper. "Five U-boats."

I try to process a word I've not heard before. *U-boat.*

"Shhh," the tall boy says, nearly smacking the short one across the mouth. "Do not use that word."

"Oh, right, sorry," the short boy replies. "Look, I know it's not encouraging news, Will, but it's what I have."

Will nods at this too. "Good work, Phillip. Thank you. The contract will be complete as of tomorrow." His eyes search the waters. "My uncle—"

Suddenly, Will cuts off and plasters a smile back on his lips. His whole voice changes, and he plants a hand gamely on the short boy's shoulder, his broad back to the ocean now. "What a delight that your parents are making their way here, Phillip! It has been *ages* since I've danced with your darling mother."

It's just then that I see Niklas striding their way. He's got the audacity to wear a slender crown atop his head and more jewelry too—a brooch, cufflinks of shining gold, even a ring of blood-red stones that burn despite the weak light. I have a strong suspicion that this boy loves to collect shiny objects, my graceful sister being just the latest.

"Ah, Will! I thought that was you, sneaking in the back and stealing kringle!" Niklas chides, doing more than simply clapping the tall boy on the shoulder—instead he brings him in all the way for a real embrace.

When they part, guilt flashes across Will's features. "There are some things I've never been able to outgrow, my friend, and kringle is one of them."

I angle myself a bit more so that I can see Niklas as he talks to his friends, but it's then that another person comes into view. Alia. She places a hand on Niklas's arm.

"Oh, boys, this is my foundling. Isn't she lovely? Did you see her dance?"

The boys nod as Niklas gives her a little twirl and she falls into him with a ridiculous smile. She's been topside for a day, and there's already more color in her cheeks, though I suppose that might be Niklas's doing more than the work of the September sun. "You've heard the story, of course, haven't you? I'm sure it's all the gossip. I found her yesterday on the beach during my usual walk at dawn. All torn up from a shipwreck and no voice. Lucky to be here, I'll say. Now she's my guest, and quite the dancer." He pats Alia's hand. "Things worked out just fine, didn't they, my dear?"

No voice? Relief floods over me—she gave up her voice instead of a life. But how? That doesn't even make sense. And why would she give up her voice? How can he fall in love with her if he doesn't even know her name? Wait, she could write it, couldn't she? Surely. But she would have if she could, right? The questions tumble over themselves as the pleasantries continue.

"Please meet Phillip—a distant cousin on my mother's side," he says, pointing to the shorter boy. "And Will, who I've known since boyhood, but, I don't know—can I still call you friend, or is cousin now more appropriate?"

Alia's slippered feet move just so as she curtsies for the boys.

"Oh, *cousins*. Don't let formalities confuse you, my lady," Will says. "Even though it won't be official for two more days, who cares? We'll be cousins for the rest of our lives." Will laughs, and I hate that I like the sound of it. "Why not start now?"

"Fine, cousin, then," Niklas agrees.

They laugh, once again too jovial as Alia looks from Niklas to Will and back, clearly confused. The joy crumbles from Niklas's face, and suddenly my lungs stutter themselves shut as I comprehend what would make these boys cousins.

Blood. Or *oh, no.*

As it hits me, the boys must realize it too and excuse themselves on the pretense of wanting coffee. When they're gone, Niklas removes Alia's hand from his arm, clutching her fingers sweetly.

"Dearest," he starts, taking a deep breath almost as if he cares, "I am to be married the day after tomorrow."

Alia's face falls. Her other hand grips his arm so tight, her fingers wrinkle the starched fabric of his tea jacket. My heart feels as if it's in her vise grip, too.

"Though it's only been a day, I . . . I feel like I know you. It's strange, this kinship that we have—both of us lost as sea. Washing ashore on the same beach, some miracle, my little foundling."

Alia nods, close to him, a look on her lovely face so pure that it says a thousand of the words she cannot. Willing him to see. Willing him to know that he does know her. That she saved him. That it wasn't an act of his God that rescued him from the wreck that drowned his brothers and father; it was *her.*

I hold my breath as I feel it coming. He's leaning into her and she's still clutching him for dear life, looking up to him with eyes that contain whole oceans of blue, her lips and cheeks rosy from dancing.

Yes. Kiss her. Please, kiss her.

For the magic to work, she needs true love's kiss—all the stories have been the same.

Their lips touch, and my arms give way as I slide down the pole from relief. It's short, and sweet—but I realize before it's over that it's not enough.

There's no magic to it. It's not transformative in the least. Whatever spell Alia has found to give her legs, this kiss doesn't have the power to keep her on two feet.

Too quickly they're apart again, all of it rushing back to Niklas—the surroundings, the people just steps away in the dance hall, what he is bound to do in two days.

"I'm sorry. I'm king now, and a king's duty is to his people. With my father and my brothers departed . . . it's up to me to do what's best. There are so many uncertain things about the world right now . . ." He trails off, and I can only imagine how the war would affect a kingdom like this. "But what is certain is that despite what's going on, I need to make the right decisions for Havnestad. And the right decision for a new king is to ensure the continuation of the monarchy."

Continuation of the monarchy. Anger singes my veins as my breath grows short. His monarchy would be dead if it weren't for the girl right in front of him.

The *king* weaves his fingers tightly in Alia's. "But please, please stay. Sofie will love you—I'm sure of it."

Sofie. I hate her name already.

He smiles softly. "Perhaps you can be one of her ladies and stay here as long as you wish."

Yes, yes, I was right—this boy just likes to collect things. His foundling on the beach. Now his dancing girl in the castle. There to entertain his wife as her own heart explodes from sorrow.

What a kind and generous king indeed.

"Your Highness," comes a woman's voice from within, "the queen mother has requested your presence in her chambers."

Niklas squeezes Alia's fingers. My sister's hand drops from his arm, obliging, as if she hasn't just weathered the biggest blow in all her life. The boy she's in love with, the one she rescued, the one she gambled her life on, cannot love her because his heart is wrapped up in a contract signed by his father.

"I will see you soon, my sweet foundling."

And then he's gone.

My sister's form slumps on the balcony, her head resting

on the cross of her forearms against the railing, her shoulders heaving beneath her tumbling hair. I slip my fingers up through the slats in the balcony floor, thin ribbons of marble crosshatched beneath my sister's feet. I touch the toe of her slipper, as light as rain. Alia's eyes flash open, meeting mine. She immediately glances over her shoulder to the room off the balcony, clearing out from the breakfast entertainment. The guests are gone, and a few servants run about shutting the open doors.

When all the doors are closed, Alia sinks to sit on the woven floor pretending she's just looking out past the cove into the tip of the sea.

My voice is low and rushed. I swing around the pole so that she can see the entirety of my face as I bark at her all the questions I can't hold inside anymore.

"How? Did Father keep the books we thought were destroyed? The ones Annemette used? Or did you ask them—Mette's daughters? Why didn't you tell me? And what happened to your voice?"

Alia takes a deep breath and holds up her hands— *watch this,* her fingers spell. When we were younger, our oldest sister, Eydis, taught us hand signals she'd devised to communicate across the room during our daily lessons while our instructors' tails were turned.

Alia signs a single word. *Witch.* We used this to describe our voice instructor, who had a habit of burying us up to our necks in the sand so that we'd learn *to properly* project without the crutch of movement.

But there's only one real witch I know. Alia didn't find the magic herself through books or rumors. She went straight to the creature who doesn't need to know the old ways—the only one under the sea dangerous enough to try something like this.

"You went to the sea witch?" My tone is appalled and disgusted at once—if there's a single being beyond humans that we've been consistently taught to fear, it's *her*. I take a deep breath and I ask, though I know what she will tell me. "And she took your voice?"

She nods.

My disgust squirms and twists into blatant outrage. I'd never sacrifice a life, but *this*. It's all I can do to keep my voice down. "So you really can't tell him that you love him? Who you are? What you did?"

She shakes her head slowly, sadly.

"What about writing? Can you do that? Tell him the story that way?"

With another shake, she confirms it. She's utterly defenseless. Able only to use her smile, her shining eyes, her graceful dancing, to get what she needs. She's done well for herself to get this far, but it's . . . so superficial. Not to mention, he's about to be *married*.

"That kiss didn't do it? Didn't appease the deal? You must earn his love," I confirm. Alia nods and I continue. "It's not the kiss that does it; it's the love behind it."

Alia squeezes my fingers and then makes our sign for human—two fingers walking. Human love.

"Or Øldenburg blood?" I whisper. Alia's face blanches, and she shakes her head violently.

No. No. No, Runa, NO.

It's the only other way to satisfy the spell. We know this from Annemette's story too.

A kiss of true love or Øldenburg blood.

But this path isn't one she's entertained—not yet. In fact, given the look she gave Niklas, it's the last thing she'll entertain at all.

"Alia, listen to me. You may not have a choice. His brothers and father died in the storm where you saved him. Everyone in the sea knows that." I think of that other boy, Phillip, but his relation to Niklas is on his mother's side. His blood will not satisfy Urda. "His might be the only Øldenburg blood available. And if that's what it'll take—"

Alia shakes her head violently again, pointing at me, then her ear, then toward the door where the king made his exit. She points to herself, and through the force of her hands, the signs she's using, the fury on her face, I understand her.

You heard him. He knows down deep I rescued him. He loves the mermaid who rescued him. That's me. He loves me.

"Alia," I say, hooking the pole with one arm and swirling my tail around the bottom so I don't slide. I grab her trembling hands, trying to still them. I've always been the one to tell her the truth when her dreams push the boundaries of reality. "He loves the *idea* of you—this girl he plucked from the same sea he survived. He hasn't said he believes in mermaids, has he? Or that he believes one rescued him? Or that you look just like her? No, he hasn't."

I reset my grip, harder, stronger, as she shakes her head. "You can't hang your hopes—*your life*—on a boy like that. The only person he's in love with is himself. He loves the idea that Urda swept him up and saved him while his inferior brothers sank to the deep. You were just the courier." The words feel like darts pouring from my lips, but I have to make her see.

Alia's shaking head gains speed, and she grits her teeth hard, a red flush gathering under her eyes.

She points to me, and I know what she's going to say before she signs it. I know her nearly better than I know myself.

You don't know him, Runa. You don't. You're wrong. That's not true.

It's then that Alia surprises me, breaking my grip on her with such strength that I teeter back, holding on by only my tail, curled around the balcony base.

Then she signs a single word.

Leave.

"No, I won't leave you. Are you crazy? You have, what,

—25

three days? And he'll be married by then. Alia, won't you—"

Leave!

She stands, red in the face, so angry she mouths the words.

I don't want to see you again. If I am to die, let me die in peace.

Then Alia turns, because if I won't leave her, she'll leave me.

And she does, not even looking back, disappearing through the nearest set of French doors and into the castle.

I slip beneath the water. All the panic I've pushed down rises, galvanizing within my chest, setting my heart a-skitter and my fingers trembling. The sudden need to do something holds tight to my skin, bones, heart, and tail.

I have to stop this. This can't happen. It can't. There has to be a way to undo this. To save Alia from herself. I can't have Alia fail. I can't lose her twice.

I must visit the sea witch.

4

Evie

THE LIGHT FILTERS IN SLOWLY, MY WORLD GOING FROM a sky with no stars to one with a rising sliver of moon. Beneath that weak glow, my body is a pile of lead, the casing of a ship sunk to this place, rusting and rotting as the urchins gut it out. The only energy I have left goes to trying to open my eyes further to see what, if anything, is left.

"Oh, good, you're alive," comes a voice.

It takes me several moments to realize it's not a voice in my head. I'm still so unused to company that it's nearly impossible to remember the sound.

I'm conscious of my lungs working, drinking in thin breaths of murk. As I work to test my faculties, the voice continues. "If you'd listened to me, I would've told you that what you need isn't in those books. That magic is for the witches above—the sea people *are* magic. You can't solve a problem like this with only land magic, you have to know the magic in the sea."

Oh, Anna. Always with the suggestions.

"I've been here just as long as you," I say, my voice sallow in my ears—nearly as dead as the rest of me. "I know what you know."

"But you don't," she responds back with all the energy I don't have. "You forget that I was Annemette for four years, *squid*."

"Don't think I've forgotten that."

Her time as Annemette is the reason both of us are here, in the dark. Her "father" all but confirmed that when he nearly killed me in my home. If I had the energy right now, I'd shut her up yet again.

I wedge one tentacle into the sand, trying to leverage myself up and around from where I landed. The pewter grind of it coats my skin in a gray rash, embedded so deep it may never come out. The tentacle gains traction, and I'm able to add two others to fortify it and push until I'm on my side. I sit up too fast, my head spinning as I screw my eyes shut and fall back onto the sea floor with a soft *whomp*.

"I know a spell that might help," Anna offers, clearly peeved I didn't jump at her hint of knowledge before.

"What is that?" I say, as I try once again to sit up. I'm more successful this time, but my head still spins horribly, my ears clouded with bells.

"*Festa.*"

If it wouldn't hurt, I'd nod. This was a spell Tante Hansa used when she'd gained the nickname Healer of Kings. It's not anything new, and I'm unsure whether it will repair the depletion I feel down to my core. Especially if I, the depleted one, am the witch commanding the magic for strength. It's not a spell I've ever tried on myself; it's only something I've seen used on others.

"Go on, then," I tell Anna. "Use that magic on me. Spell me. I gave you that voice; go ahead and use it."

She laughs, no mirth in it. "You gave me a voice, but you took my magic when you murdered me. Or have you forgotten that?" She says it like she's razzing me, but there's more pain in there than she wants to admit, and she's trying very hard to inflict hurt while I'm already down.

"No, *you* took *your own* magic when you murdered King Asger for a chance to be human," I remind her, very close to bringing up the elephant in the room between us—Nik. Neither of us has mentioned his name since I restored her voice, and I know when we do, it'll be even uglier than this. "All I did was make sure you couldn't murder again."

There's a gasp as that barb does the job. I wonder if this will be our future, wounding each other in little ways until all that's left is to bleed out.

It's silent again, and as an olive branch, I try the spell, closing my eyes and digging deep for reserves of magic that are dead or sleeping.

"Festa." The spell is meant to revive strength, though as

the word echoes through my lair, I feel nothing of the sort. There isn't much to exchange—not much strength to get when there's barely any magic within me to give.

Still, improbably, there's a twitch somewhere deep inside. Like a seedling poking through the earth, weak and reaching for the sun. Easy to snap. Easy to crush. Barely anything at all.

"*Festa.*" I repeat.

Another twitch.

"*Festa.*"

And then, Anna joins in, her voice subdued. "*Festa,*" we say together as a prickle of relief touches my heart.

We repeat it five times more, and finally I have the strength to get off the sea floor. I dust myself off. Pick at some shrimp my polypi have caught and rained from their branches. The sustenance helps, but again, I must rest. I coil my tentacles below me.

"Thank you," I say reluctantly.

"You're welcome." She laughs a little, more to herself than to me. "I need you alive—you die, and the sea king'll vaporize this whole place and those of us literally *rooted* to it."

The sarcasm sits all wrong in the little mermaid's tone, though I still recognize this Anna from our childhood, playing it off with humor because she was hurt.

I swallow a few more shrimp and gather the energy to say more, knowing that it will be a while before I can cast another spell. But then yet again there's someone who's come from the clear blue into my sunspot cove. The weak magic within me throbs a warning I might have noticed if I hadn't been concentrating so hard when the sea king arrived.

It's not him, though. There's no excess power slipping into my waters. Perhaps another brave soul who needs my help. I stack my spell books gently by my cauldron and arrange myself into the powerful creature anyone who visits expects me to be, hoping I don't look as drained as I am.

It is indeed a mermaid who appears, swimming feverishly, determination folding her beautiful face into a frown. She looks very much like Alia, though her hair has the colors of autumn strung through a base of curled blond. Her eyes are a honeyed amber unusual here in this kingdom of shades of blue.

"Send her away. Even if the knife is made, you don't have the—" Anna starts in a moment before I whisper "*létta*" yet again, and she cuts off. This makes me smile just a little bit—I probably couldn't make a pot boil right now, but I can do that.

The mermaid sees me and doesn't waste a beat, diving right in.

"Witch!" she spits with rage. "My sister will fail. That boy won't fall in love with her in four days—he's to be married. *Married!* And in fewer days than she has left!"

Now that's a surprise—he's so young. But the fire in

the girl's eyes sparks with truth.

"Give me the antidote," she demands. "I'll pay whatever the cost. Take my tongue, my eyes, my ears, hell, have my tail and fashion it for your own. Whatever the cost, I'll give it to you."

I don't reply, and the girl looks me up and down from the other side of my cauldron, her eyes glowing behind thick lashes. The fury within her is eager to escape through more than just words.

"One day is already gone. How can you just sit there like that? She has three days left to live!"

The girl raises a hand as if to topple my cauldron, that anger begging for release.

"I wouldn't do that if I were you," I say, calm in the face of her fury. This only serves to make her angrier, but she removes her hand—she's a smart one.

When she speaks again, her voice cracks, the mermaid's ire shattering into a new wave.

"Bring my sister back. You stole her from me. From all of us. You knew hers was a fool's ask—a death sentence—and yet you did it anyway." Her teeth are bared, and somehow that makes her look younger—she's close in age to the mermaid who came here. The sea king's most recent brood. "Do you know what the sea king will do when he finds out what you've done? What my father will do? Why start this again? You know the danger. Why?"

I level the girl with my gaze, and I know what she

sees—young face, dark hair threaded through with silver, I'm as pewter-toned as the rest of my world. To her, I must look every bit of my reputation. This thing she's been taught to fear—a freak of nature, tethered to my cove by her powerful father because of the things that I'm able to do. She came in here with fire and verve, angry at being left behind. Angry at what Alia's bargain may bring. But she came, despite my reputation. Because she loves her sister as much as her sister thinks she loves this boy.

"Child—"

"Runa. Use my name. You're not my oma."

This nearly makes me smile—her oma I am definitely not. "Runa, I already know what your father will do because he's come and done it. And because of that, I cannot help you."

Behind my back, I can practically feel Anna's soundless judgment—the knife is safe and ready to use. Though it was not plain in Alia's bargain, surely this girl knows her history—the magic will accept the boy's blood if her sister fails at love. I could give the knife to her now. But magic always takes an exchange, and I have done the work without promise of payment until now.

"You cannot . . . ," the girl starts, sputtering despite her clear strength. The weakness in her voice signals a sob rising, high and hard. "It's like you've torn my arm from my body. She's my twin sister. My other half. Please . . ."

"Your father depleted me of my magic. I want to help

—33

you, but your request alone is not enough, Runa."

The girl smacks the cauldron in frustration, and the metal rings out around my polypi trees, clanging to the surface, up to the sun that barely shines here. "You changed her—endangered her—for one stupid boy who doesn't even know her name. It should be more than enough that her twin sister wants her back. I shouldn't need anything else. I should be enough."

I level my gaze at her and smile, which irritates her more. "Ah, but you have what I need."

The girl's brows pull together, but she doesn't ask, waiting instead for me to plainly state what she must do.

"You see, I know about you, Runa. Famed gardener, are you not? Little Runa and her special flowers. Alia, yes, she's known for the beautiful things she can make," I say, gesturing to the red flowers the little mermaid offered me before I took her voice. "But she can't do what her twin can do. Runa, the last-born daughter by a minute, the one who keeps her father strong with all the ríkifjor he can stomach?"

Something in the girl's eyes hardens—honey frozen on a winter's day. "They're guarded. Even *I* can't go there unsupervised. I can't—"

"Then I can't help you." Runa's jaw sets as I continue. "Your father came to me, frustrated that he doesn't have the power to bring Alia back, and drunk on ríkifjor, attacked me. He attacked my power—undermining the only person alive who can save Alia. To have the power to save her, I need to build my strength back up. Surely thirty of those flowers would do."

"I can't bring you thirty flowers. Maybe one, but thirty? They're protected both by magic and by armed guards. There's no way—"

"Seeds, then."

"But—"

"Runa," I say, wrapping a tentacle around her waist, drawing her in. To her credit, the girl gives me no reaction—not a blink, no curl of revulsion, no tremble of fear. Her face is blank, hard, determined. "I cannot change my price. It is up to you to figure it out. If you want your sister to live, bring me the flowers and we will deal. Then you will have what you need."

5

Runa

A WAVE OF DREAD SWEEPS OVER ME AS I LEAVE THE SEA witch's lair. Was I really so naive as to think this creature, this slithering monster, would give me any relief?

The whole thing almost felt rehearsed, like she had been expecting me and was prepared. She stuck to her script as the actors do in our monthly moon plays, asking for impossible things in the name of love. Alia never missed a chance to show off her dramatic skills on stage, but now, what will she do with no voice?

No voice. No more plays. I shake my head. These are the least of Alia's problems.

Though I'm away from the witch's murky waters and back in the cool blue of the open sea, I'm not any more confident that I'll get my other half back alive. Loss already weighs heavy on my shoulders, and I fear I will carry this forever if I fail.

No, I will fix it. I will get the antidote. I will save Alia. I won't lose her.

I swim on, yet I have a major problem. Father counts those flowers like he'd count gold if he were any other type of king. But to my father, gold isn't power—magic is.

And my flowers are magic.

Yes, Witch, I'm *the gardener*. "Little Runa and her flowers"—the witch knows the common refrain. For all the beauty Alia can produce, I'm the one who can make the tough things grow. The important things. But I was telling the truth when I said that even I'm not allowed to go into the ríkifjor garden without supervision. The ríkifjor can't be touched, not by me or anyone else, unless Father's security—both physical and magical—deems it so on a very specific schedule.

Though I hate losing time, if I'm to get them, I won't be successful in the middle of the day—I need to wait for nightfall for any chance to sneak in. In fact, I won't be successful *at all* if Father realizes I've been gone too long.

I swim straight from the sea witch's lair to the castle grounds. The sea kingdom can be seen from miles around, shining a brilliant cerulean blue. I sweep through the front gate and into the winding hallways as if nothing is amiss. I smile at all the right people and make proper small talk. I go about my day pretending it's completely normal that Alia is not at my side.

The afternoon brings my lessons—singing, dancing,

the human arts—with my sisters. Alia's absence hangs in the water between us, each drop swelling with our growing anxiety. And yet we stay silent. If Father heard us talking, it would only make it worse.

After lessons and supper, where I looked everywhere but Alia's empty seat, a plan begins to take shape in the shambles of my distracted mind. It's perhaps the only way to get the witch her flowers, secure the antidote, and deliver it, though it won't be easy. But what choice do I have? I can't just let Alia stay there and die, even if she doesn't want to come with me. Living with a broken heart is better than dissolving into sea foam. It has to be.

I go to bed early, feigning illness, but none of my sisters buy it. When the castle is dark and quiet, Eydis spells on the light, but I'm already wide awake, going over the scenarios in my mind, eyes glued to the vaulted ceiling of our chambers. My other sisters—Ola and Signy—converge upon my bed, taking space among the blankets.

Dark blue and near black—the color of the deepest part of the ocean on the cloudiest days—Eydis's eyes fall to mine. She's usually covered in diamond dust from brow bone to chin, but barefaced in the night, she looks more serious than she's ever been in her life. "She went above, didn't she? For that Øldenburg?"

I sit up, and that's enough of a confirmation. The sob that sat deep in my throat this morning is welling up again, fat and misshapen.

Signy, the closest in age to Alia and me, already has it figured out, arms crossed tightly over her chest, the tips of her ink-dyed hair dusting the goose bumps on her arms. "And the sea witch did it, didn't she?"

I nod. Ola's eyes grow wider as she adds another question. I may be Alia's twin, but Ola looks the most like her—blond and ethereal in the way most humans expect mermaids to be. "Is there anything we can do?" Both her hands snag one of mine and squeeze. "Tell me what we can do. There must be something."

I swallow down that sob. I didn't want to include them, because the more of us who are involved, the easier it will be for Father to know.

Yet now I can't leave them out of it. "There is an antidote. But Father visited the witch and weakened her enough that she can't make it. I have to bring her something first." The way they watch me confirms they know exactly what I must bring.

"But Father—"

"How? It's guarded—"

"He'll be so angry—"

"I know!" The sob squeezes out, making my voice too loud. I close my eyes to reset. "I know," I say again, quieter and more controlled this time. "But we all know what his wrath is like—it's not difficult for any of us to imagine what he did to her. She needs the flower to be powerful enough to help Alia."

"No, no, no," Ola says, emphatic. "We need to tell Father. If we go behind his back, it will only be worse for us." She rises from the bed and heads for the door that leads from our chambers into the family wing.

"No!" I snap, jumping from bed and physically cutting her off. "We can't tell him. He's already assaulted the witch. If he finds out that she's willing to help us and not him, he won't be pleased."

"Are you kidding?" Ola says, crossing her arms over her chest, one brow cocked. Her voice is still too loud. "He'll reward us."

Eydis sweeps forward and places her hands on either side of our sister's cheeks, forcing Ola to look her in the eye. "Ola, the last thing Father is interested in is positive reinforcement. He's not going to start now."

Ola doesn't answer her, looking to me instead. "How do you know he assaulted her? How do you know she's not lying? We all know the tales—she's powerful enough to ruin the sea as soon as save it. Why would she rescue Alia after sending her to her death? Maybe she just wants ríkifjor to become more powerful. She nearly destroyed us once. What could she do with the power of those flowers?"

All of it could be true. But we have to try.

I believed the witch when she said that Father stormed in, angry that he couldn't get Alia back himself. That seems exactly like something he would do—our whole lives he's been paranoid, what with the disaster that almost befell us with Annemette. The ríkifjor augments his power, which makes him feel more in control, but it also makes him volatile. He's not the king he was the first hundred years of his reign.

"Ola, you have to trust me," I say. "I met the witch, and I believe her. I have to try."

"I want to try with you," Eydis says. "Signy?"

Behind us, she nods. Then all our eyes turn to Ola. She shoves a stray curl behind her ear. "Fine."

Eydis looks to me. "What's the plan, Ru?"

"To get the flowers, I need to go alone. The four of us can't travel in a pack through the castle. Even in the dead of night—Father will sense it."

The three of them nod as one. Then Eydis speaks. "Signy and Ola will come with me. The ríkifjor will buy us the witch's strength, but it won't get us the antidote. She'll want more." Eydis says this with certainty. At nineteen, she believes she knows more than all of us combined, and maybe she does. She touches their shoulders. "Together we will meet the sea witch's price—there's always a price for these things."

Then she looks to me. "How did Alia pay?"

"With her voice and most likely her life."

"Not if we can help it," Eydis says, and checks the night clock's swirling dial in our shared chambers. A quarter till midnight. "Let's get going. Meet us by the canyon in an hour, Ru, and we'll go with you to wake the witch. Alia can't wait much longer."

"The canyon?" I ask. It's a strange place for a meeting, this crag that runs across the strait like an old wound, cool reams of water whispering from its depths. It's also in the opposite direction from the sea witch's murky lair.

My oldest sister nods, the ends of her diamond-dusted hair sparkling like the snow the winter brings above. "By the red coral. You know the one that looks like a hammer-head on a pike?"

"Yes, I know the one, but why—?"

"Because that's where I keep what the witch will want. Where do you think I get my diamond dust from? I have a treasure trove, Ru." I always figured Father gave her the dust she loves so much, eager to marry off the next in his brood, what with all the suitors Eydis sees on a regular basis. A shiny prize for the king's second-wave eldest. "My diamonds and pearls can be replaced. If the witch demands a payment for Urda, she can have my treasures, but no one is taking my voice."

The family gardens ring the grounds, a patch for each of the sisters from the king's two wives—Queen Mette, gone in the tide long ago, and Queen Bodil, my mother, who's young enough to be the same age as our older half sisters. My patch sweeps the long way around the royal chambers, where Father and Mother's patio bleeds into the soft turquoise sand. It's the largest garden, the final connection in the ring, swinging around for the ten sisters like a short-handed clock.

My garden is nearly all ríkifjor now, blanketing the sands in their ghostly way. The only other flowers are roses with exaggerated points edging the borders, sharp enough to scare away any curious fingers on sight alone. The guards are there, even in the dead of night, planted three around, spaced like slices of pie. The public believes the security is because of the garden's proximity to the royal chambers, and that is a very good cover story indeed.

I stick to any shadow I can find, careful not to draw the guards' attention, and careful to not to disturb the aura of magic surrounding the ríkifjor—an extra security measure. My heart thuds tightly in my chest, and my swim stroke falters for just a moment.

There are so many ways my plan could crumble. The guards. The magic. The possibility that I don't know Alia as well as I think I do. Still, I push forward. Shadow to shadow, I wind my way through the serpentine layout of garden plots, thankful when I arrive at the edge of Alia's garden.

Though I've seen it a million times, my heart drops at the life there. So much life, in every color: ruby red, yellow as bright as the spring sun above, velvet purple, cloud-white. All as shiny as a new day, they're every bit as bright as she is. As romantic as she is. As full of hope and promise and sunshine as she is.

They'll die without her. If not now, soon.

There, in the middle of it all is the massive statue she acquired after rescuing the boy this summer. Like his father, brothers, and the rest of the ship, it sank to the sea floor and lodged itself in the sand. Until a day later when she returned to the scene of it all and wedged it out, using the very limits of her magic to move the thing all the way from the wreck site to this garden.

The statue is as bold as the fact that she brought it here, thumbing her nose at what anyone thought—even Father, who likely only allowed it because it shows exactly how ridiculous the Øldenburgs are. The statue was meant to make a statement on land—*Look at this would-be king! Standing tall on a ship's prow, one foot hiked up as he looks out, eyes searching for new lands to pillage!*—and it does so here as well. It's a trumpet-blast declaration of what Alia did.

I slink into the shadow of the statue and look up at *him.*

"I hate you," I whisper to his stupid, handsome face.

The statue stonily accepts my words, but there's so much more I want to say to him. That he's already broken my sister's heart and he's nearly broken mine, which is hanging on by the thread that I can save her with these seeds and the sea witch's help. That he doesn't know how lucky he is that Alia was already in love with him when she rescued him or he'd be bones like his father and brothers— one more Øldenburg fed to the sea.

That he never deserved her and never will.

Looking around just to confirm yet again that I'm indeed alone, I crouch below the statue and dig, the crux of my plan hinging on the next few moments.

Although Alia could cultivate the most gorgeous blooms, they weren't what she really wanted to grow. Not once she realized Father's penchant for ríkifjor. And so I gave her a chance to try, squirreling away seeds for her to plant. Yet, as I had suspected, nothing ever came of them. I only hope she's left the remainder where she hid them for safekeeping.

It takes several handfuls of soil pushed to the side before I feel the heat of them like the dull burn of the sun's rays at the surface, warm but distant. Suddenly, my fingers seem to know exactly where to go, and they should—they handle the magic of the ríkifjor every day. Before breakfast each morning, I tend the garden and pull the plants for Father's daily use—a shot of nectar before he begins his day. It's the only reason I was able to get above this morning—I'd prepared the ríkifjor before leaving.

Relief washes over me as the warmth of the seeds grows stronger, my fingers burning to reach them. They're here.

My sister's heart holds on to everything too long—love, dreams, hope, and things, lots of them. Her trunks are stuffed full of items, found, bought, or otherwise loved. I knew, as sure the sand in the soil, that she kept the seeds I gave her. Just like I knew where she'd be. What she'd done.

My fingernails scrape canvas. I tug at it and sand spills out, dribbling over the base of the statue, which, of course, has his whole ridiculous name and previous title on it: Crown Prince Asger Niklas Bryniulf Øldenburg V. And there in my hand is more than what I need. I release the strings of the sack and peek inside. Another sigh of relief shakes my body. She kept almost fifty dormant ríkifjor seeds.

Thank Urda.

Although Alia always played an excellent damsel in the castle moon plays, for once this damsel may not need her king after all. "You very well may have just rescued yourself, Alia," I whisper to the seeds.

"So Alia does need rescuing, then."

I nearly drop the bag and whirl around at the sound of another voice. I'd been sure I was alone, but there, right in front of me, is Oma Ragn—Queen Mother Ragnhildr—my grandmother. The woman who taught me everything I know while singing sailor shanties about mermaids and their vengeance.

Her smile is quick and conspiratorial as she swims forward. These days, her eyes are a blue so crystal clear they're nearly as white as her hair, but she never misses a thing. Not when it comes to her son, not when it comes to me, not when it comes to anything.

"Believe me, darling Runa, if your father can sense she's left the water without even checking her bed, I know it too. When magic leaves the water, those of us who've been here long enough feel it." She says it all like she's seen what I've seen above—Alia, the boy, her hopeless chance. Then her eyes flicker to the bag. "Is this how you plan to get her back?"

She doesn't have to open the bag to know what's in my hand. Oma Ragn was the one who started me off planting ríkifjor. She can sense the seeds' power just as well as I. The only one better is Father and that's because he has so much of it running through his veins, he'd likely fall over dead without it.

I wouldn't lie to Oma Ragn, and there's no use in it anyway. Not with her. "To get Alia the antidote, I need to bring these to the sea witch."

"I should've guessed that old squid would be behind this," she says with a tart turn to her mouth. Oma Ragn is two hundred years old and counting, and that time has only served to make her more direct. "She was powerful enough to perform the changing spell but isn't powerful enough to get her back without the ríkifjor?"

Her voice is too loud, and I glance around, looking to every corner and around the overdeveloped thighs of the massive statue.

Oma chuckles, her voice almost louder when she speaks

again. "Ru, calm yourself. I've distracted the guards."

She says this with such cool confidence. It reminds me of how she used to promise to spell away all the monsters in our dreams if they should appear in daylight. I can still see me and Alia standing at her bedside in the dead of night, nightmares fresh behind our eyes. She'd pull us close, and once our hearts had calmed, she'd sing three stanzas of "The Mermaid's Revenge" to send us back to sleep.

But no song is going to ease my nerves now. "Not exactly," I say, answering her question. Oma Ragn is critical of Father in ways no one else can be—especially in the years since Annemette's change—but I'm not about to offer up what the witch said he did to her. "Oma, I have to go. Please don't say anything to Father. I'll get Alia back."

"I won't and you will." Oma Ragn shoos me with a wave of her long fingers. "Go. Visit the witch. I'll be in my bed, praying to Urda that she doesn't turn you into a talking crab."

Despite myself, I smile. Oma Ragn has a way of bringing humor to even the direst situation. "If she turns me into a talking crab, do me a favor and make sure she changes me back before Father tries to fillet her for it. We need her to get Alia home."

Oma allows me a quick grin that reaches the tide-break white of her eyes. "It's a deal, Ru." She makes a move to return to her quarters, or maybe to the route of whatever midnight swim she was on when she found me, but then she stops and wraps my wrist in her knotted fingers. "Good luck, my dear. You and your sister will need it for all to turn out right."

I press a quick kiss to her cheek and leave, seed bag in hand, for the witch's lair.

6

Runa

"YOU CAME HERE *alone*?" EYDIS ASKS, A HEAVY NOTE OF big-sister protectiveness ringing out as the first strange trees surrounding the sea witch's lair come into view.

I don't blame her—it's the last place any of us would ever willingly go.

"Yes," I say, adjusting my grip on the bag in my hand— inside is Eydis's stash of shipwreck jewels, and it's heavy enough that both of us are carrying it. "Alia went in alone. I owed it to her to do the same."

Actually, I was just so angry that I didn't have the capacity to worry about swimming straight into an ancient Viking horror story.

"Is it just *her* in there?" Ola asks, nerves shaking her usually confident voice.

Signy rolls her eyes. "Of course it is. Didn't you ever listen to Oma's stories? Witches like that always live alone."

"Ladies," Eydis snaps, half whirling around, and my hold on the bag slips as she wrenches me with it. "It doesn't matter if she's lonely or popular; all that matters is that she gives us the antidote. For all the poundage in this thing"— she hoists up her end of the bag for a moment—"she can buy herself some friends."

That shuts up everyone, all our energy focused on making it through the trees. As we draw closer, the anxiety that's been swirling within me all day lessens and is replaced by a shifting tide of confidence. We're here. We're going to get what we want. We're going to make this happen.

I speed up, swimming into the expanse of pewter sand that surrounds the witch's lair. Gamely, Eydis increases her pace to match mine, determination set in her face. We haven't worked it out, but I'm the one who will be doing the talking.

Despite my middle sisters' loud jabber, the sea witch doesn't greet us immediately when we arrive. My blood pressure spikes when I realize she's not waiting on pins and needles, antidote in hand as she should be. This is her mess. This is our fight for the life she put at stake. She should at least have the heart to show up.

I hand Eydis my corner of the bounty and move in front of my sisters. Signy and Ola move in line with Eydis.

"Sea Witch," I start, and my voice is clear of any trembling, that confidence that rose in my belly setting the tone. I am the baby of the family, but I'm not to be taken lightly. The sea witch will learn that too. "I've returned with the ríkifjor. I've brought my sisters as well. The antidote, please, and we'll be on our way."

There's movement at the mouth of the cave, and behind me, my sisters stiffen.

But I'm not scared of the old squid.

My sisters may grow tense as she wakes, but I grow stronger, arms crossed—not protectively but with malice—my body one unwavering line, jaw cut.

The witch appears, slinking from her cave, tentacles a giant plume of liquid onyx. Her face is placid, and I know my sisters are immediately fascinated by her appearance— Eydis, her bare-moon complexion; Ola, her dramatic curls; Signy, the whole steely spectrum of her—because it's true: she's striking.

"Little Runa, where are your flowers?" the witch asks.

I hold up the bag. "Where would you like them?"

I don't have to explain. The sea witch is a sharp one and understands instantly. "Will they grow anywhere, or must you have light?"

I glance around her home—it's just as dark now as it was in the halo of morning. "Considering what we have to work with, it may not matter."

To my surprise the witch cackles. "I didn't choose the darkness, child, it chose me."

She waves me over a scarred shoulder and leads me to

her cave, built into the base of an enormous black rock, that must jut out and into the thick of the Havnestad night. Behind me, my sisters waver where they're planted, deciding if they should get closer to keep an eye on me. I wave Eydis back. I can hold my own.

The witch points to a spot near the cave mouth and settles back onto her tentacles, again treating the eight of them as her throne. I reach into the bag, count out thirty seeds, and then shove the rest into my bodice, hoping she doesn't notice or doesn't care that some seeds remain.

She asked for thirty, and I won't give her a seed more.

Like the flowers themselves, the seeds are milky white and so luminous that they practically create their own light in this hollow place. I sprinkle them in a half circle before sinking down to the sea floor, where I use both hands to sweep a blanket of sand over the seeds.

Next comes the magic. Mine is a spell commonly used to spark life into most anything, but there's something about the way I say it that works wonders with these finicky plants. As if they'll only take direction from me, the charge in my blood the frequency they need to behave, grow, thrive.

"*Lif. Lif. Lif,*" I say, over and over—thirty times in all. The witch watches me quietly, a smile settling into the corners of her face. She was beautiful once and still is in her own way.

As the magic warms the sands beneath my hands, I

think of how it's romantic that she allegedly gave her own life to save the future king's, except for the fact that his life led to the grandson now holding my sister's heart captive.

Nothing about these boys should make them worth saving. Not a title. Not a handsome face. Not all the pretty words in the world.

None of that should've taken my sister from me.

My anger rises all over again, along with the heat from the plants. Something about it seems to make them grow faster than I'd expected, the entire lifetime—from seed to seedling to bud to bloom—elapsing in mere seconds. Behind me, the sea witch gasps, and it almost makes me smile despite my anger.

I can do something she can't.

"You are talented, Runa," the witch says, her chin tilted upward, but this time in admiration. She sweeps in behind me and plucks up ten of the flowers—one in each tentacle and one in each hand. Then it's over to her cauldron, where she tosses them in, stems and all. The pot immediately starts to boil as I return to where my sisters are waiting and watching. The steam rises, and the witch inhales big belly breaths as the flowers' sweet perfume wraps around the lair.

It's several moments before the heat peters out, the steam dying, the boil calming. The witch dares to touch what's inside the cauldron—pure, concentrated ríkifjor nectar—with her bare hands, cupping it into her palms and bringing it to her lips. She sips it down as we watch. After she swallows, a smile slips across her face. And though she's a study in shades of gray, something warm seems to touch her—life and strength renewed in the darkness. When she opens her eyes, she's staring straight at me.

"Now we may deal."

Sensing her moment, Eydis swims forward and presents her loot. But she doesn't cut in, allowing me to continue to be our voice. "As payment for the antidote, we have brought you jewels—rubies of Rigeby Bay, sapphires of Havnestad, emeralds and diamonds of the western countries. Some free to sell or admire on their own, others ready to wear in settings of gold, silver, pewter, and the like."

At my pause, Eydis opens the bag just enough to reveal the glittering contents, bright even in this gray place.

The witch looks but doesn't seem to see the beauty flashed before her. Her tone is level and matter-of-fact, her voice stronger than any time I've heard it. "Jewels are not what I require."

"Pearls, then," I say, gesturing to the one hung by golden thread at my throat. All of us—including our mother and half sisters—have them, a favorite gift from Oma Ragn. "We can easily obtain a large number of pearls in a matter of hours."

A flicker of disgust moves across the sea witch's face. "Definitely not pearls."

My confidence begins to slip. Inside the safety of my

rib cage, my heart stutters and teeters. "I returned with the ríkifjor. We refuse to make the same deal our sister did—you shall not make our entire generation voiceless. We've brought you items of great value that could buy you freedoms you haven't seen in decades," I say, frustration and exhaustion making my voice thick, yet higher than I'd like. I can't sob in front of this woman. In front of my sisters. I look her dead in the eye. "What will be enough for you?"

The sea witch's answer is immediate. And I wonder if she always knew I would return with my sisters, just like she knew I would come in the first place.

"It's not much that I require, and it means more to me than it does to you." She could say the same thing about our voices, so I do not find comfort in this statement, clamping my lips shut, waiting impatiently for her to go on. "All I want is the same thing from each of you: your hair."

At this, Eydis's breath catches. "Our hair? But why our hair—it's not precious; it'll grow back. *You* could magic it back."

The sea witch's face remains placid—no reaction. Simply a tilt of her head. She's nearly the definition of bored, settling on a throne of writing black.

"That's exactly right; it is of no consequence to you. Hair grows. But that is what I request for what you want me to do."

This can't be right. It can't be. From all of us? Something that isn't precious, endangered, or rare?

This has to be a trap. A trick. Wrong.

The sea witch just watches us, no concern crossing her face or posture, as she waits to be paid.

Unease growing in my belly and in my teetering heart, I nod, telling myself it's not what she wants; it's what she needs for the antidote. Maybe she needs a piece of us to return our missing piece.

The witch seems to sense the tide turning her way. She extends a hand to me. "Come then, let us take your hair."

One by one, the witch seats us on a sandstone block next to her cauldron and, using a plain knife fashioned of razor-thin coral, slices our hair up to our chins. Eydis sits first, and, without planning it, we go in birth order. Ola next. Then Signy. Then me. Every lock is tossed without a second glance into the cauldron.

When she's finished, I straighten, nose to nose with the sea witch, awaiting our antidote. The murky water feels cool against my neck, and I tell myself it's simply a new sensation and not my nerves settling in. We've done our part; now she will do hers and then we'll save Alia from her quest.

"Very good then, my girls. You'll have what you need, along with instructions as to what must be done."

I expect the sea witch to return to her cave, rifle around,

and come back to us with another little glass bottle filled with a shimmering liquid.

Instead, the witch hands me the knife she used to cut our hair. I stare at it, the words dying in my mouth. The witch brings a silky tentacle to my chin and tips my head up so that I can do nothing but stare into her dark blue eyes.

"Find your sister at the waterside and give her this knife. If she does not gain the boy's love in return by the end of her fourth full day on land, she must plunge this knife into his heart, letting the blood drip upon her feet. When his life-force is gone and his blood has anointed her new body, she will be human for the remainder of her days."

"She can't come back to us?" Eydis asks. "She can no longer be a mermaid?"

The witch's voice is level and clear. It's a dagger to each of our hearts. "Oh no. Never. That isn't how the magic works."

No. That's not right. The words tumble out as I try to grab a breath.

"But Queen Mette—"

"Queen Mette's magic was something else altogether— the joining of this world's magic with the magic above."

She says it like it's a fact. That Father's first queen was able to achieve something we can't. My guts sour and pucker. I glare at the knife in my palm, wondering whether, if I murder this witch right now, my sister will automatically sprout fins and be called home. The weapon is sharp enough to slice a finger straight through with barely any pressure. There's definitely magic in it, but it isn't what we asked for.

What's more—it won't work.

Alia's face on the balcony when I suggested this as an option flashes through my mind. I know my sister, stubborn and romantic to the core. She won't murder Niklas under any circumstance, even if it means she'll rot from the inside out.

This was supposed to be an antidote—an alternative to get her home.

"But that describes your magic too," I say, lobbing the sea witch's logic back to her. Reminding her of who she was. I move from my seat to my full height, daring to bear down on this witch, reclined on her stupid tentacles. "Which means you have the antidote. You have what Mette had. We kept our end of the deal. This isn't an antidote; it's a murder weapon. We agreed on the antidote."

The witch straightens herself to her full length, giving me a taste of my own medicine, staring down her nose at me. Her presence is more than her frame—the entire cove seems to join her in staring me down, the weight of it all pressing into me. On all sides, her strange trees seem to curve inward, their skeletal limbs reaching out for me, my sisters, our anger.

"You know nothing of my power. And it was *you* who said the word *antidote*, Runa. I did not," the sea witch says. "I told you I'd give you what you need. And what you need is this knife."

7

Evie

OUR CONVERSATION IS OVER, AND THE MERMAIDS swim away, their new chin-length hair streaming lightly behind as they navigate my polypi forest. But our visit is not over. I can feel it from the tip of my tentacles to the very ends of my curls.

"Why do you need their hair?" Anna asks.

"You'll see," I say, hoping that will stop the questions. The Anna I knew wasn't full of questions, but that seems to be who she's become since I gave her a voice. I suppose if I'd been left as a silent polypus, I'd have many too.

"You're not . . . you wouldn't . . . you can't. If you leave us, we'll be turned to rubble. Father—the sea king—he'll decimate your lair."

"I can't leave unless he frees me, Anna," I say, fishing the hair out of the cauldron before tying it all together with twine. Once wrapped, I tuck it into the remaining ríkifjor blooms, ensuring that it's snug and hidden. "No spell of mine will change that."

"That doesn't mean you aren't preparing to leave. Why else would you need that hair? I know you're not going to use it to bring *me* back."

"*Létta.*"

I silence her not a moment too soon. Runa has returned. I can only hope she believes she's imagined her twin's voice.

Runa has my knife clutched carefully, tightly between both palms before her chest, like she's praying. The confidence has faded from her features, but here she is again. Unsatisfied with the bargain. She looks to me, eyes shining, and I know before she speaks that her voice will be the weakest I've heard it.

"She won't," Runa says, bottom lip rosy and trembling, her voice barely loud enough to be heard over the near-stagnant tide of my home. "She's loved him since the moment she first saw him last year. She's the only reason he didn't die in that storm this summer. She wouldn't let him die then, and she won't kill him now . . . even if means her death."

My breath catches. "*This* summer?"

The girl nods. I knew Alia had lied about the boy already loving her; she all but admitted it, but I at least *thought* the details of her story were true. I cock a single brow and ask a question that's already been answered in the pit of my stomach. "And I don't suppose she's had a statue of him in her garden since she was ten?"

Runa glances down at the knife in her hands and then back to me. "Alia does have a statue, but only for the past few months. She pulled it from the wreckage and dragged it over to her garden like some sort of altar."

I inhale deeply, closing my eyes. Beneath me, my body becomes perfectly still, tentacles like cut stone. Even my uncut curls feel weighed down by whatever is moving through my belly. Anger and revulsion—both directed at myself, not the little mermaid. I should've known the girl was trying to manipulate me. I've had sixty-six years on this earth to know better.

Finally, after a long moment, I open my eyes. "Alia told me she saved him a year ago, on the first night she saw him. She told me she'd had a statue of his likeness in her garden since age ten. And she told me that when she left him on the beach, he was found by a girl—one he believes rescued him, and therefore loves. She said she'd watched that love for a year."

Runa's lips drop open, color coming again to her cheeks, the fierceness in her eyes returning.

"That story isn't correct—he's marrying a girl from somewhere else. *But*"—her voice is trembling along with everything else—"if you knew all that *and* what she had to do in four days—why on earth did you say yes? Why on earth did you send her up there knowing she'd fail? That she'd die?"

Because I believed her love was worth it.

Because I saw myself in her. And his grandfather in him.

Because I still believe in happy endings, even when I'm a nightmare.

Runa is staring at me, and I wonder if she can see it in my face—the girl behind the years. The one who gave herself for Nik more than once and who would do it again.

"I thought her heart had had enough," I say, and now my words are weak and threaded with all the exhaustion I don't have the strength to hide. "I thought that she deserved a chance at love."

"A chance?" Runa advances on me, what's left of her curls swirling around her like a lion's mane. "You heard all that, with all your fabled wisdom and reputation, and *you knew* she didn't have a chance."

"None of us knows anything for sure, Little Runa. But your sister was resolute. She sought me out, willing to fight for something she believed in. Whether she wins that fight or not, it wasn't my place to tell her she shouldn't try." I clench my teeth, my fists, my tentacles. "Love is worth suffering and sacrifice if it's true."

"Love is worth *nothing* to a life if you aren't around to live it!" Her face is screaming at me: *Why can't you see this?*

Haven't you lived long enough, suffered long enough, to see that death is permanent? Haven't you lived long enough, suffered enough, to see that death is death? "Alia should've been here for three hundred more years. How many times could she have loved in all those decades and not paid so dearly?"

Runa is heaving now, the knife deadly in her grip. I'm not afraid of her, but suddenly I am afraid *for* her.

"You don't believe in love, do you?" I ask.

Her fingers clench white-tight around the knife. "I love my sister."

"Runa," I say, wanting very much to lay a calm hand on her heaving shoulders, though it won't help dull the abandonment she feels. "If you truly love her, the best you can do is give her that knife and accept her choice."

"*No.* I won't *accept* that. I gave you my father's flowers, endangering him *and me* in the process. We gave you our hair—and you didn't even use it for anything." Runa raises the blade. "And now I have a knife but a sister who would die before wielding it on the only damn Øldenburg available."

The mermaid isn't done. She's pausing to make sure it sinks in for me. Everything she's lost, laid out plain.

"I only have one more thing to give you, and if you don't take it right now, you'll find out how talented I really am." Her nostrils flare, and she advances on me, knife out. "Change me. Change me and I'll do it. I'll kill the boy if it means she'll be saved."

The girl's amber eyes bore into my face, her shoulders and chest heaving.

I truly believe she will kill the boy for her sister to live.

I am both impressed and completely heartbroken over this. No matter what she may think of me, my motives were pure in sending her sister above. I firmly believe my heart was in the right place when I gave Alia legs. Though now I realize I shouldn't have worried as much about her lying on land as lying to me, though either way her manipulation may be Nik's grandson's undoing. Somehow, I wish Niklas were anyone else. Maybe he is—maybe the little mermaid told me one more lie to get her way, knowing my history with his family and how I loved Nik.

"You've seen this boy above, and yet you will do it?"

Runa nods, fury hot in the set of her shoulders. "Oh, I saw him. He acts like she's a prize pet. Something shiny he found on the beach. A nice complement to his stupid sapphire crown or dumb red ring."

My breath catches. "Red ring?"

"Yes, it's not rubies or garnets but something else. He rubs it like a two-bit moon play villain."

I work to keep my face plain, though at my back I can feel Anna yearning to scream. When Nik was alive, he would visit often. He'd dip the toes of his oxblood boots in the water, rear end in the dry gray sand, and tell me about his life. Within a year of my absence, he told me how a maid had found a red crystal rock in the old dresses

I'd left at the castle the night that my time above ended. It was the stone the sea had given me when I practiced my first exchange spell—Annemette's life for what the sea had already claimed. He remembered me wearing that dress when he'd spotted me while readying Iker's boat for the Celebration of the Sea.

My heart lurches for all the things I would've done differently that morning on the dock. I should've kissed Nik when he brushed a curl from my cheeks, his fingers lingering long enough that we both turned nearly as red as the stone in my pocket. The stone that Nik fashioned into a ring, that now sits atop his grandson's finger.

"What else do you know about him?" I ask the girl.

I'm worried I've gone too far and that her frustration won't stand it, but Runa bites her lip, her interaction above running through her mind. Though she's thinking hard, I find it difficult to believe she's forming a lie. She badly wants to save her sister, and it's enough to keep her honest. It wouldn't do to exaggerate.

"These other boys, they were talking about something called a U-boat."

My heart stops. U-boat? It had been invented when I was a girl—it wasn't common, but Father had done his research on them for King Asger, believing he might be able to better spot whales while working in tandem with them.

They weren't widespread then, but now, with time and

improvements in technology? They might be. That possibility looks much different to me from my vantage point under the sea. The danger they might pose to the merpeople is great.

"They're ships that can stay underwater for weeks at a time," I say, my memory shooting back to drawings Father got from a sailor near the mouth of the Rhine in the North Sea. Runa startles. "Yes, what you're thinking is correct—they'd be extremely dangerous to your people in the water." A shock of realization goes through me. "And the kingdom is building U-boats for the war effort?"

Havnestad always put its people to work on boats in times of famine. Times of war may be no different.

The girl nods. "All of Denmark, including Havnestad, is officially neutral, though boys in the southern regions are close enough to Germany that they're being conscripted. So, Havnestad—all of Denmark, really—is in the war, whether it wants to be or not."

Boys, stolen for war. They're just bodies. Bodies upon bodies. I don't think it would be much of a stretch to believe Niklas or any other ruler losing civilians to a foreign power would want to make sure that power succeeds.

"Niklas is king of Havnestad now, not simply a prince." More news to me—news that would explain his impending marriage. "So, he would have to approve these U-boats—I don't know how it works above, exactly, but here Father would have a say on anything that could be a potential pain—or profit."

Profit. In war? I can't reconcile this thought with my Nik. Though his grandson is not the boy I loved. "And you believe he could be making a profit?"

"Why else would he help without declaring war himself?" she says, anger flaring, though it's not for me. "He's probably even making a profit on the mines he's set in the waters."

I know all about the mines. They go off daily outside my lair, a sign of what rages above.

Runa shakes her head. "They're meant for enemy ships, but they're dangerous to all of us down here. There's something unsettling to me about a man who would place live bombs in the sea without a care for who or what might detonate them."

"And your people have died from this practice."

"Not yet, but there have been injuries. Whales, sharks, and fish from the smallest to the greatest have been killed. If a ship explodes, the projectiles can wipe out anyone or anything in their wake." She takes a shaky breath. "It's bad enough already, and who's to say how long the war will last?"

The meaning of all of it piles between us, shadows dancing in the almost-dawn. In some ways I'm protected here in my prison, protected from the outside by buoys Nik erected long ago, my cove off limits to anyone who would want to wade out into the black tide. They do toss Sankt Hans Aften dolls into my waters each year though. Not everyone, of course. Only those who believe the tale of the witch, the prince, and the spell that plucked him from the brink of death.

The mermaid stares at me. "Let me do it. Help me save her. Change me." She dares to grab my hand in the one that doesn't hold the knife. "Please, please. Please let me make this right. I can't lose Alia."

Something Tante Hansa once told me breaks loose from the memories of old, falling into the forefront of my mind.

Loneliness is the weakest excuse for magic there is, and it mixes horribly with pride and ignorance.

She'd meant it as a rebuke of me while I tried to help Annemette, yet I know this is different. This girl is lonely because this is her sister. Her twin. Her other half.

She's not prideful. She's not ignorant—she knows much more about the situation than I did about the girl I once knew. That much is for sure.

And she's given me every indication she will go through with murdering the king to save both her sister and the merpeople endangered by the U-boats and the mines.

My mind churns with all the possibilities. Who might live, who might die, what might become of the magical imbalance with another mermaid on land. With another exchange. It's a long shot, but we all might get what we want.

I add my other hand to the top of hers until we're holding each other like fish skewered through the belly on a pike. Her hand is warm and reminds me a little of home.

"I will change you, but listen closely." The girl's eyes widen with relief. "Here is what you must do. As I told you before, dying Øldenburg blood must fall on your sister's feet, shed by this knife. If that happens by the last moment of the fourth day—at sunrise, because that is when she ascended—she shall live. Though she can never become a mermaid again."

She swallows. "Never? Not even with this knife?"

"Not the terms of her deal. The magic is serious about exchange—the sea cannot take her back." I wrap a tentacle around the girl's waist. "Now, your deal is different."

I watch her eyes as I let that sink in. Her lip begins to tremble, and I don't blame her—she feels as if she's failed already because her sister can never again be a mermaid—but the girl's eyes remain fierce and steady.

"Your deal, Runa, is one of very specific action. You are there to help your sister, but still, Alia must kill the boy with this knife. I can't change that either. Her life was her bargain, not yours." This truth seems to puncture Runa's resiliency even more. "But having you there by her side, like you've always been, is the greatest power you have to give. Do you want me to go on?"

Runa swallows a sob and nods.

"After Alia allows the blood to fall on her feet for her survival, these are the things you must do to return to the sea: You must gather the boy's red stone ring and retrieve the knife. Then you must sprinkle the boy's blood on your own toes. Fail to do any of that by the close of the fourth full day after your arrival, including sending me the ring and the knife, and you will remain human forever."

She swallows. "I . . . I won't become foam in the tide? I'll become human if I fail?"

"Don't assume you will fail—you didn't come here to fail." She squeezes her eyes closed for a second and then she's right back with me. Good.

My tentacle slinks off her waist and my hands drop hers as she runs it over in her mind. It's a lot, true. And I gather that unlike Alia, the very last thing Runa ever wanted to be was human. But that was before she knew her sister might die. "Now, do you agree?"

She's nodding before the words are out. "Yes, I agree."

I watch her, making sure she means it. But she's unwavering under my hard stare. "Give me the knife."

Without a word, she extends the weapon. There's a little hesitation as I transfer the hilt to my hand and draw it close, inspecting the serrated edge, the coral so finely cut, it's almost translucent in its sharpness.

"Give me your hand."

The mermaid extends her left hand over my cauldron,

clever girl. She'd been holding the knife in her right, dominant, hand. She may trust me to change her, but she isn't so sure I won't send her topside missing an important appendage.

As a measure of good faith, I put a tentacle around her wrist instead, silky smooth and delicate. The cauldron is as deep and dark as the night, yet there's a heat rising from it—part of my particular magic. I place my own arm over the cauldron, so that our arms are side by side. Then, without warning or hesitation, I drag the knife over the skin of my palm. Blood, onyx dark, oozes into the flat gray of the water, molasses slow and sparking with the magic I hold within.

The girl's eyes stay on the knife as she waits, knowing that it will be her turn next. My blood drips onto her flat white palm in the moment before the knife breaks her skin. She doesn't move, recoil, or even wince, though blood as red as the flowers her sister gave me swirls into the gray. I smother her hand in mine and squeeze, our blood dripping into the pot's belly below as one.

With each drop, the cauldron softens with an inner light. It has the same silvery glow of a full moon on shallow waters, flashing mesmerizing rays into the starbursts of the girl's amber eyes. I take a deep breath, and then I let my voice echo off the polypi, deep and commanding, with all the power her flowers have afforded me.

"Líf. Saudi. Minn líf. Minn bjod. Seiðr. Seiðr. Seiðr."

As I say the final word of the spell, the cauldron trembles with light—blinding and brilliant and enough to turn this whole pewter-rendered world stark, shocking white.

When the spell is complete, the light recedes in an instant. From the depths of the cauldron, a silvery liquid swirls, as if the best pearls in the ocean had been melted down.

I bring a tentacle up before the two of us, a small bottle grasped there. It's much like the one I gave Alia. This one is light green in color, bringing all the power of the new spring sun. I dip the bottle into the potion, fill it to the top, and then stop it with a bit of cork.

"Take this draught in the shallows, so you shall not drown," I say, and then I give her one final reminder. "You have four days for yourself. Two for your sister. Ring, knife, blood."

With careful fingers, the girl seizes the bottle and the knife, pressing both to her heart, and repeats back what she must do. "Ring, knife, blood."

As she turns to go, I swear I hear her voice again, whispering a single refrain.

"I'm coming, Alia. I'm coming."

8

Runa

TOPSIDE, THE FIRST FINGERS OF DAYLIGHT SWIPE ACROSS
the horizon, a bright white light across the Øresund Strait,
the promise of the sun coming fast. The morning glow
touches the beaches of Havnestad, the mountains behind
the town lit only at the very tops, the rest in the steely tones
of the sea witch's lair.

The play of dawn would be beautiful if it didn't signal
another day gone for Alia.

I'm coming, Alia. I'm coming.

I cling to the shadows falling from the rocks that hug
the sea witch's black cove, the draught just as heavy in one
hand as the knife is in my other. I need a place to change.
I believe the sea witch that it would be best to take the
draught in the shallows. It's easy to picture Alia two dawns
previous, changing on the main beach, timing it just so to

coincide with the morning walks in which the king likes to indulge. She'd skipped breakfast for weeks on end just to watch him wander around, tossing sticks with his dogs, surveying his kingdom.

But from where I am, my view of Havnestad's main beach is already filled with townspeople. The docks beside the beach are alive with the sounds of men, cargo rolling along on horse-drawn carts tinkling with lantern light that won't be needed in a few minutes' time. Many of them carve a path straight up a skinny brick road that lines the ocean and leads up to Øldenburg Castle, carrying preparations for the wedding, I'm sure.

The rest of the beach is an ode to that occasion as well. Tiny paper lanterns are strung from poles in a regal square closer to the castle, the skeleton of a bonfire pit to one side, an altar to another. I'd once been told the Øldenburgs loved to be married at sea, on the decks of their great ships, but I suppose it would be rather disastrous if the wedding party struck a mine planted in the waters its groom believed he owned.

I don't see the boy on his morning walk, not yet, though he will likely be there soon. And maybe with Alia, if I'm lucky. I tuck the knife and bottle safely within my bodice, tight against the beating of my heart and the ríkifjor seeds I placed there before returning to the witch's lair. My precious cargo safe, I swim around the black cove and to the other side of Havnestad, toward the sea entrance to the castle with its marble balcony. Cliff faces meet the waters here, so different from the rest of paper-flat Denmark, this little kingdom.

Around this side, not yet to the castle's channel, there's a strange arch of stone, yawning over a fissure between the rocks. The water streaming under it is deep and sure, and I swim through, coming up onto a little lagoon. On a sliver of beach, between two large boulders, standing sentry at its mouth, is a tiny cave. To one side is a steep stairway of stone and switchbacks, leading up to the cliff. I strain my eyes in the low light to see exactly where it leads, but there are only trees, shading the clifftop from view of the castle above.

Yes, this will do.

But first, I'll need clothing.

The witch gave me nothing to wear, so I must make it myself, using what is around. Which isn't much. Sand, rocks, and water. But under the surface—that's something I can use. And so, I spend the rest of dawn pulling seaweed from the lagoon. It's not much, but it's just enough for a skirt to go with my sea bodice.

My bodice is a salt-water ivory, the color of a seal tusk, spelled together with the sheen of a thousand pearls by Eydis, who won't have any of her sisters wearing everyday canvas. Considering the silks and stays that Alia was wearing in the castle yesterday morning, it's a good thing Eydis has such exacting standards.

—77

Once I have enough seaweed—dark green and thrumming with the closing summer—I lay it all out on the beach and close my eyes.

"*Snúa. Efni.*" I command.

A cool whiff of magic settles against my skin, my confidence spiking.

My magic works here.

My eyes fly open, and I watch, repeating the spell over and over, as the magic does its job, weaving each length of seaweed upon itself, twisting and braiding, each piece drying lacquer-hard once put in its proper place.

"*Snúa. Efni.*"

"*Snúa. Efni.*"

"*Snúa. Efni.*"

Soon enough, the seaweed has thatched itself into a skirt that is actually quite beautiful—as deep and shiny as the best emeralds. I wind it around my waist, securing it with one last fat piece of seaweed that finishes the dress like a silken ribbon. It feels a little strange—having something besides water flowing over my tail. There's some seaweed left over, and I set it aside on the beach as I come into the shallows—someone will surely have a use for it.

Pleased, I remove the knife and the draught—half of me above water and half of me below. The bottle catches in the light streaming over the rocks, the sun that much higher now, though the light is still blue with the receding night. The potion within glows like the moon on a clear night—so opaque as to be nearly white, shining as if it has a life of its own. Maybe it does.

I take one last look at my tail fin, sighing in the sand here beneath the hem of my new dress.

"Don't look at me like that," I tell it. "I'll get you back."

I pop the cork and let it fall into the water.

Bottoms up.

The liquid is cool to the touch but burns going down— fire water coating my tongue, throat, and belly. The warmth spreads across my body in the length of time that it takes for a bullet to explode from a pistol. And, suddenly, I'm the sun itself, pulsing and strobing with heat we rarely feel in the sea.

I cling to the knife in my hand, willing myself not to drop it, my fingers sweltering themselves numb, the bottle already dropped, my concentration only enough for one. I'm melting. I'm as liquid as the sea—hot, warm, steaming. Only the knife is solid; fire is what it bends to and I am fire. Fire and fury and nothing at all.

All of it is intense enough that I wonder whether, in my anger and desperation, I've made a huge error. If the sea witch concocted a potion to end me, not aid me. Some old grudge mingling with a new one for Father's recent attack, killing off two of the sea king's children in one easy swipe. But just as that thought crystallizes, the heat backs off. The warmth cools into something hard. Solid.

Legs.

Bones and muscles and tendons and arteries and veins. Ankles and toes.

My lungs sputter in my chest, no longer suitable for both worlds. Made for only one, and it's not my home. I gasp in as much air as my lungs can hold, suddenly in need though I haven't been underwater for several minutes. Somehow without my mermaid body, the air temperature is much colder, and I immediately begin to shiver, the adrenaline coursing through my veins notwithstanding.

I push myself up out of the lapping tide, new legs wobbling under my weight, my toes digging into the uneven sand below. It's almost stunning to me that I'm whole and solid. I look down past my seaweed skirt to those toes, flashing white. I am human. And now my clock is ticking right along with Alia's.

I test out my stride, taking a few uneasy steps. The shifting nature of the sands under my feet doesn't help before I nearly fall over. And then I realize that even if I figure out how to walk, I still won't be right. I need shoes.

I backpedal and retrieve those extra wisps of seaweed.

"*Snúa. Efni.*" I say the spell, but . . . something's *distant* about the magic I've called forth.

"*Snúa. Efni.*" I repeat, thinking it might improve things.

It does, but the distance stays, even as the seaweed begins to obey, weaving itself into one slipper and then another.

I keep reaching, reaching, reaching, for the magic as

it works. It hears me, but it's from across the room, not within my veins. After much longer than I'd expected—several minutes longer than it took the magic to create my entire skirt—my shoes are made. They aren't durable in the least, but they should do for now.

When I'm finished, the sky has evened out into a lush blue, the warmth of dawn gone. Another day begun. Two days behind. Time to find Alia.

9

Runa

THE STAIRS AND SWITCHBACKS ARE AN IMMEDIATE test for this strange new body of mine. Nubby rocks and wayward roots tear at the soles of my slippers. My calves and thighs stretch and constrict with the movement as I climb, the lagoon growing smaller with each step. There's no railing of any kind, so I balance with my hands out, the knife and the little ríkifjor bag cinched safely against my breastbone.

By the time I reach the top of the cliff, I'm breathing hard on my unfamiliar lungs. I pause for a moment to catch my breath and stare out at the Øresund Strait twinkling in the sunlight. But I don't have time to stand around. Once my breath settles into a more normal rhythm, I turn my back to the ocean and pick my way along the path leading from the stairs.

I've been taught that autumn brings leaves to the ground,

but here they still cling to their limbs, green but on the cusp of turning, dense and content in the new day's sun. Through them, I can only view snatches of the castle on the hill. Still, I'm not yet skilled enough to walk and look up without tripping, so I point my eyes to the ground, watching each step for an errant root. The brush snags at my dress, and it occurs to me that I must be very careful here—entering the king's company as a stranger will be hard enough, and if I look as if I've been spit out of the forest, that most definitely will sound the alarm.

As I walk along, I try to fix my hair, knowing a cut this short won't help me in the least—it's unusual, and not in a good way. But with every spell I can think of, the magic doesn't change it. Nothing changes it. It'll have to do.

I soon come to a cottage, sitting squat under the trees. It's small and old, and I know without even peeking through the shutters that it's abandoned. For some reason this makes me think of Niklas and his shiny objects—how can humans love things so much when they're alive and then let them rot when they're gone? Do they treat their people this way, or just the other things they collect in a lifetime?

Past the cottage is a more defined path of cobblestones gone slick with time, zippered together like crooked teeth, padded on either side by overgrown grass. Where the cobblestones meet the road, heavier bricks run all along the waterfront—along the beach, past the lighthouse and docks—and wind up the hill toward the castle and the town proper, with its witch-hat roofs and cheery paint.

I hesitate for a moment, thinking of Niklas's beach walks and the possibility that Alia might attend. Even without knowing the terms of Alia's magic, the king must not be daft enough to believe he can enjoy beach walks and sweet kisses with his "foundling" after the arrival of his bride-to-be. If he can't or won't understand that, his wife might kill him, unless Alia and I get to him first.

I turn for the castle. It sits heavy on the hill, perfectly square, with turrets on each side. Manicured lawns of an almost otherworldly green bleed out from the base, stopping only for forced boundaries—the sea lane, the ocean itself, and a row of rather stately looking homes that butts up against the grounds like a doorstop.

The castle guard is out in force on one lawn, shoes shining and hair smooshed in place, as they run through a formation that I can only imagine is intended for the wedding.

For all the guard's organization, everything else is abject chaos. People are running every which way, unloading carts from the docks—bolts of fabric, hand trucks of out-of-season fruits, taper candles by the armful. They're even unloading people, uniformed valets rushing to guide silken ladies and starched gentlemen out of motorcars and up manicured paths.

Chaos provides cover, and for this I am extremely

grateful. Swallowing a deep breath, I plaster a smile upon myself and fold in with a school of men and women in fancy dress. My attire is light compared to what they're wearing—I need to find something with sleeves or a shawl fast—but I say a little prayer again to Urda for Eydis's sense of flair. The pearls on the bodice save me, as does the magic that wove my skirt.

The procession of wedding guests slows to a stop just past the doors, where castle guards check each name on parchment. A flurry of titles in multiple languages streams past their lips. Most are Danish and German.

Hertug. Markis. Greve. Friherre. Baron.

Herzog. Pfalzgraf. Markgraf. Reichsfreiherr. Herr.

I tuck in behind two maids heading in the direction of the marble balcony. I don't know where Alia will be, but if the king truly is the man of habit that Alia witnessed, it's as good an assumption as I can make.

But an assumption, a smile, and a passable dress only get me so far.

"May I help you?"

I freeze at the sound of a man's voice, calling to me from the intersection of the hall I just passed. I reset my smile and check that my chin is held high before presenting myself.

I grit my teeth and turn . . . and it's him.

The boy from the balcony with the nice smile and hushed tones.

Will.

Light brown hair, combed nicely to the side. Blue eyes like the tide in dusk. Broad shoulders that remind me of Father more than they should.

I brace for an admonishment, the story I'd prepared on my journey here ready on my tongue. But then Will tosses that handsome smile at me, and I realize I'm not a suspect—he's trying to be friendly. My luck is so stunning that I fumble over my words for a second. "I—I, yes," I say. "I'm looking for Alia."

His mouth wavers a bit, and I recognize my error. I swallow and try again. It would help greatly if he didn't look at me like that.

"Excuse me, let me try again," I meet his smile. "My friend," I start, because I know Alia can answer yes or no questions, and she might have said she was without a family. "She's been missing two days, and I've tracked her here. She's unable to speak, but her name is Alia."

The boy's eyes light up, and there's a devilish crinkle to his nose. "Oh, yes, I know exactly who you're talking about—I think everyone this side of Lille Bjerg Pass knows." To my relief, a small laugh escapes the boy. "The king will be pleased that you're here . . ."

He trails off, and I realize he wants my name. "Runa. I'm Runa."

"Runa the rescuer," he says with another little laugh, and a warmth spreads across my belly because he doesn't know how right I hope he is. "I'm William, but you can call me Will." He extends an arm, his jacket dark and perfect. "Come with me. I just left them."

I take his arm, and for some reason that makes it more difficult to walk. As if I'm thrown off-balance by the mere closeness of him. I'm not the type of girl who prances around on a boy's arm. It strikes me as for show, and maybe it is—a castle like this and a king like that and maybe everything is put on like a moon play.

Will walks me through the castle, all the while making small talk, and I'm grateful because he's inadvertently giving me hints that are enough to adjust the story I have in my head about who Alia is and where she came from.

"He found her washed ashore two days ago, wearing this old ball gown. Niklas—the king—said it looked like she'd stepped right out of an old photograph and onto the sand."

The warmth in my stomach grows when I realize that maybe the sea witch hadn't sent Alia into the lion's den completely unprepared—she hadn't given me clothes to cover my own nakedness, but the witch must have shared a relic from her day to keep Alia from stumbling onto the beach nude. I suppose that was a kindness.

"She has a particular love of yesteryear fashion . . . and dancing."

"I'd say Niklas appreciates both." He laughs again, but then lowers his voice to a conspiratorial whisper. "Honestly, if it weren't my own cousin marrying him, I'd have mistaken her for the bride. He's quite taken with her." I work to keep my features calm—if only the magic had given her forty days and not four. "But don't tell Sofie that or she'll toss me off the balcony."

Will guides me up a staircase and down a hall, and just as we're about to head into what looks to be yet another ballroom, Alia sweeps into the hallway too. Her face is pointed toward the floorboards and is a wreck—unprepared for company, and definitely not for me.

I warn her the only way I can. "Alia! Oh, my darling *friend*, I was so worried about you!" I untangle myself from Will and rush to her as her head flies up. I catch her in an embrace, and, before a reaction can spread across her face, it's buried in the crook of my neck.

"I'm here. It's going to be all right. Please don't be mad." I squeeze her one more time. "Smile."

We part, and Alia presents herself to Will. Suddenly her eyes are alight—animated.

"As soon as I heard where you were, I came looking. Did not a one of the hofdames make it?" Will perks up at the court term for ladies-in-waiting.

I'm unsure if they've asked Alia of her heritage, but I know one thing—if she's in love with a king and staying at his castle, we must make sure she's invited to this stupid wedding. A whiff of nobility is the best way to go.

Alia shakes her head, and I moan dramatically at the

loss of the ship and the people, and that my friend was alone for so long. I really should've heeded Alia's pleas and tried my hand at acting with her. "Oh, no. Dear, I'm so sorry." I hug her again, and catch eyes with Will, who seems genuinely touched. "I am so glad you are safe."

"I'll get His Highness," Will says, walking past us and through double doors into the ballroom.

When he's gone, Alia extracts herself from me and pins her eyes on mine, pointing quickly to her lips. She wants to use a word we don't have in signs. *Sacrifice.*

Like the day before, Alia makes the sign for *witch*, and then presses her hand to her throat. Then, she touches the ends of my wrecked hair in question.

She wants to know what I gave up to be here. If not my voice, then what?

The questions continue, pieced together in signs and mouthed words.

What else did you sacrifice? Your hair? It looks stupid. Why on earth would you let her do that? Why on earth would you come here at all? Runa, this is too dangerous. What were you thinking? Were you thinking?

"I—"

A peal of laughter stops my explanation dead in its tracks. "Alia! Her name is Alia? Bring her here—I must see her."

Will appears and leads both of us into the ballroom, and toward a titter of amusement. The chandeliers glow though daylight streams in through more double doors that lead onto a balcony. The king is surrounded by maids, setting up the room for a grand feast.

"My foundling does have a name!" His dimples flash, and he takes Alia by the hand, twirling her under the twinkling lights. His amusement is enough that no one in the room can avoid it. After the spin, he crushes her into a quick embrace. It seems more intimate than the kiss on the balcony, and I catch Will looking away as I do the same.

When they separate, he places his hands gently on her shoulders. "And it is a lovely name indeed." My sister can't help it, a smile melts across her face—whatever had made her upset when we saw her in the hallway is gone. Niklas seems pleased at that. He turns to present himself to me.

"And you're her friend? Runa, is it?" His delight flashes my way, and it's nearly as blinding as the sun. "I'm King Niklas, but please do call me Niklas—there's no need for titles among friends."

I didn't expect him to be so warm. I really didn't. Not from any look I've had at him—far away, up close, nor through Alia's moon-eyed descriptions.

I clear my throat. "Runa—yes, Your Highness," I say, and he seems to like the title even though he just shrugged it off. Men always prefer titles that make them sound important, and anything else is a lie. "I came in search of her when her party didn't arrive, and I've been so worried. It's very fortunate that you found her and took her in—thank you for your kind hospitality."

"Oh, Runa, you'll have to answer all the questions that Alia"—he pauses on yet another chance to say her name, before continuing—"has been unable to answer for me." Then something occurs to him, and his eyes shift from mine to Alia's and back. "Oh, please tell me she can stay for a few days more. You won't be stealing her back to Helsingør right off, will you?"

Helsingør. They must have had Alia point at a map. So that's where we're from, then.

I glance at Alia to make like I'm double-checking, and then I say, "We'd love to stay, but we don't want to be a bother—I hear you're to be married. Congratulations."

When Niklas answers, it's to Alia, whose hands he holds in both of his. The joy has softened in his voice, and it seems as though he's momentarily forgotten that both Will and I are standing there. I look at my hands. I can't watch him be so caring—not with the knife meant to murder him pressed against my ribs.

"Please stay. And please come to the wedding."

Oh, Urda. He *is* charming. With his stupid eyes and his stupid dimples and his stupid broad shoulders. It's true.

And maybe he does really care for Alia.

But even if she had her voice and could tell him what she'd done and how she loves him—even if I could betray our kind by telling him myself—four days to love relies on him. He must love her. He must feel enough that the magic has no choice but to bend to the will of his heart. Not hers. The burden of proof is on his stupid head, and Alia's picked a man who may never see it.

I hate it, but my mind jumps to our father. Despite his now monstrous ways, he was once a man who fell so deeply in love, so quickly, that he changed a woman in the minute before she drowned. But that sort of instant, powerful love is rare, and sadly, that love isn't this love. Niklas's love won't be powerful enough—not in an instant, not in four days, and most certainly not with the roadblocks of duty, war, and obligation. Still, Alia nods, and he pulls her into yet another heartbreaking hug.

There's a commotion behind us. I turn, and Will is offering his own embrace to a woman escorted by the other boy from the balcony. Phillip. I hear a girl's sweet voice say, "They told me you were coming to greet me, Cousin!"

When he releases her, it's to present her, his hand holding hers aloft, and I can already sense Alia's heart sinking. Will smiles at the girl and then at his friend and soon-to-be cousin. "My good king, Komtesse Sofie of the Duchy of Holsten has finally arrived."

10

Runa

ALIA AND I DO OUR CURTSIES AND HOLD OUR SMILES AS the three of them catch up.

Cousins Will and Sofie have the same rosy cheeks and light brown hair, but it's clear right away that Will and Niklas know each other much better than either knows Sofie. Still, they've existed in the same constellation for all their lives, some upper echelon of culture not hampered by kingdom lines. The right name, the right blood, and immediate trust is given. It's the same below the surface.

I wish to hate everything about this girl just like I do Niklas, but she's so enthusiastic, it's almost impossible not to be moved by her energy. She laughs with her whole body, her Danish touched by the German so common in Holsten. Plus, she has a book in her grip—by the look of it, *Effi Briest*—and honestly, there's nothing I love more than reading. But this girl is not meant to be my friend. And certainly not Alia's.

It isn't long after Sofie's arrival that Alia's features falter. Tears threaten, and she tosses me a sign by way of explanation. *Garden*.

"If you will excuse us," I interrupt the reunion, "Alia tells me you have a beautiful garden on the grounds, and I'd very much like to take it in."

Alia snatches my hand and pulls me out before either boy can offer to come. But just as we hit the relative darkness of the hallway, we hear Sofie's voice. "Ladies, you don't mind if I come along, do you? I am in need of fresh air." I force Alia to stop her determined pace and play polite. Sofie catches up. "I still feel like I'm in that motorcar. My head is simply spinning from all those winding roads over the pass."

"Of course," I say, both of us grinning wide. "Please come, Komtesse Sofie."

"Thank you. My room is not quite ready yet—my hofdames are quite particular." She shoots Alia a knowing look. "And I think the boys could use some time together."

Alia nods, but it's not convincing. We need time alone, but we can't make Sofie our enemy any more than she will be after she matches the embrace she must have witnessed with the castle gossip about Alia and Niklas. I paste on the smile Sofie is seeking and grasp her hand. "And so could the girls."

This appeases Sofie, and we wander down the stairs and through the halls, Alia mostly leading the way. She's always had a fine internal compass, and using it on land seems to be no different. Maids swirl around us, minnows flitting down a stream. They run about, hanging grand twists of fabric from the bolts I saw earlier. Others fill each sconce with a fresh taper, and replace rugs just beaten in the breeze. Nearly everything is the same shade of blue as their uniforms. The decor is overpowering; they've nearly re-created the blue cast that sits over the sea king's palace, one scrap of fabric, yard of rug, and taper at a time.

"What do you think of the wedding decorations?" I ask as means of small talk. "I hope you like *blue*."

Sofie's green eyes snag on a rope of velvet being hung over the door facing the garden. "I do . . . ," she says as we head under the new rope and out the doors to a small landing. "But it's a bit much. I fear everything will be blue—the rings, the cake, the wine. If the fish at dinner tonight is blue, save me some extra rolls, will you? Because I just can't eat that."

"Got that, Alia? Bread for the blue bride." Alia gives a thumbs-up as we pick our way down the steps.

Despite the end of summer, the garden is still lush, the rosebushes mature and thick with blooms of all colors. Red, pink, white, and yellow dominate, patterned throughout the garden like so much lace.

"Now this is colorful," I say, mostly because I have to

keep this going—it's too early to send Sofie away. Next to me, I can feel Alia's unease. There's a pinch in her brow, and I know she's thinking about how much I haven't said.

Sacrifice.

But we must play this game.

"They once had tulips here, I'm told," Sofie says, inspecting a bush of pink blooms, still striking, their thorns thick and deadly. She smiles at us. "But a past king ripped them out because they reminded him of a broken heart."

The sea witch's face plays in my mind. Her prince, who became king with her sacrifice. Annemette.

"Niklas said he wanted roses because they show all of love's parts—the beauty, the longevity . . ." She snaps one off and holds it up, one pristine finger hovering over a rather jagged thorn. "The pain." Sofie smiles, and something stirs within me.

"But there should be no pain for you; you're to be married to a king!" I say, trying to keep things light, though I want nothing more than to end this conversation right this very instant. Next to me, Alia squirms.

"Isn't there pain in a choice that is meant to be forever? Forever is both a promise and an end."

An end. Her eyes linger on Alia, and it's clear now this girl already knows the castle gossip. She knew it before she set foot in the building today. And she's not about to let Niklas's relationship with Alia go a second farther.

We come to a bench, shaded from the noon sky by a

large tree. Sofie sits and invites Alia to her side with a little pat. When she does, I hover over their shoulders like the ghost that I am as Sofie takes my sister's hand in hers.

"Your father is a titular baron, no?" She smiles as Alia nods, and then her eyes fall to Alia's hand, soft in her palm. "Even so, you'll be in my place soon. It won't be your choice to make—fathers like ours retain and expand their power by promising away their little girls."

This is true. I still refuse to like Sofie, but I can relate to her. Alia's lip quivers—she can relate too.

"And though I don't necessarily appreciate my lot, I plan on being successfully married in a day's time." Sofie's grip tightens, and I have a sudden urge to take Alia and run. If only. The komtesse's eyes flash up. "The king may like your face and your silence, Alia, but he likes the money and connections from my father more. Let go now, or the pain will be so much worse."

Alia visibly jerks at the bluntness of it all, her shoulders sweeping back as she rips her hand away. She's standing before I blink, and she bumps me, off-balance.

Alia runs toward the garden gate and is through it without a second glance.

Sofie doesn't rise to chase down Alia, which is simply fine by me. I pick up the length of my dress to free my feet and try my best at a run. The feeling is even worse than walking, this strange, unsmooth propulsion forward accompanied by a pain similar to being stabbed over and over with each step. I careen through the gate, lucky it didn't latch and stop me dead in my tracks. Alia is already far ahead, and I need to sprint. With each breath, I picture the children I've seen on the beach, running with such surety that their legs won't tangle and instantly drop them in the sand. It's a slow start, but I soon catch up, a much uglier runner than my sister, but just as quick, as it turns out.

"Alia." I catch her just as she's turned for the town proper, her hunched shoulders and sadness-flushed cheeks all wrong against the bright colors of the buildings. "Alia, she's not wrong. It was cruel but it's true. You know it."

She spins around to the hand I've placed on her shoulder, her face a mess and lips trembling. She looks me dead in the eye, and I know she doesn't hate me for what I've just said.

Alia knows it's true too.

I expect her to say it but then she signs something else. *Why? Why are you here? Why, if it's true, did you do this? Why did you see the witch? Why did you make a deal?*

Yet another "why" in the shape of her fingers, she finally falls into wracking, silent sobs, and collapses into me. The heaviness in her heart pulls her off-center. I nearly fall back under the weight of her, but I will my new legs to be strong. Her shoulders heave and shake as I lean us against the nearest building.

I kiss her hair with all the love and fierceness I hope

she can see. "Alia, listen to me. I didn't sacrifice my voice, no. But I did make a deal with the witch."

She pulls back and points a finger to her chest.

For me.

"Always for you. Without you, there is no me."

Alia shakes her head hard enough to rip free of my embrace. She falls against the wall.

No. No. No—you shouldn't have.

"It's done. I'm here." I grab her hand and will her to look at me, not to get stuck in the weeds of guilt. "You want me to survive? You need to survive too."

Alia draws in a breath as big as the sun, closing her eyes as her lungs fill and then release. She opens her eyes, and they're on mine—ice blue on amber, two pieces of one whole. Alia remains still long enough that I wonder if we'll spend the next two days like this, in a silent showdown. Finally, she pushes my hair behind my ears, and I can tell she is distracting herself from this decision by focusing on my haircut.

What must we do?

And so I tell her. Of the knife. The ring. The blood. When I'm done, she raises a brow, still trying to make sense of the exchange. Of how what she gave equals what I did in the witch's magical equation.

It's then that I tell her the rest. Of Father's wrath. The injured witch. The ríkifjor seeds from her garden. Our sisters' sacrifices—surely if I can't magic my hair back, neither can they . . . and Father will notice.

Your hair really does look stupid, she says, but it's just a deflection.

With each passing detail it all seems to sink in. The flush in Alia's cheeks pales, her lip trembles. The cords of her neck tense and release. She signs a final question.

If we fail, you won't die, like me? Instead, you'll be human?

I thought Niklas's rejection would hurt her the most—that I came because I knew she wouldn't be enough to gain the love she wants so badly—but now my opinion wavers. By the looks of it, the fact that I will be human if I fail when she would be human if she succeeds is just as heartbreaking.

"Yes," I say softly. "If I fail, I'm doomed to be human. But if you fail, I won't want to live—above or below, it will all be too painful."

When I'm finished, she's looking me straight in the eyes. And maybe it's because she's realized now that we've always been together and always should be. Maybe it's because she knows there's no other way. Or maybe it's just because she loves me. But she nods.

King Asger Niklas Bryniulf Øldenburg V must die.

11

Runa

WE MUST SATISFY VERY SPECIFIC MAGICAL CRITERIA. IF we do anything else, we're murderers plain and simple. Maybe we are anyway. I don't know.

All I do know is, we don't have a choice.

Still, it's not easy to think about. If I break it into its components—murder, blood magic, theft, fleeing the scene of the crime—it becomes hard to see the good in it. The point. The ends, justified by the means.

If we fulfill the magic's requirements, Alia will live and I will go home. But a man will be . . .

I can't—we can't—think of it as anything other than what we must do.

All that remains now is *when* the deed will be done.

If I'd thought we could've gotten out alive, I would've grabbed Alia's hand the second she nodded, marched into the castle, and made her end it. But that would've been a mistake—we returned to an impossible parade of banquets and teas and beach bonfires with literally everyone in the kingdom, witnesses all.

Yet the longer we wait for just the right moment, the longer we spend with the people who will suffer once we're successful. Each kindness, each smile, each minute seeing a little of ourselves in them curls at the edges of my determination.

So we decide to wait until the sun goes down, take the king in his sleep that night.

With any luck, his chambers will be bare beyond his beating heart, his ring will be close at hand, and an exit will be available.

But that plan is scattered after the supper bonfire, when we learn something more about Havnestad culture. It's tradition for the castle and all its rooms to be left to the bride the night before a wedding. Good luck or something. It certainly proved to be for the groom, who would instead board a motorcar with his groomsmen—Will, Phillip, and other laughing lads—for a property in the valley beyond Lille Bjerg Pass.

In fact, because tradition insists, we won't even *see* Niklas until the ceremony.

So, now as the new morning turns into the afternoon, we've lost an entire day. Our only chance at success is tonight—the bridegroom's wedding night. Mere hours before the sunrise that will take my sister if we fail.

Despite what the sea witch thinks, I do believe in love—I've just never experienced the romantic kind. Still, I know Alia's heart as well as my own. I know her love is intense, and so taking a knife to Niklas will undoubtedly be heart-wrenching, though doing so as he lies next to his new wife I fear will be even worse.

But again, we have no choice. By the time the sun comes up tomorrow, the king must be dead, or Alia will be.

I take a deep breath in front of the mirror in Alia's room. I'm trussed up in a modern human gown—Havnestad blue, cinched by a rib-breaking corset, courtesy of our hosts. I might as well be yet another one of the decorations. The knife is still tucked against my breastbone, thin, cool coral pressing on my skin, and the ríkifjor seeds lie flat in their pouch against the small of my back.

While Alia is dressed just as I, she wears her heartbreak heavily in the set of her shoulders, the line of her lips, her downcast eyes. Even her hair seems to droop toward the earth, her curls lying limp down her back.

"We have to go to the wedding," I implore her. "There will be too many questions if we're not there."

Alia shrugs exaggeratedly and flops back on the bed, fully dressed thanks only to the maids assigned to each guest's room. Her hands fly through a flurry of frustrated gestures. No translation needed.

It doesn't matter. Who cares if there are questions? We'll murder him and then disappear. It will help us not to be around.

"No. No. If—when—we succeed, you will still be on land. And when you disappear, you'll certainly be a suspect."

No one will suspect a woman.

"Are you kidding? Were you not paying attention during our lessons? No one fears a woman when she's a docile, dancing object, but the second she's scorned? She's a hysterical danger to herself and others."

From her bed, she shrugs violently yet again. *Let them think that.*

"They will see you as a girl so in love with the king that if you can't have him, you don't want anyone to have him. You'll be suspect number one."

Who cares?

"It isn't a victory for you to live the rest of your days and spend them hunted." I sit down beside her. "We need to ensure you're safe."

Finally, she doesn't shrug. But she doesn't react at all except to shut her eyes.

I place a hand on her leg. "What do you want to do with your life once you're human?"

I expect another shrug. Maybe some renewed blubbering about how there's nothing to live for without Niklas at her side. Instead, she pushes herself up onto her elbows, and then shoves back against the headboard, freeing her hands.

Again, she signs *witch* but points at herself. She's not talking about the sea witch. She runs through gesture after gesture, more animated than I've seen her since I've been here.

In a minute, I've got it.

Alia wants to be a powerful witch. Under the sea, she's the ninth daughter of the sea king. Something to be married off for an alliance—like Sofie. She wants the freedom to make a name for herself. For her magic to thrive in a place that's been systematically stripped of its power for hundreds of years—the witch-hunter king; Sankt Hans Aften; burnings, drownings, banishments. For all the magic in every drop of sea water, there's almost nothing above. She could change that.

I smile down at her. "Yes, you'll be a great witch. To do that, we must survive this first."

I don't have the heart to ask her if she's tried her hand at magic without her voice. To see if it affects her, if it only adds to the distance I feel—or if she can do it at all. I also don't have the heart to remind her that Annemette lost her magic the second she became fully human again. Though perhaps that was because her true human form, Anna, was never a witch at all, and Annemette's mermaid powers were not hers to keep.

Alia takes a deep breath and swings her legs over the edge of the bed. Ready to go.

Finally. We're late.

We quickly wind our way through the empty corridors. All the guests have surely already gathered on the beach. Alia points me down small hallway, a shortcut to the courtyard, when a voice rings out.

"I don't. I don't have to. It isn't necessary. You heard Father, it's all set up anyway—"

Sofie.

Then another girl's voice meets hers. "Dearest, they're all waiting for you." The hard-edged lilt to the girl's consonants tells me it's Agnata, one of Sofie's hofdames. We were seated across from each other at the women's feast yesterday. "You can't disappoint them."

"The people won't care if he marries me or anyone else. In fact, it might be best if I don't show up. Then this is purely a financial transaction."

Alia's eyes meet mine, and suddenly they're shot through with glee. On her lips is a particularly human question: *Cold feet?*

There's some rustling, and a footman appears. Alia greets him with a wild smile, and I wave, and hope he didn't see us standing there, still as stone, listening in. We burst out of the doors, all but running. Our hearts are pounding as we hit the cobblestones of the sea lane that leads down to the main beach. The wedding canopy comes into view, and the smile falls off Alia's lips. She grabs my hand and repeats, almost as a silent chant: *Cold feet. Cold feet. Cold feet.*

As guests of the castle, we're placed on the groom's side, in the very last row of the covered seating, new friends that we are. Around the edge of the canopy, thousands of citizens mingle as if they're at a sporting match, the lot of them sprawling out onto the beach, seated on woven blankets and the sun-warm sand.

Not two minutes after we're seated, Niklas reappears, no worse for wear from his boys' night. His hair shines dark and is styled with care, a crown fat with sapphires upon his head as he smiles from the altar, dimples flashing along.

Alia spots him before I do, and everything about her goes still and rigid beside me. I know she's seeing the boy she's dreamed about for more than a year exactly as she hoped he'd be someday with her at his side. Again, she mouths her refrain, hope in her eyes for the first time since it died on the marble balcony. *Cold feet. Cold feet. Cold feet.*

Niklas settles in next to the chaplain and turns to face the crowd. My breath catches as he immediately finds Alia in the crowd. Though we're in the back and dressed in Havnestad blue like the majority of the groom's guests, he can't help but be drawn to her. To look at her. He meets her eyes, and for a moment, my heart flutters, just as it did that day on the balcony.

Maybe there's a chance.

Maybe he really does love Alia.

Maybe that love is enough that he'll stop this wedding farce and bring Alia up there instead, marrying her with a kiss so fierce, the magic has no choice but to be satisfied.

Maybe the only sad part of the story is that I will remain human against my will. If Alia is happy and survives, that will be enough for me.

But then, as quickly as their eyes met, Niklas forces himself to look away. His gaze finds the tips of his polished boots. His hands remain crisply folded behind his back. And that swoop of hope in my heart crashes into the sand. He's going to go through with it.

As if in confirmation, Niklas's eyes sweep up again, and he smiles. The whole crowd gasps, and we don't need to turn to know what he sees. What they all see. Sofie has arrived, cold feet and all.

At my side, Alia begins trembling hard enough that I grab her hand to steady her in her seat. Suddenly I hate Niklas so much that in that moment I wish we had time to make him suffer. To experience an ounce of what Alia feels in her heart right now. Alia's whole body shifts toward mine, words ready to be formed without sound. Her eyes are big and round, purple shadows of her sleeplessness carving moons beneath her lashes.

He loves me.

I shake my head and force my voice to stay a whisper,

hundreds of ears around us now. "If he loved you, he wouldn't put you through this."

Alia's mouth sets into a tight line, her brows pulling together hard and quick. She shakes her head and then her hands and lips and the entire hang of her body is throwing herself into what she wants to say.

Look at how he watches me. Look at how he's drawn to me. He. Loves. Me.

"Alia," I say, my voice barely above a whisper. "Whatever he may think of you, it's not enough."

Her lips quiver in response.

"It'll be all right, Alia," I insist, gripping her cool fingers tightly. "We'll be all right."

I hope I'm not telling her a lie.

The band strikes up, and Alia's eyes squeeze shut and she resets our hands so that she's gripping me as hard as possible.

Sofie sweeps down the aisle on the arm of a man who must be her father—Baron Gerhard—but who seems so slight that a strong gust might blow him all the way to Rigeby Bay. It's hard to believe this man holds so much power over Niklas—his heart, his love, his life. But there he is, same moss-green eyes as Sofie's twinkling in the salmon light of dusk, as he deposits her beside the young king.

The ceremony is blessedly short. And then comes what everyone is waiting for. Niklas removes Sofie's veil, pushing it over her hair to reveal her face. It's polished with a smile, no ounce of the doubt and frustration we heard from her before. Then he bends down and, without hesitation, plants a kiss on her upturned lips.

Next to me, all the tension in Alia's grip fades. I tear my eyes away just as Alia's body goes slack.

12

Runa

"ALIA," I WHISPER-BEG INTO HER EAR. "WAKE UP. YOU
can't do this. Hysterical woman, remember? Fainting
is most definitely high on the list of hysteria symptoms.
Please."

Her head knocks heavily on my shoulder. She doesn't
hear me. She doesn't move. Everything about her has given
out; that moment of hope made everything worse.

The audience is standing, clapping—another dagger.

The king and his bride turn, newly ringed fingers
pressed together and raised aloft, as they present their
union to the masses. I'm partially pleased Alia won't see it
and be completely horrified. Around us, everyone shoots
to their feet. We can't be seated.

If someone hasn't noticed her out cold by now, they
soon will. I yank her up, wrapping an arm around her

shoulder blades. Her head lolls into the crook of my neck. Niklas's attention is shifting from Sofie to the crowd, and I know he'll look for her first. He can't help himself.

He can't see her like this. No one can see her like this— if a physician is called, Alia will be under observation all night. The king will see to it.

I lean into her ear. *"Vaka."* I whisper the spell softly, but deliberately. Wake.

Alia's eyes flutter open with a start. Her head jerks off my shoulder, and I plaster a smile on my face as an order to her. A veteran of moon plays, she knows exactly when to take a hint and improvise, quick wits and all.

Her face mirrors mine just as Niklas's eyes find hers.

Yes, your foundling is still here. Still looking at you like that. Still wanting you.

The boy king smiles, and next to him Sofie does too.

They head down the aisle, and when they hit the last row, so close that Alia could reach out and touch the fine cut of Niklas's suit, her body grows light again. Liquid next to me, as if she might dissolve right there, taken by the sand into the other world.

Yet my sister holds fast. Strong thing that she is. Brave thing. She meets his eyes with all her beauty and love and promise, and for a moment, he can't look away. He watches long enough that Sofie's gaze follows his. As they pass us, they're both looking at my sister, holding her ground.

Still here. Still in love.

Per tradition, the bride and groom lead their wedding guests—the seated attendees only—up to the castle. The common people line the sea lane, pressing in thick layers against the progression. Even at a distance, the mass joy among them rattles my teeth as they sing old sailors' songs that we know even under the surface.

All the smartly dressed guests flow up the brick-lined paths and into the castle under the indigo of a new night, torches as old as the castle itself ringing the great stone walls of the place.

But we wait them out. Though revived, Alia is still wobbly on her feet. When we're finally ushered out of our seats, we split off through the masses and cut onto a lonely corner of the beach to sit for a moment under the stars.

We face the sea. How I wish to be back there. Up here everything is too bright, too loud, too much. Even in the new night. Alia won't look at the blue waters, shimmering against the falling night. She watches her hands instead. But I know she smells the brine and life. She makes a sign: *Can't.*

And then she's to her feet. *Can't.*

I scramble up after her. I'd like to convince myself it's the sea, our home, that she can't handle, but I know it's what we must do tonight.

"We can," I say. I grab her hand as we turn for the castle.

She takes a deep breath. *I know.*

We make slow progress up the now-empty sea lane, through the rose garden, and into the castle. I hold fast to Alia's hand as we climb the steps to the ballroom I first saw her in that day, the one with the marble balcony. Music streams out into the hallway, the thrum-and-thump of dance testing the ancient castle's foundations.

"There you are," Will says, appearing in the hall. "Niklas said you seemed ill. Are you all right, Alia? He's been so worried about you."

Alia is gripping my hand so tightly that I can't even pretend to be affable. "So nice of the king to spare a thought about how Alia is feeling."

I expect Will to snap back. To stand up for his friend. His cousin. But instead of flat platitudes, he takes my sister's hand. "A broken heart is a burden unlike any other." I'm so shocked my lips drop open—meaningful balm for her pain is the last thing I was expecting from one of Niklas's cronies. "I'm sorry, Alia. If you'd like, just give me a nod and I will help you to your room. I'll see to it that dinner is brought to you, too." He smiles. "I can throw in two slices of that ridiculous cake as well."

I wait for Alia to respond. Though I'm the one who made her attend the wedding, somehow after surviving that, this justification suddenly feels okay. She sat and smiled through that broken heart of hers, and the weight of what we must do, and suffering through one final party isn't necessary. We can retire with this alibi and prepare, completely excused by one of the king's closest confidants.

Maybe her illness, the heartbreak that even the bride herself has noticed, coupled with a note from me, the girl who arrived to fetch her home, will be enough that we can leave the palace with no good-bye more than a simple note of thanks. No one thinking twice about us in the chaos that is sure to happen in the minutes and hours after the king is found dead.

Will and I wait, both our eyes left watching Alia. Allowing it to be her decision alone.

Alia shakes her head—*I'm fine*—and takes Will's arm.

Alia is strong. Alia loves pageantry. These are the reasons I tell myself that she said yes.

Not that she believes we will fail. Not that this dance might literally be her last.

Inside the ballroom, men and women whirl in time, their movements all tightly choreographed. The pieces of modern society depicted in a churning metaphor of hand touches and elbow hooks, curtsies and twirls.

"Ah, les lanciers," Will says. "You will be magnificent at this, Alia."

Her eyes shift, watching the happy couple twirl by. Sofie is a cloud of ruffles and glistening skin, and the sapphires in Niklas's crown catch the chandelier light with every twist and step. Again, he's encrusted with pretty things he's collected—the sea witch's red ring on his right hand, more eye-catching than the new slim band of gold on his left; yet another gilded brooch; a pocket watch.

The dance floor is padded with onlookers several people deep, cups aloft. Summer wine, fleeting as it is, coveted at this final hurrah before autumn. Hvidtøl—white ale, like Father prefers—flows freely to mugs as big as my head.

Food—so much food. If there's something that needs mending in our lessons on human culture, it is the fact that food has an unparalleled role. An entire whale filleted and presented on a spit, roasting low and slow until the meat and blubber is falling off the bone, caught before plummeting into the flames below. The last of summer's fruits, ripe and glittering with sugar and syrup.

And, in the corner, as Will hinted, is a massive cake, the icing the requisite Havnestad blue, one side of the cake emblazoned with a sugar-made depiction of the Øldenburg coat of arms, and a red-and-white nettle-leaf coat I assume is the coat of Holsten.

The song ends, and the dancers line up again, switching partners. Niklas's gaze finds Alia in the crowd. I expect him to call to her. To ask her to perform, even though he knows she's ill, his pleasure at watching her dance greater than his concern for her physical struggle.

I'm about to yank her ear to my lips and inform her if she goes to him like his pet, I will end him myself right here. But then Will pipes up again.

"Alia, if you'd like to try it, I'll be your partner."

Another kindness from this boy.

Alia glances to the dancers, lining up again. Behind them, the musicians reset. Niklas and Sofie exchange sparkling glasses of summer wine. My sister nods, and Will extends his arm.

Alia's arrival on the dance floor is something grand, the revelers parting for her like water around a ship's bow. All eyes go to her, knowing that they're about to see something truly special.

Of course, Niklas notices too, looking up too quickly from his pull of wine. He gulps and sputters, coughing. Sofie jumps back, pressing the ruffles of her dress into the curve of her body, hoping to keep the fabric clear. Someone pats him on his back and a handkerchief is produced. He holds up a hand—*I'm okay*—while pressing the handkerchief to his mouth with the other. The music starts up again, and he waves off anyone who descends on him, watching the next round of dancing with watering eyes.

Serves you right.

There's an odd number of male suitors, and Sofie is drawn into the fray. She goes without a second glance at her husband, melting into the song.

Almost immediately, her father takes the bride's place next to Niklas. The older man leans into the king's ear. Niklas keeps the handkerchief up to his face but is clearly saying something to the man. Sofie's father points his chin toward the French doors and the marble balcony. It's almost imperceptible, but the king nods.

And then something strange happens.

They break apart.

The king going one way, his father-in-law going another.

I check on Alia and Will—mid-song, and pink-cheeked—and shoulder through the crowd bordering the dance floor. As I pass, I snag a plate of cake from a waiter's platter, hoping that my movements appear natural. I smile and gesture to the confection as I pick my way across the room. There are a few small round tables pushed up against the wall, and I am able to land my plate on one that looks out the open door to the balcony.

There, as expected, is the king, leaning against the railing, breeze off the water testing the hold of the pomade in his hair.

I take a forkful of cake . . . and immediately gag.

How in the name of Urda can these humans eat something as sweet as this and still have their teeth?

When the foul bite is safely spit into my napkin, I wrench my eyes back to the balcony.

Niklas is still there, facing the water. Another man comes to him—not Sofie's father, but someone dressed as a palace guard. Placing a hand inside his jacket, the guard fishes out an envelope and presses it into the king's waiting palm. Niklas says nothing to the guard, who, duty done, turns and heads for the ballroom.

As the song comes to an end, I search the room for Baron Gerhard. He's right where Niklas left him, clapping politely as the song ends.

The king comes in, smiling and clapping as if he never left. And, for once, instead of seeing Alia first as he enters the room, he zeroes in on Sofie, all smiles.

13

Runa

THE RECEPTION ROARS UNTIL MIDNIGHT. THE KING and his bride retire, but Alia and I make sure to stay a few minutes longer. The more people who see us here—happy, smiling, and dancing—the better.

Alia is exhausted when we make it back to the gilded confines of our room. She's failing now, the fabric of the spell that keeps her in this body fraying at the edges and growing weaker with each moment. I help her into bed, shooing away the maids who have come to help us undress. She needs all the rest she can get.

Yet, somehow, her fatigue energizes me. I can't let her fade, the weariness building upon itself until she can do nothing but wait for her bones to dissolve into sea foam. I can't. And so, though it's minutes until morning, I stay awake, preparing.

I summon a maid, asking her to gather parchment,

an ink pot, and pen. When she returns with my items, I request that she find another home for the gowns, under-garments, stockings, and slippers that have been gifted to us during our stay. All of this is an alibi—hopefully enough to buy us time before they come looking for us.

When she leaves, I sit at the vanity.

Thank you for your kindness, King Niklas.
I will never forget you.
Alia of Helsingør

Our alibi fortified in ink, I test my magic again, stand-ing in front of the long mirror.

"Blakkr," I whisper to my reflection.

Again, the magic, once so forcefully present, streams in from a distant place. Listening, but having to journey to answer the call. I reach for it, begging it to stay close. I'll need it tonight. Still, the spell does its work, darken-ing the blue of my gown to the deepest black of the night outside.

I repeat it, hoping to change my hair. The short cut makes it far more recognizable than I'd like, but the spell won't change it. I repeat it once more, but still, nothing.

"Damn witch."

My eyes snag on the ink pot on the desk. I dip the pen tip into the pot until ink beads and drips off the point, and then run it in a streak through my hair. A ribbon of black immediately appears, the witch's magic not immune to the powers of ink.

Excellent.

When I'm finished with my hair, I decide to test out my magic on Alia—her hair wasn't affected by the same stubborn spell as mine. *"Blakkr."*

In less than a minute, her hair is as black as night—and we're suddenly much less recognizable. Satisfied, I wake her—and she's not happy about it, eyes blinking open heavily. Alia holds up a single pointer finger.

One more hour.

"No. There's less than five hours until dawn. We can't wait any longer. I'm sorry."

Alia doesn't protest again, but she's slow to move. Everything she does is at a reduced speed. The resistance of it all weighs on her movements as I help her swing her legs over and stand. Her eyes catch in the mirror and suddenly her half-closed eyes spring open, starfish wide.

Her fingers fly to her dress, her face, her hair. She gasps soundlessly, her hands moving furiously as she finds more than enough energy to march over to the mirror.

She twirls around to better see what I've done. Whirling to face me, her hands move again in a flurry of signs.

I look like I'm playing the sea witch on the stage!

I nearly laugh. "Okay, you're right, but if you look like her, then you don't look like yourself. See? Perfect disguise."

Alia grumbles soundlessly, bringing a hand to her hair once again.

I pull the knife from where I've hidden it in my corset and offer it to her. Alia's eyes fall to the serrated blade, her retort dying on her lips as she extends a hand and takes it.

"Ready?" I ask her as she weighs the knife in her palm.

Her eyes meet mine, her hands calm. *As I'll ever be.*

~

Alia has been to the royal chambers. I can tell by the lack of hesitation in her steps as we slink through the shadows of each corridor, winding our way to a part of the castle where I have not been.

I don't ask her why. How. When.

Whatever the reason, it didn't result in the love she needs. There's no point in making things worse with questions.

The knife hangs heavier in her dress than anticipated; even with her fluid, lithe steps, it creates a hitch in the fabric. It's hidden, but it is undeniably there.

We turn a corner, and there's a guard stationed outside the outer chamber door. The man is awake, a newly shined pistol catching the weak light of a single sconce.

We don't need a mouthed order or hand sign between us. I know exactly what needs to be done and do it before she can inquire.

"*Ómegin. Rata,*" I whisper.

Warmed up, my magic feels closer, and the guard

immediately falls asleep where he stands, his body thudding softly into the wall behind him.

We don't hesitate, rushing past him, careful to close the door gently behind us. Although the spell works to induce sleep, one's slumber can still be disturbed.

As in our own home, the king's chambers are massive and consist of rooms upon rooms—a private library, study, meeting room, parlor. At the end of it all is the bedchamber, doors swung wide. The moon hangs heavily in the sky, its silvery light falling in from a large private balcony that takes up one side of the room, overlooking the same slip of water seen from the marble balcony. The energy of the sea charges the room, salt heavy in the air, and I almost feel that we're about to enter the witch's lair—steel-toned and haunted by near-ghosts.

Alia can feel it too. She takes a single step over the threshold and freezes, her gaze locked on the bed.

Niklas lies on his back, in a bed piled with furs of great animals that roam the topside earth far from Havnestad. Sofie is next to him, her hair splayed out across the pillow in shards of tawny, unspooling pin curls messy against glorious silk.

They aren't touching.

Not that I'm surprised. It's hard to put on a good show in the unconscious mind.

I nudge Alia forward.

The ring. The knife. The blood.

She won't move, so I do, tiptoeing to the vanity, where the king's crown rests on a pillow, and his other shiny objects sparkle in the moonlight. The red ring is there, awaiting his finger in the morning light. I slip the ring on my thumb.

Deed done, I turn back to my sister. She hasn't moved. The knife is in her hand, but she's still at the foot of the bed, her eyes pinned to the rise and fall of his chest.

The moon is lower now, and I know we're that much closer to dawn. We've got maybe four hours, but the way she is now, she might stand here all night.

Her eyes flash to mine, the blue a stormy sea in the silken light.

I can't. I won't. This is wrong.

All of it plays across her face as she drops the knife and it clatters onto the bare marble. The parchment-thin tip chips off, marring the only thing that can keep our futures intact.

I scramble for the knife, and though broken, its cool magic seems unaffected. The noise, though—it's enough that the king stirs in his bed. I look from his fluttering eyes to my sister and dare a whisper. "It's how it must be."

I'm here to save my sister. This is what I must do.

I get behind her and wrap her in my arms, forcing her hands around the knife hilt. She's struggling—elbows flying into my ribs, jerking away. Using every ounce of strength, I get us both to the edge of the bed. The king

—125

twists ever so slightly, and the sheet drops, exposing his chest.

It's now or never.

I raise the knife above our heads. And whisper one final reminder into her ear. "It's what you must do."

Then I plunge the knife toward his heart. Alia's hands follow with mine . . . and then they're not. My hands are left alone on the knife hilt as they break the skin, the blade straight through his heart.

The boy's eyes fly open, jolted by the sudden pain.

We lock eyes, Niklas and I, and . . . the tiniest speck of remorse crumbles loose from my rage, before his eyes close for the last time.

Alia grabs my arm in that moment, trying to yank the blade free—as if it can be undone.

Oh, Urda, I wish it could.

I killed him, not Alia.

I press Alia forward, trying to shove her feet onto the square of marble where his blood will surely drip any second now. But she finds another wave of fight within her and uses my momentum to wrench us both back. The knife dislodges, more in her hand than mine.

Alia and I both hit the marble, her full weight landing with a crunch onto my body. My head whips back and bangs off the diamond-hard floor, my vision going blurry as a hot prickle of my own blood trickles somewhere from my scalp.

My sister scrambles off me, knife in hand—most of the blood sprayed off the knife and onto the marble when she hit. I try to find the words to tell her to wipe the blade on her feet, just in case Urda will accept my sacrifice in place of hers, but my tongue won't obey my mind. Before me, Alia vacillates between trying to help me up and reaching for Niklas as if she can repair him.

And then there's a howling cry.

Sofie.

She's awake and wailing, hands covered in her husband's blood, which she wipes furiously on her nightgown. I expect her to dive for us, believing her own life is in jeopardy, and go for the knife.

But instead she hops from the bed, taking a book from the nightstand as she lunges to get past Alia and to the threshold.

Alia blocks her, knife out, trying to stop her from leaving, but Sofie shoves Alia away, and they both stumble toward the balcony. Alia falls backward, slapping her wrist on a chair drenched in moonlight. Her fingers fly open, and the knife sails backward.

Sofie grabs the book again, and rushes past where I lie, broken on the floor, working to get to my feet. As she goes, I can't tell if the pounding in my head is from the blood leaving my body, her footfalls on the marble, or the press of guards.

Alia gets back to her feet, rushing to the edge of the

balcony, peering over the side. I know by the immediate hang of her shoulders that the knife is gone beneath the waves. Even if the sea witch can retrieve it, our fates are sealed.

She turns around, eyes taking in Niklas, face up in bed, his blood soaking the sheets and furs.

I get to my feet, woozy. "They're coming." I can't tell how loud my voice is. It could be a scream; it could be a whisper; it could be no real sound at all.

Alia grabs my hand. I don't know where we'll go, but we can't be here.

The footsteps are growing now. Several men running.

Alia yanks us back out of the bedchamber and into the parlor, over to a bookcase. She pulls hard on a slim volume of dusty green leather, and the whole bookcase moves. At least I think it does—my vision is double now, a starburst of purple blotting out most anything I can see.

Then we step into the dark and begin to run.

14

Evie

I HANG OVER MY CAULDRON, FINGERS DRILLED TO THE edges, knuckles turning white. Before me, everything's gone to hell.

Nik's ring is on Runa's thumb, but the girl is wounded, bleeding from the head.

Beyond her, Alia lunges with her knife in hand at the boy's bride, who's screaming her pretty little head off. There's no sound to my picture, but I can only imagine the entire castle and half of Havnestad are blinking their eyes open to the noise.

On the bed, Nik's grandson takes his final breaths on the linens and furs. Somehow, I can't look away from him. Despite the years, he reminds me more of Nik than I expected—dark hair, coat-hanger build, ears that could pink at the tips for the right girl.

Maybe with the right spell, I could fix all this. Heal him, bring them back, and not upset Urda. Maybe—

"Come out, you old squid. Explain yourself!" A booming voice echoes throughout my lair. It's ancient and feminine, but no one would accuse this sound of being weak.

Conflicted heart in my throat for Alia, Runa, and Nik's grandson, I erase the swirling scene in my cauldron and hastily straighten myself, preparing for the hurricane to come.

A woman appears, much older than I. Much older than the sea king, too.

Queen Mother Ragnhildr.

She's spry, with tail-length hair so white it glows, straight and light enough that it swirls around her body like a halo. The ancient mermaid is swimming at me, full-speed, toward where I stay firm.

Fury is in her movements, her face, her hair. She raises a hand, ready to topple my cauldron into the nearest polypus branch—very much like Runa, days prior.

Before she lays an aged finger on my pot, the cauldron bursts into stark red flames. Her ancient reflexes do their job, snatching back her hand from the scalding heat, and—impressive—she doesn't lose her focus.

"How dare you, you washed-up witch!" she hollers. "Endangering two of my granddaughters by giving them legs and filling their heads with hope."

I meet her rage with a colorless, calm voice. "Everyone knows your granddaughters grow on trees. You still have eight left."

"Bah! Eight is not ten. Or can you only count as high as your tentacles?"

I cock a brow, voice still cool. "Schoolyard taunts from a woman over two centuries old? I expect better from a woman of your reputation and stature, you *old* fish."

The woman's eyes spark, and I know she's taken the bait.

"Does this look *old* to you?"

I brace for a display of brute strength like the one her son threw at me, but where the sea king prefers a meat cleaver, his mother employs a razor-edged scalpel.

"Færa!" she screams. A searing bloodred light streams point-blank at my forehead.

I dive and hit the sand hard as she shouts the command again and again. The second my shoulder smacks the sea floor, I roll back to a crouch, pewter sands swirling around me like smoke.

"Reykr!" I yell back. The gray sand responds, lifting into a cloud as thick as a village on fire, and blows toward the old mermaid in a choking, blinding mass.

She is more than mature, and she is ready, the breadth of her powers and years at her fingertips. As the first tendrils of my sand bomb reach her, she's already shouted out a command. *"Vaxa bálkr!"*

In the blink of an eye, the whole foundation of my lair begins to shift and shake. A wall of vines shoots out from the dead sands, thick and protective. The wall repels my own spell, sending the sand plume straight into my face. As I begin to hack and cough, the mermaid screams again from behind the wall. *"Vaxa hellir!"*

The sea floor gives another furious shudder, and from its depths, one more wall shoots up, this one a great circle, surrounding me, the cauldron, and Ragnhildr. As the vines lace tightly together, the sounds of the ocean grow quiet. Even Anna has been cut off, the polypi tree excluded from our cocoon. The wall between us withers.

"Alone at last, old friend." Ragnhildr extends a hand, her skin near translucent with age. I take it, letting her help me off the sea floor—and then I offer her a smile.

"I let you win, you old fish."

"I hear we had a close call." The woman's voice is softer now. "I'm glad you're all right."

"I almost wasn't. Your son's power is unstoppable under the spell of ríkifjor."

Ragn shakes her head, the necklaces piled around her neck tinkling. "The ríkifjor could've been a gift, but he's used so many of the flowers, I wonder if he can survive without them. Too much of a good thing can be a worse curse than almost anything else."

She says this, and once again, I'm reminded of my fatal

mistakes with the Tørhed. I made everything worse by trying to heal the drought with my spells of abundance. Yes, too much of a good thing can mean death just as easily as not enough. Balance is crucial for all living things and the structures that support them.

Ragn goes on. "Yet, even with the ríkifjor and all that it's cost him, he's not powerful enough to do the things he wants. He can't get his daughters back. Only you can do that. And though I know somewhere in that thick skull of his he loves them, I believe he loves more what they can *do* for him."

"I agree," I say. "He seemed hurt by Alia's betrayal, but he would not have come for me because of a broken heart."

"No, that tear we felt hurt him something terrible, even if the ríkifjor has masked his magical decline. That drug will only work for so long, especially now that Runa is gone too. With each missing piece, he grows weaker, their magic escaping him."

It's not a perfect equation, but I can't help but picture the sea king's magic streaming out of him like the lifeblood out of Nik's back.

Out of Nik's grandson's chest.

"What will he do?" I ask her. I'm not worried the sea king will kill me—not anymore. He's hoping he can keep me on the edge of fear long enough that I'll do as he commands. But there is so much worse he could do than end my life just by *using* what's left of it.

"You mean after he's done having me do his bidding against you for sending Runa away and leaving the others with chic bobs?"

I smirk a little. "He doesn't like their new look?"

"You're pushing him, old squid, and I'm worried," she says. "Even trimming their hair . . . that loss is painful too. It'll take forever for their hair to grow back."

Yes, I know. They can't magic it back. The hair is magic itself—and it is immune to whatever they'll try.

Oma Ragn pulls in a long, steadying breath. When she speaks again, the weight of her two hundred years colors her voice. "The humans are weak from the great war above—war always does that, you know. War airs the worst in all of us and lets it fester in the light." The old woman draws a sad smile. "And while their ugliness rots in the open, their human magic is nearly nonexistent to stop it. What better time than now to attack and shift the balance of magic permanently?"

The sea king will attack humans. I never thought this would happen. For millennia, the merpeople have survived as legend. Attacking humans means decimating the legend and the safety that comes with it. The ríkifjor has made him drunk with ambition.

I blink and I see that boy king dying on the bed. Perhaps if there was magic on land, he might not have needed to commission U-boats or lay those mines, all things that have surely set the sea king on edge. Yet, still, striking first and destroying our shroud of mystery will bring nothing but more death to us below.

"But who will fight alongside him?" I ask. "He's spent the last fifty years ensuring the common merpeople are terrified of the surface."

Her answer is immediate and firm. "He's planted fear within them. He knows how to sow it and grow it into what he needs it to be."

My mind drifts back to the Sankt Hans Aftens of my childhood—a bonfire on a beach meant to renew fear and hatred of my kind, to prove we're devils, that we don't belong, that burning, drowning, or banishment was the only fair way to go. Things are different now in the years since I saved Nik, but the seeds of that fear were sown deep enough that it took a very public, traumatic act of love to change any sort of perception.

As that truth settles over me, Ragn speaks again, this time as quiet and uncertain as she was commanding and sure just a moment ago. "What should we do, Evie?"

"He sent you here to weaken me again. Threaten me again. Make me think he's winning so my powers will be his to use as he sees fit." I pause because I hate what I must suggest. "We need to make him believe he's succeeded."

Ragn nods. "He's a hard man to convince. I half believe he sent me here as a test—he knows we've had contact without direction."

Of course he does.

"You can't keep coming back here." I hold up a tentacle. "I have an idea."

Yes, this might work.

I grab a fresh swordfish spear and sterilize it over the magical fire I keep hot under my cauldron. Then, before I can think about the pain, I slice off a rabbit's-foot-sized piece from the tip of a tentacle. Blood black as night streams out, and I cauterize the wound with the hot swordfish spear before turning to hold the tentacle tip out to Ragn—my one true friend in all these years.

"Bring this to him as a gift. A trophy stolen by his mother's abilities." She takes it, but before she can slip it onto one of the many golden chains around her neck, I stop her. "Hold it out and still, please."

She does just that, my blood trickling onto her hands. I dip a finger in it and run it along an upturned sucker. Then, I swirl the same finger in the contents of my cauldron, whispering nearly the same spell that brought me my view of the fight in King Niklas's bedroom just minutes earlier. Though the sea king has blinded me from viewing the sea floor, he has no control over what I see on the land.

"*Lita. Heyra.*"

The sucker sparkles with the golden light for a quick moment before fading into the same onyx monotone of the rest of the tentacle tip.

Ragn's feisty smile is back. "Clever witch."

"See to it that he wears your trophy proudly and often."

"I'll thread it from his belt myself."

Ragn places the tentacle safely around her neck, and I know she must get back. The last thing we need is the sea king following up and surprising us.

I pull her into a long hug. "Take care, you old fish."

"You do the same, my friend."

When we part, I dissolve the vines, leaving us in the open. The old mermaid leaves without a word.

When she's gone, Anna can't help herself. "Evie, you're hurt."

"It's nothing," I say, and turn my back to her. I nearly spell her silent again as I hear her draw in a breath, but she stops when she realizes what I'm doing.

I lean over the cauldron, swirling the contents as fast as I can with a clean swordfish spear. Then, when the storm within spins on its own, I spell the king's bedroom back into my sight.

"*Lita.*"

The room is filled with men in matching uniforms and shocked expressions. The king is dead, his blood spent.

The girls are gone.

15

Runa

THE FIRST PEALS OF THUNDER SHAKE THE GROUND AND sky as we hurtle from the belly of Øldenburg Castle. An unmarked panel delivers us onto a wisp of land balanced between the castle and the cliff face tumbling into the gray, churning sea.

A crack of lightning rips through clouds, and for one stark moment, we're completely exposed. Black dresses, clearly in disguise, clearly out of place and on the run. We have to get out of here. My head is fuzzy and bloodied, and I know my coherent thoughts right now are running on adrenaline alone, but our options are not good. We can't go back into the castle. It's easy to imagine the news of the king's death spreading like wildfire through the king-dom—windows light one by one, signaling yet another person who knows. Another person looking for us. And we can't make it to the water. From here, even as mermaids, we wouldn't survive a dive into the cove or the sea proper without breaking a bone or several. In these human bodies, we might just break our necks and drown. Our only choice is to run.

Straight onto the open lawn that spreads in front of the castle.

It's not yet crawling with men; it will be soon.

I grab Alia's hand as the sky coughs and sheets of rain pour down, plastering our hair in our eyes. "We'll have to lose them in town. Did you ever go there with . . . him? Do you know your way around?"

Alia shakes her head.

No matter. We'll find our way. I tighten my grip on her hand and take a running step, but she stops me with a hard yank, her heels digging in. Then she's signing.

Witch.

"I know, we didn't satisfy the sea witch," I whisper in a hurry. "We'll work that out later. We'll find a way, but we can't talk here. Come on—"

I'm cut off by another peal of thunder loud enough to steal the words from my tongue. The whole sky lights up like the middle of the day—bright enough that we both instinctively shut our eyes.

When I blink back into the rainy present, it's to the loud bark of men's voices. Up on the balcony, a pair of guards point directly at us, tangled together, still in plain view below.

"Run!"

Just like that first day when she tore out of the castle's rose garden, Alia is quick and graceful, charging forward in a rush of wet hair and black silks. I stumble along after her, more sure than two days ago, but I hesitate more than I'd like with each footfall.

"There they go!" A man screams, running down the same grand steps where I'd entered the castle searching for Alia. "Get them!"

I don't know how many men he's commanded, but the boot strikes on the stairs and then the pavers are terrifying in number. Yet even worse is when they go silent, each man's progress swallowed by the soft cushion of lawn.

Now it's Alia, swift Alia, grabbing my hand. Pulling me on. We snake to the end of the lawn and hit cobblestones again as we come to the row of stately courtier homes that abut the castle grounds. Alia doesn't hesitate, her stride strong and sure as she yanks me down a flower-lined easement between two of the houses, towering and quiet.

I steal a glance behind me, and there must be twenty uniformed guards running in our direction as more people—guards, castle staff, guests—pour into the rain as if all of Øldenburg Castle is aflame.

Somewhere, bells toll, screaming the news. *The king is dead! The king is dead! The king is dead!*

When I turn back to Alia, I nearly smack into her

shoulder as she realizes we've met a dead end. A ship-sized boulder stands in our way, a sheer, imposing wall of stone. Rainwater streams down the eroded face—it would be impossible to climb in our current state. It curves to our left, swallowing any option we would've had to go around that way.

Our only choice: scale the garden fence to our right and hope we can make it to the cover of town before the guards realize which way we've gone.

Alia is already yanking me toward the iron fence, its spirals spiked and imposing. She begins to climb—smooth and efficient, despite the rainwater making slick work of her grip. My sister: graceful, agile, athletic.

My head is pounding hard enough that I'm not sure I can get my hands and feet moving in the same direction. I grip the fence below her, feeling completely uncoordinated.

Alia waves from where she's already scaled the fence. *Stay there.*

Then she disappears.

In a moment, she's reappeared, wrenching open a hidden privacy gate and grabbing my hand. I'm moving before I command my legs to do so.

We snake through a side yard as shutters open and lamps burst on beside us. A woman begins screaming at us like we're vermin in the pantry. "Out of my garden! Out!"

We push through her front gate, hoping for a free moment to wind around the fence's corner and head straight into the adjacent town.

Instead, we come face-to-face with a pair of guards. There's the slightest hesitation as one guard can't decide if he should yell an alarm or tackle us. As the other starts to scream, his hand fumbles for the pistol at his side. In my wooziness, their reactions play out like the last tendrils of a song, and it gives me just enough time to find a spell on the tip of my tongue.

"*Ómegin! Rata! Ómegin! Rata!*" I cry, pointing my words and my effort at the idiot with the gun and then to the other the moment his hand snags a length of Alia's skirt.

Blessedly, the magic comes again, just as it did outside the king's quarters. It's enough that they're both falling to the ground, sound dying from the one guard's lips. Alia grabs my hand. Her dress is ripped, white skin of a leg flashing in the night. The fuzz clears from my head, a close call making everything suddenly sharp enough to draw blood anywhere I look.

We're running again, this time on an actual street, pointed toward the slope of town as it climbs up Lille Bjerg Pass. Shops stream by as we gain speed. Alia is my compass, picking her way across the cobblestones, through the shadows, and dodging down alleys. Behind us, voices ring out. We're not moving fast enough, but I can barely keep up this speed. My head is throbbing now, and the blood is sitting, matted in my hair, despite the rain. Again, my senses go woozy as my adrenaline wanes. Head down, I watch the path before me and Alia's feet as she navigates. I have to see each step before I take it, or I know for sure I'll fall facedown on the cobblestones.

Impossibly, Alia quickens her pace, dragging me like a downed whale. When I blink up from the ground, I see why—we've reached the place where the street ends and the mountain trail begins. Past the trailhead, there's an immediate curve into the trees. We've finally reached some cover. I gulp in a huge breath, heart hammering in my throat. But we can't stop now. Up we climb, sprinting through the rain over rocky paths rife with sticks and brambles cut loose from the storm, until the world is a thick canopy of brush and trees.

From our spot above, we track the guards' path, peeking through the brambles to watch streetlamps flicker on as they knock on doors and search for anyone who's seen us.

As I take the first step toward the countryside, Alia grabs my hand—this time to stop me.

I meet her expression, and I know I'm in for it. That anger building as she kept it locked away long enough to get us off the grounds.

I loved him.

It's a statement but there are only questions in her eyes.

How could you murder him? How could you murder the man I love? How could we think it was the right thing to do? We just killed the king!

My pounding heart flutters with every recrimination in those questions. That I'm a monster. That I wasn't clever enough to find another way. And the worst, that we failed, so he never needed to die. Yet, my anger and frustration and the helplessness of it all compounds until I explode on her, my voice a whisper but deafening in her accusatory silence. "You agreed! And you know he didn't love you!"

Runa, she signs, and I nearly fall over because she hasn't actually used my name since I've been here. The sign is simply two fingers—one, Alia; two, Runa.

There's no me without her.

In all the years since we came up with these signs, I never knew how true that was.

He didn't deserve to die.

I swallow. No one deserves to die. But, but, but . . . I grit my teeth.

"How could you still have any love in your heart for him after you knew he could build a weapon of war and sell it to the highest bidder? One that could destroy our home, our people too?"

I walk away from her, taking those first steps down the other side of the mountain. The air is heavy with rain that's begun to let up, and my dress sticks to my skin, its grip growing stronger with each step. When it dries, it'll be a part of me.

Alia catches up and grabs my arm to get my attention, and then her hands are flying through one sign and another, her lips moving furiously in the weak light.

I didn't know at first.

But you heard Sofie; he was marrying her for money. For his subjects.

This war has already disrupted trade. Who knows how long that'll go on.

Those boats were a transaction meant to feed his people— plain and simple.

I keep walking, and she runs ahead of me and grabs both my hands in hers, blocking the path so I'm forced to look at her. She uses the two inches she has on me to the best of her ability as she glowers down—logic and heartache and our failure in the defiant set of her shoulders.

Niklas was a good man.

Alia drives that knife in and waits for me to explode again, just like she knew I would. I'm the sister who tells her the hard truth, but that doesn't mean I want anyone to toss it back at me in kind. Especially not about this.

I grimace and slap her hands away. "Do you know how foolish you sound? I know you're a romantic, but how can you be so blind? How?"

The cords of my neck rise, and Alia lets my anger roll

over her like pain she'd been waiting for. Yearning for. Like picking at a scab that you know will bleed. Want to bleed.

Fine. Let it bleed.

I bare my teeth. "That money would only line his pocket, kill his people, and make our kind vulnerable to discovery, capture, imprisonment, and murder."

She shakes her head, emphatic.

You've listened too much to Father!

Humans are not the root of all evil.

How do we know that they'd destroy us if they discovered us?

I stomp away from her, tossing my words over my shoulder, higher pitched than they should be. "They'd treat us exactly like anything exotic they've come across. Our kind would be locked behind bars at the zoo, forced to perform in circuses. Some might even take our fins for prizes to display—mermaid-skin pillows to rest atop pelts like those in your own lover's bed."

Alia stops dead behind me. I turn around to pull her forward. We have to get going—our lead will evaporate before we know it. With each step toward the countryside, we're losing our tree cover. In mere feet we'll be naked targets under the clouded stars, just as we were on the open lawn. But now the guards are ready with their pistols and likely orders to cut us down.

They won't need to question us—Sofie witnessed the whole thing. They just need us to pay.

Alia's standing there, shoulders shaking, head lolling

back. She doesn't make a sound, but I feel the sob radiating out of her, the sound of it seeping into my bones.

Oh, Urda.

I take her hand now, softer than before. I don't snatch it or grab it, but handle it as I would the most delicate little fish.

"Come on . . . let's keep going. Wherever we're going . . ."

She sniffs. Another sign.

Witch.

My head pounds with her making that sign in the courtyard. I'd thought she wanted to talk about the sea witch and our failed deal, but here, where we can't even see the water, it strikes me another way.

"Wait. A human witch?"

She nods. And then grabs my hand, spelling out letters on my palm. She has to do it twice for me to form the word on my lips in the weak light.

K-A-T-R-I-N-E.

"Katrine? A witch named Katrine?"

She nods again. And points down to the valley as it must angle back toward the coastline. Then, she makes another singular sign.

Help.

I hesitate. "Do I have to remind you the last time a witch helped a mermaid? No, this Katrine will not help us."

I can't believe you. You think I'm foolish, but you regurgitate

—147

Father's words like you don't have a brain in your own head!

She thunks me hard upside the head to prove her point, but then almost seems to regret it, forgetting my injury as I sink to my knees, off-balance. She helps me up but doesn't apologize as I squeeze my eyes shut and wait for the ringing to clear. It doesn't, and it seems like it might never, so I turn and try to get past her to go back toward the mountain pass—if we skirt down the edge away from Katrine's, we could lose them in the lands north of the kingdom's seat.

But Alia plants herself in front of me.

Your flowers—he used you to suck up every ounce of power in the sea and strip the land of everything the humans and their fear of witches didn't. It's corrupted him. And you know it.

I swallow hard and stop attempting to pass her. I do know it.

There's no more balance.

She needles in on that word again: balance.

But by working with the few remaining witches on land, I can help. I can make a difference. I can restore the balance— restore Father to the amount of power he can handle.

Magic is needed here to save the ocean. Save Father from himself.

I add her words together until the pieces lock into place. I think of everything she told me back at the castle, of her plans to make a difference here. My own words ring in my head—*Yes, you'll be a great witch. To do that, we must survive this first.*

I draw in a deep breath and measure my words. "And this is why you know about Katrine . . . you were doing research?"

Alia nods.

I knew I would have four days. I wasn't going to go to the surface unprepared.

I don't point out that she was most definitely unprepared if her research didn't include the fact that her love was already engaged to be married. Or that he was building weapons of war for profit.

Urda, this is such a mess.

Alia presses a hand to my face. Her energy, her life burns against my skin.

She's alive. So present.

The thought of losing her again scrapes at the edges of my heart. The panic that led me to the sea witch after confirming what she'd done rises again within me.

If you think I would have those U-boats in our ocean, you don't know me at all.

Then, a tug of my hand. *Come on.*

I don't know that this Katrine can save my sister. I don't know that she won't just murder us both the second she smells magic on us. But I do know that I love my sister with all my heart. The sea witch told me that supporting Alia was my greatest power, but maybe I can do more. I yank back on Alia's hand hard enough that it not only stops her momentum but also shifts her back. My sister bumps off my shoulder. I take her face into my hands on the rebound.

And kiss her.

16

Runa

WE STAY THERE FOR A LONG MOMENT, MY LIPS ON HERS.
I've got my eyes squeezed shut, waiting for the magic to do
its job.

I love my sister.

True love is all that matters to this damn spell, and
considering I flubbed my end of the bargain so spectacu-
larly, I'm basically human now.

So. Work. You. Stupid. Magic.

Despite her fire and fury, Alia's light in my arms, and I
wonder if this is her leaving me, the magic tethering her to
this body, to this side of the deal, almost completely eroded.

When my eyes fly open, they meet Alia's.

We part, a question on her lips.

What are you doing? she mouths.

I explain my logic and she laughs soundlessly. I miss its

—151

bell-like quality, and the jolly shifting of her shoulders is not the same. She waggles her eyebrows and makes a sign that makes me blush a blue streak.

Calder.

Then, to make it worse, she mouths out the sentence so I can't ignore it.

Now I know what you were up to with Calder at the hot springs.

I cringe but laugh and toss it back at her. I may have a special friendship with a certain first-year guard, but she's well-known to be immediately and furiously smitten with any merman lucky enough to costar with her in a moon play.

"Nothing you haven't done already with Svend, Balder, Hammond, or Geir!"

She laughs soundlessly again, shoulders quaking. Then, she takes my hand. The rain has stopped, and a breeze twists through her hair, drying it in pretty waves around her shoulders.

Another sign.

I'm sorry.

"I'm sorry too. I shouldn't have yelled. I just—it's been so difficult."

She smiles softly and tugs me along. We start again in the direction of Katrine's home, and I don't protest, traveling to the south and west. The grass is soft beneath our feet, and though the trees are few and far between, it's easy to believe it's simply us, the summer-ruined grass, and the stars.

When she looks to me again, it's to mouth something else.

I do feel better.

"Really?"

She nods.

Alia plants a kiss on my cheek. *I think it worked.*

"Really?" I ask again. There wasn't anything I could feel on my end. I don't know what I expected—maybe a shock like a lamp taking flame or lightning coursing through the sky.

But I'm a vessel for the love. Maybe it only matters what *she* feels. My uncertainty is most certainly annoying to her.

YES, she scream-mouths, arms wide to the sky.

"Okay then, it's just so—"

A pistol shot cracks through the calming night around us.

We both dive for the ground, unsure where the bullet came from or where it's going, knowing only that it's meant for us. Rainwater clings to each blade of grass, and when my face hits, it's like a spray of cold water to my temples. The back of my head throbs accordingly.

I lift up enough to see a flash of fire just before the report of another shot. They're close. Much closer than expected. And coming fast. We can't stay on the ground.

Our hands find each other at the same time, and we get to our feet, running perpendicular to the shot. They'll have to change course and aim to get us now. There's a stand of trees in the distance—clearly a marking for where one farmer's land meets its neighbor.

Another bullet rings through the air. This one is so close, its white-hot heat burns past me. I brace for its companion, the other guard lining up his shot, but I have to keep moving. The trees don't seem to be getting any closer.

The guards are too far for me to spell them asleep like the ones at the courtiers' garden. What can I—

The second shot finally cracks through the air.

I turn, and again, it's like time slows, the image of the bullet and its trajectory clear in my mind—the last one came for me, so this one will come for Alia.

I throw a hand out over her back and scream the only spell I can think of that might be of any help at all. *"Skjoldr!"*

Invisible, yet solid, a shield spreads out from my hand, despite the distance I've felt from my magic. The bullet hits, just above my hand. Right between Alia's shoulder blades. And then it falls to the ground.

I stop running and turn to these faceless men in the dark, both hands out now.

"Skjoldr! Skjoldr! Skjoldr!"

The men are moving in fast, but the shield does its job, standing warm and strong the whole length and width of my body. It's not perfect cover, only working on one side, but it'll do.

Behind me, Alia has stopped running and circled back, crouching within my wingspan.

Several shots ping off me, falling dead on the grass. The men are close enough now that they appear blue instead of black in the dark, their uniforms meant to look sharp and intimidating in a castle setting, but imperfect for tracking prey in the countryside.

Dumbfounded, they exchange a word I can't hear, and then they lunge for us. Sprinting full speed. They're smarter than they look. One dives for my feet to knock me over. The other tackles Alia.

I'm blinded by the man on top of me. He's got both my hands locked over my head and is fumbling for his pistol.

I can't see Alia; I can only hear the grunts of the guard demanding she stay still. The man on top of me gets a hand on his gun, and rather than drawing the trigger, he flings it back, ready to slam the cool metal down on my temple.

"Villieldr!" I spit in his face. The man hesitates. But with his delay, my skin grows hot with wildfire, turning purple in the night.

"Yeow!" the man yelps as welts form on his palm where he was pinning my wrists together. He rips his hand away and falls back, sending his pistol flying into the grass.

—155

"*Ómegin! Rata!*" I shout at him, spelling him to sleep like the guards before.

Skin still sparking with flame, I roll onto my feet and survey Alia's situation. She's kicked the guard off and disarmed him of his gun and hat. There's a huge rip in her dress, bigger than before, and both her legs flash white in the dark as she stumbles up from her knees, clearly trying to go for something in the grass—the pistol.

The guard, sloppy on his feet, goes for it too. He's longer in every way than Alia—taller frame, lankier arms—and I know he'll get there first even with her apparent speed.

"*Ómegin! Rata!*" I shout at him. But he's too far from me—the new breeze grabbing my words and lifting them away—and stays upright.

I sprint after him. "*Villiedlr! Vindr!*" I thrust both arms out in front of me, aimed at the guard.

A wind rustles up within me, and it takes every lick of concentration I have to funnel that strength so that it blows the wildfire from my skin, through the space between us and to the broad back that lurches for the unseen pistol in the grass.

The fire scalds his back in a jet of purple flame. The man screams and falls to the ground, desperately trying to extinguish the fire from the tip of his head to the soles of his well-heeled boots—now likely binding with his skin.

Alia grabs the pistol and shows it to me over her head. She's trying to scream something, eyes frantic.

Stop. Stop. Stop.

She can't see someone else die.

But I need to make sure she's free.

When she's clear of the guard and running my direction, I call off the spell and hex him with the sleep spell I've used on the other guards—"*Ómegin. Rata.*"

The guard stops writhing on the ground, his mind drifting off, away from the pain I've caused.

Alia doubles over, catching her breath. She raises a hand to show she's all right, and I realize I should do what she did—grab the pistol off my man. Any ammunition too.

The guard who attacked me is facedown in the grass several feet away. I crouch gently, breathing hard, and considering how loud we've just been, I mutter another round of "*Ómegin. Rata,*" to reinforce his sleep. I grab his pistol, and we begin our trek again.

Alia's previously smooth stride has an inescapable hitch in it, blood staining her leg through yet another rip in her dress. She still moves better than I do, all things considered. We stay silent as we move toward the copse in the distance. It's clear now that no more guards are rushing down the side of the mountain for us. Most likely, if any of them witnessed that, they're doubling back for reinforcements. I know this might mean we have someone tailing us, but I need this silence. I need to believe we're alone. Beside me, as we slow, Alia's breath has grown shallow. Light.

The stand of trees breaks the silence between us and around us. Gulls call to low gray clouds as the morning tide sweeps in, the ocean roaring to life with its endless, undeniable movement. Just feet from where we stand, the rolling countryside abruptly falls away, giving itself to the ocean in the form of a steep cliff face.

I don't negotiate as she sits down on the edge of the cliff. It's a wonky, south-but-east rotation to this jut of land, and beyond it is a deep blue line, separating where the water meets the sky, the night meeting the day. Alia pats the ground next to her, exposing the gash on her leg to the salt air. A lump forms in my throat. When I sit, Alia smiles and tears a piece of cloth from her dress, attempting to tie it around her calf. I add my hands to the problem and eventually take over as her fingers fumble—I have a much better angle to tie such a thing.

How are you feeling? she asks and places a careful hand against my head, turning it so she can see what happened to me. Her fingers are gentle as she inspects it, not pulling on the hair that's dried over the wound, blood clotting it all into a bird's nest of black-red and ink-ruined strawberry blond. She nudges my chin up with a crooked finger. There's a smirk on her lips. *It makes your hair look better, actually.*

I cough out a laugh and sigh. The heaviness pressing down on my shoulders is enough that I think I might sink through this cliff, through the ocean, and melt into the core of the earth. When I can't stand it anymore—the silence, the hope—my lips begin to tremble, and I can hear my voice going high enough that it threatens to erase itself into mere mouthed words too. But Alia presses a finger to my lips before I can begin.

I forgive you. I know you thought killing Niklas was right. I'm sorry I'm the reason you will live in this body.

I hope you come to love it.

"No! No, we can fix this. No. Don't say that. You're just tired. You've lost blood. The sun is coming up and it'll be all right. You'll be all right. Two sides of a coin—me and you. That's how it's meant to be."

Alia brushes a strand of hair off my face.

Runa, she says, and I wince again at the sign—two. The two of us. I'm the second. She's the first. *I love you.*

She signs it as that blue line between the sea and the sky flashes white. I read her eyes and I know she can feel it.

It had to be romantic love. Our love was strong enough, but it wasn't what the magic needed for this exchange. I take her hands into mine and say exactly what I wished to tell her the moment I realized I'd lose her like this, to this boy, to this dream. "Alia, I love you."

The light changes again, the first fingers of dawn slipping up from the horizon. They sweep across us, iridescent. Alia's hands grow lighter in mine until they're nearly nothing at all. Pressure builds in my chest until the whole of me trembles. Her hands don't shake in mine. Nothing moves her, serene as she is. Alia closes her eyes, and I know with complete certainty that I've seen the blue there for the last time.

I draw in a breath—a long pull of the brine air with lungs made for it—and watch as Alia becomes nothing but sea foam.

My sister, my twin, my other half, gone.

17

Evie

"She's failed. She's gone—can't you feel it?" Anna asks in her stolen voice.

Yes, yes, I can feel it.

Even though the dawn does little here, it's definitely risen, the morning tide changed. The magic has shifted yet again. Alia didn't make it.

Nothing went according to plan. Though she captured Niklas's eye, his whole heart was not hers. She wasn't the one to kill Niklas—Runa did that, and the blood didn't even drip on her feet.

She's gone, and the sea king knows it. He felt it just as surely as we did. And his rage will be worse when he realizes not only is his one daughter dead, but the other—and the power he gets from her special skills—is staying top-side forever.

Yet Anna's babbling on like we're getting Christmas decorations rather than another body dead from magic. "She'll be here soon—a baby tree! Won't that be fun?"

I'm beginning to regret giving her a voice.

"You know what you must do now?" she asks with conspiratorial glee.

"Enough, Anna. A girl is dead." I'm tempted to silence her not with just a quick spell, but for good.

Why did I bring her back?

Yes, I missed her. Though there's no undoing what she's become. What she did and what she tried to do. It's only been four days now, but it's clear that this Anna is not my Anna. She never will be again. Still, somehow this Anna, in all her earnestness to make up for lost time, by forcing her opinions on me, has torn a memory loose from the brambles of our history.

My Anna was always keen on advice too. Always suggesting another way. Something else to try. Most of the time it was because though I lived in the literal shadow of royalty, I would never think like them, and she knew it. Nik and Iker were different from most, the people's princes, as it were, but my outlook on the world was still different.

That Anna was trying to help—I know it. Trying to nudge me in an acceptable direction. Fit me into a little box so I could last longer in our trio. She knew I didn't belong, and she used what influence she had to keep me around, safely protected from any calls for my removal from Nik's orbit.

Her advice meant something then, and I always wanted to return the favor, but she never sought me out until that day when I dared her to go into the ocean.

"How . . . how do I get him to look at me . . . the way he looks at you?" Anna asked, shoulders slumped on the steps of her home, the day before her shared birthday with Nik.

I sat down next to her and pulled my knees tight to my chest, the other hand on hers. The three of us had just spent the day together, as always, before Nik had to leave for finance lessons with the royal treasurer.

Anna's question was an awkward ask, but it was one that could be made from a position of power, if not age. A fisherman's daughter must always answer a friherrinde. Yet I didn't know what to do with her question any more than I knew what to do with how Nik looked at me.

I thought of all the things I'd done that Nik seemed to like best—working a ship like a boy instead of a girl, swimming into the depths without fear, and then there was the time we never spoke of, when I saved him. I'd thrown myself onto a rock to break his fall, leaving me with a collapsed lung, a dead mother, and yet a healthy, safe Nik.

Finally, I said, "He wants you to be brave."

Anna's lips pursed, tears sparkling in her eyes. "I'm just

as brave as you. That's not it."

"You are just as brave as I am; we just have to prove it." My mind wheeled for a chance to cure her desperation. There was a way to make Nik see. There had to be. "A race. Tomorrow, we can go to the beach and swim against each other. And make sure you win."

Anna's nose scrunched up. "That doesn't sound very brave."

"Did you see the ocean today? The current's fierce. It should be the same tomorrow."

She inhaled deeply and looked up, blue eyes scanning the beautiful lawn and the towering turrets of the castle beyond. After a long moment, she nodded. "It's a start."

It was. I just didn't know it was the beginning of the end.

Now, I sigh and look to where this Anna is rooted, here, forever with me. Because of me.

"What should I do?" I ask, finally.

If she weren't tethered to the sea floor, Anna likely would've leaped into a grand twirl for all the joy that's in her voice when the suggestion she'd kept deep inside bursts forth into the murk between us. "You need to become human, Evie! Go home. Restore the balance. It's the only way you can stop the sea king."

She's so happy I nearly feel bad cutting her down. "I can't do that. You know I can't. You know I tried to leave long before I asked him to free me."

"Yes, long before. You haven't tried *now*." She says it like it's the most obvious thing in the world. "You just sent two mermaids to the surface. If the sea king is that upset about losing a fraction of his magic with two of his brood on land and three others with missing hair, you know it would make his fins curl to know you'd escaped above."

She's made her case.

And she's still going. "Besides, you've used your land magic and coupled it successfully with sea magic. Urda has made you strong in ways no one has ever been, Evie."

It's a compliment, and I let it seep into my bones, because I can't remember the last one I received. Still, what she's saying is an impossibility.

"But I have nothing to give Urda for the exchange," I say, piling my tentacles beneath me. The one abbreviated tip sits nicely on top. "My hair, my voice, I'd need it all to weather the trip above and survive whatever the sea king does to retaliate."

"What about the ring the girl has? It was Nik's, no?"

I flinch at his name on her lips. I'm unsure if she can tell, though. I keep my voice colorless. "Runa has no need to bring it to me now."

Anna laughs. "And you're going to let a little thing like that get in your way?"

The ring, the knife, the princesses' unused hair—Anna has a point. It could work.

18

Runa

As THE GOLDEN RAYS OF DAWN SWEEP INTO MY EYES,
the memory of Oma Ragn singing hits me like a cannonball to the chest.

> *Come away, come away—*
> *O'er the waters wild.*
> *Our earth-born child*
> *Died this day, died this day.*

> *Come away, come away—*
> *The tempest loud*
> *Weaves the shroud*
> *For him who did betray.*

> *Come away, come away—*
> *Beneath the wave*

Lieth the grave
Of him we slay, him we slay.

Though it was sad, I loved "The Mermaid's Vengeance." Because I knew it was from above, there was a little measure of guilt within me for its appeal, Father's constant refrain about the dangers of humans, *the evils* of humans, in my ear.

Once, when I was older, I asked Oma Ragn about it, and why she'd sing it at all if a human wrote it. Her answer was immediate.

"My dear Ru, I've sung it to all my girls for a simple reason: we cannot forget what humans think of us." She paused and gave a little smile. "Or what we can do to them."

The light shifts from gold to salmon, the sun crisp against the waters, and all I can do is watch the spot where Alia once was.

"Or what we can do to ourselves, Oma," I say, the song swirling in my head.

For once I wish I could cry the way humans do. I can't, not yet, not until the exchange has been made for good. I may cry then, but it doesn't help me now, my sorrow having no real means of escape. A sob isn't enough. Beating my fists against the ground isn't enough. Screaming at the sky isn't enough.

Though I've never felt them, I imagine tears as a release. When a body has nothing left to give, it can only will its anguish back to the earth. Much like Alia just did. She became tears a thousandfold and returned to Urda.

"Runa?"

I startle at my name spoken aloud, wrenching my head around to look over my shoulder. My hand crawls to the pistol in my lap.

Will. He's standing there, his body protected by the stand of trees. His hands are raised in the air like I'm pointing the pistol at him already. Despite the shock on my face, he takes a step over the brush protecting him and comes into plain view, his hands still up. "Runa, I'm not here to hurt you. Or capture you. I promise."

He takes another step, his body fully exposed and mere feet from me. It's enough that I shoot up to standing, barring him from coming closer.

"What do you want?" I ask.

He lowers his hands a little, but still keeps them out. His eyes flit to the gun in my grip, but there's something about his hesitation that isn't about what the pistol can do.

"I saw what you did to those guards. Back there. I . . . the fire, it was a spell I'd never seen."

I say nothing.

This boy is Niklas's friend. His cousin by marriage for a few brief hours. He's not an Øldenburg, but he's adjacent enough that the last thing I need to confirm for him is that I'm a witch. I shift on my feet. I don't want to kill another human today, but I find my finger sliding to the pistol's trigger.

"Oh. Look. No—I mean, I can only do this."

A little sheepish grin curls at the corners of his lips as he bends down and plucks a blade of grass from the earth. He holds it up and swipes his hand over it like the magician at one of the pre-wedding parties we attended. I'm about to roll my eyes, when he says something that makes the hairs on my forearms stand straight up.

"*Vaxa fagrliga lágr kappi.*"

The blade of grass shivers for a moment in the dawn's light before spilling out of itself—stretching down and up and out until, in two blinks, it's something else entirely. A flower—thin white petals and a sunny yellow center.

Will bows and presents it to me. "William Jensen, at your service. A very serious wizard who can only make daisies."

I don't take it. I'm too stunned. "A wizard?"

He nods. "It's a big term for what I can do, but yes, I have some measure of magic. Not like you—or Alia."

I suck in a deep breath. "Did you see her go?"

He nods and after a long pause, he speaks again. "I'm sorry."

That thick feeling of release presses hard on my chest again and suddenly I either want to tackle this boy and whip him with the pistol in my hand the way the guard had hoped to do to me or sink into the ground and sob until my voice is raw and used. I sweep my finger off the trigger because I don't trust myself not to actually use it, and hold the grip tight in my fingers. "What do you want?" I repeat.

"To help," he says simply, still holding the flower out for me.

"I don't believe you." I haven't been in these legs long, but they stand sturdy beneath me. Unflinching. "How do I know you won't haul me back to the castle for imprisonment or worse? Your cousin has told everyone in the castle that we're the reason her husband is dead. I don't know you, Will, but I know your loyalty bends toward her and the dead king."

He places the flower in the front pocket of his coat. "Don't shoot me. I have something I need to show you."

"If it's more flowers, there's no need."

Will steps over the brush and into the trees. My hand slides back up to the pistol trigger as he squats down. When he stands, there's a man under each of his arms, both clad in uniform of Øldenburg Castle. More guards.

"My cover," he says. With a grunt, he raises them up higher and presents them to me. Each man has a giant goose egg at the temple, raised enough to make their heads appear deformed. "They won't remember what they saw in the valley. Heck, they might not remember their own names once they open their eyes." He drops the men in a heap. "Now do you believe me?"

I don't. Not yet. I shake my head.

"I'll take you to Katrine."

At the witch's name, I gasp. "You heard us talking about her. You probably don't even know who that is."

To my surprise, he laughs. "She's the most powerful witch in Denmark—of course I know who she is. Who do you think I asked to help me learn to spell anything beyond daisies?"

"She's not very good if that's still your only trick."

His cheeks pink and his nose crinkles in a very becoming way. "That has more to do with me as a student than her as a teacher."

I don't say anything more. Will takes a deep breath. "Runa, listen. Katrine's place is a safe house for our kind. It'll be your best bet."

Eyes on me, he reaches down to the guards' bodies and tosses each man's pistol and ammunition across the grass to my feet.

"Think it over. But I'm unarmed, and I know the way." He stands again, this time with his hands at his sides. "And if what I've said has led you astray, shoot bullets or fire, and that'll be that."

I stow the weapons and ammunition in my pockets. Will seems to sense this means he's convinced me, and he stands on edge, waiting for me to take the first step. But first I have some questions—I'm not as trusting as Alia.

"Why are you doing this? Why do you want to help

me? Why would this Katrine woman want to help me? A murder suspect is a murder suspect, most especially if she's a witch."

Will isn't flustered by my questions. He answers plainly, blue eyes never straying from my face. "Because I've spent the last three months of my life doing whatever I could to keep Havnestad's U-boats from getting into the hands of the Germans."

"Why?"

"Because they will be the single most deadly weapon of this war." He pauses and lets that sink in before continuing. "A plane can drop bombs, yes, but there are warning sirens and bomb shelters and the like. U-boats come at you from the deep with no warning and no mercy. Just this month, one sank the HMS *Pathfinder*. Split the hull in two, sank her within minutes. Two hundred fifty-nine souls lost to the sea."

My breath catches at the number—two hundred fifty-nine.

I've just lost my sister and it feels like the end of me too. How many dozens of people felt that way after their loved ones were slaughtered at sea?

And if that's what humans will do to each other, what will they do to us?

"You can imagine after that success, they want as many boats as possible. And though Denmark is neutral in this war, Niklas saw an opportunity for his practically bankrupt kingdom to pay off some debts and maybe make a buck. They've been secretly building boats here with plans to set them to sea in the Øresund Strait for Germany." My mind pages back to our schoolroom map of pinched waterways and open seas. "Sink soldiers, sink cargo—murder men on their decks, and starve out Great Britain: that's Germany's plan."

I'm flabbergasted. I don't have a stake in what these humans do—Germans, English, Danes, they're all the same to me. But the sheer loss of life and the cruelty of it all is almost tangible.

"Sofie's father encouraged Niklas to build U-boats. Waved money in his face and whispered promises in his ear. This war ruined the summer whaling season, and his coffers were already looking lean, so he took the bait." Will glances down and away now, the memories flashing behind his eyes. "I tried to convince him he could make money another way. And Sofie worked on the baron, but a daughter can bend her father's ear only so much."

Well, that's something I do know from firsthand experience.

Will continues. "When it was clear convincing wouldn't work on either end, we made alternate plans. I don't want—and the witches I know don't want—these weapons in the hands of anyone. They have to be destroyed, and we're going to see to it that they are."

I was always taught that humans were our own worst

instincts put to souls, but maybe there is some good here. "And Katrine is one of the witches who is against the boats?"

Will nods. "Like I said, Katrine's home is our safe house. When I say you'll be safe there, I can guarantee it, because though we're not murder suspects, if we fail, we'll likely be captured by a bunch of angry Germans before Havnestad can banish us for witchcraft."

He catches his breath and meets my eyes. "If you'd like to join us, we could use a witch like you."

For effect, he holds out the flower once again. A peace offering.

This time, I take it.

The sunny little thing shines in my hands. There's no root to it, but it'll do. I place it gently on the spot where my sister once was. *"Vaxa. Líf."*

The daisy warms in my hand, straightening, strengthening itself until it's become one with the ground below, its sunny heart lifting for the heavens above.

"Dveljask," I tell it.

Stay.

Though I didn't create it, somehow this little flower is the perfect sentry, standing tall so I'll always know where Alia left me.

～

Will and I walk in silence, the only sound between us the *thunk thunk thunk* of the pistols slapping my legs with each step. While I'm grateful for the respite, after a few miles, even the silence is getting to me.

"You're different than you were at the castle," I say. "That boy could talk my ear right off my head."

"I am different when I'm in a setting like that," he concedes with a brisk laugh. "People with titles always want a show. They don't want the farm boy from Aarhus who wakes before dawn to feed the chickens; they want the boy who cleans up nicely and bows and chuckles at all the right times."

"Well, I'd like to get to know the boy from Aarhus. Who is he? Besides a daisy creator."

"He talks like a common person and looks like one too. The distance between the nobility and the commoner has grown slimmer than is comfortable for someone who's been born into a title their family's held for hundreds of years."

It's strange thinking of things in human years—hundreds of years under the sea can mean one ruler. Like Father.

"If I were to show up to a soiree straight from chores, they'd shoo me out, terrified. I'm a walking warning that class lines are blurring. The people like their nobility accessible and human—the Øldenburgs are particularly good at that—but they don't want them dirty."

"You don't want the title that came with your name, William Jensen?"

—175

Will shrugs. "Doesn't make me any better a person to have it. I'm still the same boy with chicken shit on his boots. The real me is in the name, not the title."

I think that's true, though until my time on land I've never had the opportunity to live it. "So this is the real you?"

"It's the me I know best." Then, he looks me square in the eye. "Is this the real you?"

I tell him the truth. "At the moment, yes."

"Fair enough, Runa."

We stick to the coastline, the massive cliff angling down, down, down, until the beach meets the line where the sheer face of rock once was. Then, the coastline is flat as far as the eye can see, summer-stale pasture thick and rolling.

"It's just up here," Will says. I look ahead but see nothing but more than grass meeting the shore.

We come upon a hill that's molting a bit. Instead of going up it, Will goes around, and I follow.

But as we swerve around the mass, I realize it's not a hill at all—it's a house, built into the countryside. From this vantage, an old stone foundation peeks out beneath thick hatches of hay disguising the front. There is a small brown shutter covering a window, and an equally brown door beside it. From a distance it would look like nothing of consequence worth exploring.

"Stay here," Will says. He steps up to the door and does a very specific knock—two slow and measured taps, one pause, and then four quick raps.

The window shutter creeps open.

"Who's the girl?" a feathery voice asks.

"A friend. She's one of us."

It's strange, the non-use of names, the level of trust missing. If I weren't standing with him, this exchange would be different. Maybe. In wartime, trust is something else altogether than in peace.

But that's enough for the woman inside, and we hear the sound of locks twisting. The door gives, and Will enters first. I follow, my eyes adjusting poorly to the shadows; the whole place is nearly dark as night.

Somewhere, a light flickers on, a match meeting a lamp. The woman with the whispery voice is awash in light. Her hair is that of a lion's mane, Viking blood deep within her, and her face isn't as old as her voice would suggest.

Katrine.

I can smell the magic on her—spicy, earthen. She is powerful indeed.

Katrine raises the lamp to my face, and I stiffen, knowing the illumination isn't for me to see her; it's for her to inspect me. I force myself to smile, though the heaviness in my heart can't make it genuine. Now that we're inside, Will begins to rattle off my better attributes.

"This is Runa. She's of Helsingør, and I've seen her work spells that I didn't even know were possible—"

The sound of the lamp slamming to the table cuts him off with a clatter. Without hesitation, Katrine grasps my upper arm and wheels me toward the open door. With strength that can't all be human, she gives me one final shove.

"Get out!"

19

Runa

THE DOOR SLAMS SHUT AS MY BODY SMACKS THE ground.

I shoot to my feet, as embarrassed as I am angry. Through the shutters, Will's voice carries. "Katrine, why did you do that?"

Yes, *why*? I want to know. I nearly stomp away, but now I'm mad, and Will has seen too much.

I lunge for the door handle. My fingers immediately burn, and I snatch them away.

The witch spelled the door.

Well, I can spell it right back.

"Frijósa." I spit at the door. Frost immediately piles on the knob, so cold it begins to smoke.

"Brjóta." The knob shatters into ice pellets no larger than grains of sand.

"Styra mót minn rodd." The door nearly swings off its hinges toward me. The room is exposed, the door wedged open by magic, and there's no way they're kicking me out again without answering my questions or hearing what I have to say.

I enter the cabin. Will and Katrine stand stunned still at the table.

"Villieldr." This time, when my skin goes aflame, I limit it to my left arm. It crackles like a torch and I hold it aloft, dangerously near the dry sod wall. Everything in this place is flammable. Katrine's eyes grow wide, and she gasps, her understanding of my threat clear.

"Promise me right now you won't tell the guards I've been here, or I promise *you*, there won't be a place left for them to find." The words roll off my tongue, threats I never thought I'd utter—burning down this house is the last thing I'd want to do to survive—still, I don't take them back.

"We won't," Will says. Hurt flashes through his eyes, and yet he's calmer than I'd like. But I suppose he's seen my fire before.

My attention shifts to Katrine. "I want to hear it from you."

"Fine," she says, chin held far too high. "Now, leave. We don't need your kind here."

I shift a brow. I'm not exactly sure what my kind is

these days: murderer, mermaid, failed sister, part human. There are many reasons to despise me.

"It was her sister who murdered him, not her," Will says to Katrine, deciding that murderer is my most abhorrent title, though I can't say why he believes my innocence.

"No, *she* did it."

Another voice.

My sturdy legs quake beneath me at the recognition of it. Heart lodged in my throat, I swing my arm wide toward the sound—coming from the shadows of the corner.

Sofie.

Still in her bloodied nightgown, a ratty blanket draped across her slim shoulders. The girl stands and steps into the light.

I wield my arm around the front room to make sure there's no one else hiding in the shadows. Along the back wall there's an entrance to another small room, but the door is flung open and it is empty. The shadows everywhere are clear, save for an orange tabby the size of a wild turkey.

"She's the one who murdered the king." Sofie drills her brilliant green eyes into my face, suddenly a much harder girl than the one I met in hair ribbons and lace. "Though not for our cause."

"No, she has her own reasons to fear Niklas and his U-boats," Katrine says, finding her footing. "She's a mermaid."

Both Will and Sofie gasp.

I look to Katrine. I don't ask. I don't confirm it.

She tips her nose into the air again. "Your magic smells of the sea."

I expect she'll ask me how many days I have left. After what happened with Annemette, the remaining witches likely know more about us than before. I should have guessed. Yet they have centuries to go before they know as much about us as we know about them. Our vast knowledge of humankind is the merpeople's only advantage beyond being made of magic.

"Where's the other one?" Sofie asks, her eyes combing the curves of my dress, as if I have Alia hidden in the folds.

"My sister is dead."

I swallow hard and pretend Katrine isn't watching me, those questions about my exchange thick on her tongue.

"I'm sorry," Sofie says. "I had a sister once too." She seems to turn into herself for a moment, and Will puts a hand on her shoulder. "Outright murdered, though no one will ever admit it." By their lack of reaction, it's clear Will and Katrine already know what happened to this sister, and I don't ask. Sofie shakes the memory out of the present. "Did the king's guard get her?"

"No." I meet Will's eyes and hope he'll keep what he saw to himself. Something tells me he will. Repeating it—or even hearing him repeat it—would be akin to living through it again and I can't do that now. I don't know if I ever will be able to. "But the king's guard is most definitely still after me . . . and I suppose if you're here in the dark, they're after you too."

Sofie nods. "Yes. I ran out of the room, screaming my story to anyone who'd listen, but when the guards entered and you weren't there, I had to leave. Even with your beds empty, my story wasn't sound, since you'd left a note one leaves when they're departing." Her eyes darken. "And now we're all suspected. I had this handled—Niklas was listening to me. He *was.*"

Her face blanches, and I wonder if maybe she felt a little differently about him for those few hours after the wedding than she did that day in the garden. Again, Will seems to feel this with her, his head dipping as he rubs a hand across his brow.

"Now the kingdom will go through with the sale for sure. No king, no heir, no money," Will says, calm and clear. "Chaos."

Sofie's eyes flash to mine. "It was ridiculously stupid to kill him."

"We had to . . . she had to . . ." The witches stare at me, waiting for more. I swallow. "To save her. To go home. But it all went wrong."

Alia's singing face hovers against the back of my eyelids as I let the wildfire dim from my arm.

Come away, come away—
The tempest loud
Weaves the shroud
For him who did betray.

Sofie and Will share a look, but Katrine's eyes tighten on my face in a way that makes me feel completely naked. She sees what I'm not saying, and maybe—just maybe—she might help me go home. No matter what, I must make the days I have left here count. Alia would have demanded it. If the U-boat sale goes through, we are all in danger.

"Yes," I finally say to Will, careful with the word on my lips. "But if we take advantage of that chaos, we could not only destroy the boats but ensure the whole program is shut down. The boats that are built won't be sold, and they'll stop making them."

"We?" Will asks, a quirk of amusement across his lips.

"If you can handle *my kind*," I say, and Katrine purses her lips. "I'd like to help you finish the job. I came here to save my sister, and I was unable to do that. I'd like the chance to help you with your cause and protect my people. It's what Alia came here to do."

A true grin spreads across Will's face. Sofie doesn't smile but nods. They both look to Katrine, who finally tips her chin in agreement. Once she does, Sofie rushes in to confirm my thoughts on the program.

"What Runa said is true. We can destroy the current crop, but without any moles in the castle"—she points to herself and Will—"we can't cut off the construction and sale of more." Her eyes flash to mine. "What did you have in mind?"

Burning it all to the ground.

"We strike not only the boats, but the supplies, the workspace, the storage. Everything," I say. "We destroy it all at once and make it impossible to rebuild."

A guilty look crosses Will's face. "That would mean taking out the livelihood of half the port."

It's true. It would. But it wouldn't kill them.

"There's no king to approve payment for their hard work anyway," I say, wincing. "What if we remove the drifting mines within the strait? Make it safe enough for them to sail to finish the season? They'll be able to catch enough to survive winter and the succession plan."

Will frowns much like he did on the balcony, working through my line of thought. His eyes flash to mine, and his face scrunches a little. "You're not just a mermaid; you have access to royalty, don't you?"

I don't answer. Instead, I look to the group. "If we're going to take advantage of the chaos, we must work fast."

One by one, they nod.

Good.

I pull up a chair and take a seat, the others following suit.

Everyone glances to me. But this is not my plan. I look across the table to Katrine.

"Tell me everything you know about the production of U-boats."

20

Evie

THE WISH THAT THINGS HAD GONE DIFFERENTLY FOR
Alia presses on my lungs, heavy and leaden.

I can't live with regrets, not with all the years I may
have left. But I do wish I'd given the magic something
besides her voice. I had my reasons, but now I can't help
but play the whole thing over again in my mind. If I'd
done something differently, maybe the magic would've
been kinder.

For all the grief and guilt hanging hooks in my chest,
the sea king has fire and anger. It's been building all day,
this gurgling, unstable pressure from him—a volcano
threatening to erupt. It sits like a slow-moving storm on
the horizon, warm, waiting, violent. All his mercurial
power and the magic that goes with it teeters on the cusp
of disaster.

I've been expecting the sea king and his anger to pay me another visit.

It worries me more than anything that he hasn't.

Because if he's not threatening me, he's threatening much worse.

And so, I lean over my cauldron and call to my missing piece.

"Minn moli, líta."

The swirling murk within the pot bursts into a bright, shining light. Eyes forever used to the shadows, I blink—I haven't seen a blue like that since the final disastrous boat ride with Nik, Iker, and Annemette.

The effect is enough that I check the night above. The sky above my lair is most certainly black, pulled through with stars and a fat moon.

That peculiar blue radiance of the kingdom erases the night as much as it erases the darkness that comes with depth. The kingdom is a beacon under the waves—only the sea king's magic can bring light.

Ensconced beneath the cerulean bubble, tens of thousands of merpeople mingle in a massive amphitheater fashioned of sea stone. An array of flowers of immeasurable elegance and color rings the very top level of the stadium in a vibrant rainbow. I can't identify them from this distance away, but strangely, I can feel Alia's magic in them.

"Each daughter has a magical gift reflected in her garden," Anna says from over my shoulder, as if she knows exactly what I'm thinking. "Alia's was clearly the ability to make anything beautiful—and possibly to see the beauty in others."

I feel deep in my bones that this is true.

"And Runa's is the ability to grow difficult things," I answer.

"Yes, and she also has the gift of properly handling difficult people—her father and yourself included."

I laugh, though she's not wrong. A lifetime ago I was far easier—and more eager—to please.

"What was your talent, reflected in your garden?" I ask, because I'm genuinely curious. When Anna grows quiet, I add, "Or maybe it's best I reframe that question as—what was the talent *they told you* was yours?"

Now it's Anna who laughs, but it's so bitter it almost doesn't qualify. "Luck. My garden was a bed of four-leaf clovers. It was only later that I realized *they* thought I was lucky to be there at all."

There's nothing constructive to say to that.

In the cauldron view, the merpeople fall silent. Expectant. Anna and I grow silent too, waiting.

I shift the view to confirm Ragn did me one better than attaching it to the sea king's belt—instead, he wears it clasped on a chain of sea pearls around his neck. A token for the world to see. And one that lets me both see the crowd and hear him—sound I couldn't get when summoning a view of the girls above.

The sea king twists, and the view shifts to the stage behind him. Sitting there, lined up in a formidable row, are his daughters—the first five with their long hair and children of their own, the three younger ones wearing long strings of pearls atop their heads as if it will disguise their shorn hair. It doesn't and they know it, their faces colored with nerves they're trying very hard to disguise along with their bare necks. Between the groupings are the queens—Ragn, sitting proudly as queen mother, and the sea king's second wife, Queen Bodil.

The view changes again as the sea king positions himself at a large, cut-coral podium, its red strands reaching for the stars like the antlers of a twelve-point buck. Applause greets him. From the way my tentacle is tilted, the swell of his cut-marble chin comes into view. He nods and gestures, and I can just see the tip of his eel-mouth crown—sharp and shiny as he tosses out his thanks until the ruckus dies back into silence and expectant stares.

"Dear citizens of the sea kingdoms, you honor yourselves, your fellow citizens, the royal family, and your king by gathering here tonight."

Predictably, the crowd applauds itself for showing up. Then, the sea king pauses for a key change.

"Citizens, your sense of urgency is important in this crucial moment because, make no mistake, we are a people terrorized."

Again, the crowd shifts, from self-appreciation to stern nods.

"Humans have always made our world dangerous—threatening to murder us, expose us, exploit us. And now they attack each other, poisoning our waters with bombs that explode daily—littering our precious world with both their dead and the moral decay of humanity. Though we all know morality has never been humanity's greatest strength."

I roll my eyes. This is a man who magically changed a human into a mermaid and then married her. Hypocrite. Moreover, his sense of empathy is nonexistent.

"There have been numerous close calls since these mines appeared this summer—we've been fortunate that merperson injuries from these weapons have been scarce."

He pauses. Behind him, his daughters white-knuckle their chairs.

"Today, our fortune ran out." The sea king lets that news sink in. The silence sits leaden over the crowd.

When the sea king has wrung the most out of that pause, he speaks again—if anything, he is quite the orator. "A human-laid mine went off this afternoon, killing a humpback whale and injuring ten merpeople who'd been hunting it to provide food for their families."

There's a commotion and then applause—the king rotates toward the clatter, and the injured merpeople enter stage right. They're bandaged and bruised, the worst one helped along by two others, clearly missing the majority of his tail fin.

When they're settled, the king returns to the crowd. "Pray for these brave souls to heal. And pray that we do not lose another whale this way—we cannot feed our people on animals riddled with shrapnel."

The people clap gently as the injured are shuttled from the stage.

"Many of you knew of the mine explosion before tonight and urgently gathered your family, friends, and neighbors to this arena to pay your respects—it is best that we seek each other in times of great suffering." When he speaks again, the sea king's voice has grown quiet, heavy. "Yet what you may not know is how much more we have suffered this day. How much my family and I have suffered this day."

There's an audible gasp from the crowd. I gasp too, his intent crystalizing in my mind in a way that I hear the words before he says them. "No, you can't, you wouldn't . . ."

But he would. The bitter man he's become. He definitely would.

"Today, we had our first death from a mine explosion, and it unfortunately hits very close to home."

People in the crowd are craning their necks now, counting the women behind the king. Murmuring.

"There is no easy way to announce this . . . Princess

Alia has died from her injuries in a mine explosion."

The crowd inhales at once, their faces stunned.

"I am told her death was almost instantaneous. She didn't suffer. She may not have even known what happened. And I take solace in that. I want you to take solace in it too."

He pauses, and now it's pin-drop silent.

"Unfortunately, that is not where this story ends. As you may have guessed from the presentation of the royal family tonight, my Alia was not alone when those humans tore her limb from limb. No, she was with my youngest, Princess Runa."

White-hot anger shivers loose in my gut. Lies on lies on lies. Explaining away a truth—two daughters unaccounted for—with a story meant to feed the fear he's worked so hard to build in the last fifty years.

The crowd whispers panicked questions.

"My Runa was lucky enough to survive the blast that took her twin sister, but she is badly injured and unconscious. She may never wake up."

The crowd reacts, unquestioning. They believe every word, though curiously, no one had heard of *this* mine explosion before. No rumor made the rounds. There wasn't an eyewitness account. Not even a well-placed hero dragging the girls' bodies into the castle, relaying the story.

Nothing.

He just says it and they believe him. No critical

thinking. Not even a question.

I nearly wipe my view right then. I can't watch a man lying to his people. Using untruths to work them into a caustic froth of fear and vengeance.

"The royal family will bury Princess Alia in her garden at dawn tomorrow. The funeral will be closed to the public, and I ask that you respect our privacy in this time. Meanwhile, I would be honored if you would pray to Urda to return Princess Runa to us soon."

He expects to get Runa back.

He'll visit again.

And if she stays on land, he'll kill her off, too, using her death as another strike against humankind.

"The loss we as a people have suffered today is great. But hear me now: it will only become worse. This war above has the markings of being the greatest, most devastating war the world has ever seen, and the mines are not our only danger."

The people sit up, spines straight.

"Great warships are already patrolling our waters, new cannons at the ready. Flying ships have appeared in the sky, dropping bombs a hundred times as powerful as the floating mines. And if a threat doesn't come from a mine or a cannon or a great flying ship above, it may very well come from *down below.*"

There's another collective gasp.

"Yes, down below. The humans have created ships that

sail underwater. U-boats are what they have named them, but what I call them is the greatest threat we have ever faced from humankind."

Feverish, the crowd is in motion now, tails flapping, sending plumes of violent bubbles swirling.

"The U-boats are meant to destroy large warships before being detected. They're stealthy metal beasts, loaded to the teeth with ammunition. One has already sunk a large British warship, killing more than two hundred human men—a mission so successful it is sure to lead to a swarm of these boats in all waters from here to the Atlantic."

The crowd grows louder, and the panic on their faces makes it all come clear. Everyone is setting up scenarios in their heads—for the lack of thinking they did when accepting his story of Alia's death and Runa's "injuries," the wheels are really turning now.

"A swarm of these U-boats means not only more explosions, but, for the first time, we face a real, immediate threat of discovery. Humans can live on these ships underwater for days at a time. Reach depths no man can swim. They have equipment that can sense our settlements in a way no human has before."

He pounds on the podium, the coral spires threatening to snap.

"If they can see us, they can capture us. If they capture us, they can prove our existence. And then we all know what comes next—mass imprisonment, enslavement, extinction."

The crowd has risen off the stadium steps.

"Humans have always been our enemy. The most dangerous threat to our kind. We have lived in peace for millennia, but the time has come when we can no longer hide. We can no longer sit quiet. We cannot wait for them to find us. To save our kind and our way of life, we must act."

The stadium roars in approval. It's loud enough that I not only hear the booming applause through the cauldron, but in echo as the tide carries it from the sea kingdom straight into my waters. The polypi tremble with the vibration of hundreds of thousands of voices yelling.

The king finishes, his voice no longer thunderous but heavy and grave. "Go home, my dear citizens. Go home and hug your loved ones tight, have a good meal, and get a solid night's sleep. Because the day is coming soon when we will fight back."

⌇

Ragn was right. *He's planted fear within them. He knows how to sow it and grow it into what he needs it to be.* Yes, yes, he has. And what the sea king needs is war. He could have easily blamed Alia's death on me. It would be true, and they've always feared me. But if he turns the merpeople against me, he'll never get his Runa back.

Still, there is no way he will win a fight against man.

With magic or without, if humans are good at one thing, it's destruction.

I swivel the tentacle to capture the sea king's face as he returns to his chambers after the big speech. Only Queen Bodil is with him, the other members of his family stripped away. She leans into an embrace that seems somewhat forced, his stance cold. "Don't stay up too late, my king. Heed your own words—even kings must sleep."

"I'll be along shortly."

The queen tips her lovely head in acknowledgment and then disappears without another word.

Bodil gone, the sea king closes the door to his study and pulls out a tightly corked bottle—what looks to be hvidtøl, pilfered from a human vessel.

"Hypocrite," I mutter.

He settles into a chair at a great desk. Books and ledgers press in from the walls, heavy with centuries of information, though if I look closely, I can spy the empty slip of space where the ledger containing the details of Queen Mette's change once was. He destroyed them after Annemette nearly revealed and ruined them all—Ragn has told me this much. I wonder if behind me, Anna senses this.

The sea king takes a long pull of the hvidtøl, whispering magic that keeps it free of seawater—the same spell I use with my potions. When he retires the bottle to his desk, it's as if he's aged a hundred years more. His skin seems thinned, showing every line, wrinkle. Veins run crosshatch under his skin. The blue of his eyes seems to fade. Even his hair, usually long and flowing, has gone brittle and split at the ends. Weak. That's something I never thought he'd appear.

Yet, even as he looks as if he might dissolve into a pile of dust, the man takes another deep gulp of hvidtøl and then casts a summoning spell. *"Koma,* Svend."

In the space of another swallow, there's a quick, efficient knock on the study door.

"Enter, Svend."

A young merman with the polite posture and efficient movements of a favored servant sweeps into the room. "You called, Your Highness?"

"I need a dose of ríkifjor serum tonight."

This servant isn't the type to even remotely sass back, but his expression flickers just long enough to count as a hesitation. "Certainly, Your Highness."

He's answered correctly, but his reaction isn't lost on his king. "What is your concern?"

Svend draws himself up. "I have no concerns, Your Highness."

"Ah, but you do. Out with it, Svend. However, if you take a cue from my mother and chastise me for my ríkifjor consumption, I will be sorely disappointed."

The young man shakes his head. "I would never presume to suggest such a thing, Your Highness."

"Good man."

The sea king nods for him to speak.

"Your Highness, the ríkifjor flowers are . . . suffering."

"Suffering, how?"

"This morning when I retrieved your dose, nothing was amiss. But over the course of the day, they've begun to shrivel."

The king's eyes go wide. "Shrivel?" He spits the word with disbelief.

The boy confirms it with a curt nod. "Yes, sir. At least half the crop is damaged."

The sea king runs a hand through his hair. "Are they salvageable? Can we retrieve serum from them somehow and store it?"

"The flower keepers—we've tried. But the shriveled flowers produce no serum."

I'm impressed when this king, as awful as he's been to me, as controlling as he is over his daughters, doesn't lash out at this boy. He doesn't even demand to inspect the flowers for himself. Instead, he settles heavily back into his chair. "They're dying without Runa."

The boy doesn't presume to nod, though he does have a question for his master. "Your Highness, would you still like me to bring tonight's dose?"

"Yes, Svend, the usual amount."

The boy bows and leaves.

Alone, the sea king allows his anger to surface. In a

blink, he's smashed his bottle against a bookcase across the room, sparkling shards littering the space where the boy just swam a moment earlier.

I turn from the cauldron, looking over my shoulder into the mouth of my cave, where Runa planted my ríkifjor. A handful of petals has fallen from the remaining plants and onto the seafloor. The flowers will be gone by the time Runa's four days are complete.

If he doesn't get her back, the withdrawal from the ríkifjor might be enough to kill him.

I shudder.

The sea king, as bitter, furious, heartbroken, and sick as he is, will have nothing left to lose.

21

Runa

MORNING DRIFTS INTO NIGHT AS I LEARN EVERYTHING this small coven of rebels knows about the Havnestad U-boat program. Which turns out to be quite a lot—they know dates, places, the program's organizational structure.

What they don't know is much magic. Even Katrine, despite her reputation and her clear knowledge. Worse, there aren't many of us. There isn't a network of covens working together on this plot. Our army is solely composed of these three witches plus two more—Phillip, the other boy from the balcony, and Agnata, Sofie's handmaiden. And neither of them made it to the safe house when things went south last night. Neither numbers nor magic are in our corner.

It's one thing to learn in daily lessons about the ways nonmagical humans, especially those in power, went about extinguishing the witch community—Hypatia in Greece, over a millennium ago; Salem, across the Atlantic; the Pendle and Chelmsford witches in the British Isles; and here, King Christian IV, the self-styled witch-hunter king, and all the women he tossed in a fire—but to see how it has left those who remain is quite something.

I'd thought that maybe Will's singular ability to fashion daisies was simply because of a lack of practice, but how can he be expected to learn when even his teacher's skills are rudimentary and self-taught through the faded pages of ancient texts? Katrine can sense magic, and spell a door, but her magic only has practical applications.

Like her cousin, Sofie has a finger on the thread of magic, but she can't properly use it. Even now, I can barely recognize a whiff of her magical scent, it's so weak. It's not surprising, then, that she hasn't successfully completed a spell—not even Will's daisy-making one. Still, she can sense magic like the others—she smelled it on me and Alia, though she did not discern it was from the sea—so there is some small hope we can make a real witch out of her yet.

It's decided that we'll take a quick break, wash up, eat something, and then I will work with these witches to see if I can teach them something of my magic.

Which is another small problem. My magic is tied to the sea, even more out of reach than their own magic. If

I am to be useful to these witches, and to myself in this body, I need to learn to tap into the magic of the land.

I come up on Katrine as she's clearing bowls and spoons from the soup she made, something hearty of clams she pulled from the shore the day before. "Katrine, may I speak with you alone?"

She tosses a glance over my shoulder to Sofie and Will, who are adding new kindling to the small fireplace built into the house—something we're only able to use at night to avoid detection. Drying her hands on her apron, Katrine nods and leads me into the small room at the back of the house.

Earlier, I learned that this is her sleeping quarters. It's not much more than a bed surrounded by trunks of clothes, and items meant for earth magic—craggy-edged gem-stones, corked bottles of various potions, the dusty books containing all the magic known to her. This is where she found me a clean dress. It's a rough-spun cotton thing that, though plain, fits me nicely after I wash the blood and the disastrous night from my hair.

Now, Katrine lights a lamp on her bedside table as I close the door tightly behind us. She nods for me to speak.

"Before I can instruct you tonight, I need your help," I say, and then reach for a way to say what I feel. The fat orange tabby, Tandsmør, sways against my ankles, maybe trying to help. "I don't know how to describe it, but my magic seems *thin* in this body. It still does as I ask, but it's unlikely that I can do the sort of big spells we need reliably."

To my surprise, Katrine chuckles. It's a gruff sort of thing that has more weight to it than her natural voice. "You lit your arm on fire after busting down my door. If that is thin, you're being a tad harsh on yourself."

Okay. Yes. Compared to what she does, what I do is impressive. It's just not . . . right.

"Since I've been here, my magic has felt distant. It still comes from the sea. Is there anything I can do to make myself feel more connected on land?"

Her lips press into a line, and she gestures to my hand. "Is that not why you have that ring?"

I look down—I almost forgot that Niklas's ring is still on my thumb.

Katrine taps it with a fingernail. "Stones ground us. This ring is made of mahogany obsidian—a very good choice to connect you to the earth. It's made of the same iron that's said to be at the earth's center. A ring fashioned of this stone is meant to support integrity and courage— even under the most difficult circumstances."

My mind flashes back to my assumptions about Niklas that I spit into my sister's face. *That money would only line his pocket, kill his kind, and make our kind vulnerable to discovery, capture, imprisonment, and murder.*

She'd fought me on that, and then Will had confirmed it. *This war ruined the summer whaling season, and his coffers were looking lean, so he took the bait. I tried to convince him he could make money another way.*

Maybe Niklas wasn't lining his pockets, maybe he really did think he was doing right by his people. But it was a narrow-minded view that would affect so much beyond Havnestad.

I blink at the ring. It may be mine now, and it may have helped me during our fight with the guards, grounding my magic in this place in a way I didn't realize, but it also connects me to Niklas's murder, and if we're to go back into Havnestad, the last thing I can be caught with is this ring.

"Do you have another stone that might work for me? Something that will help ground me in another way?"

Katrine sinks to the chest nearest the bed and flaps it open. Within are pounds upon pounds of stones, all rough and jagged. She comes out with a purple stone about the size of a chicken egg.

"Amethyst is the traditional way to go—one of the most magical stones we have. It's meant to balance fear and manage emotions."

"Perfect."

I accept the amethyst and let it warm my palms. It sits there, heavy as a heartbeat, intense and alive. The magic within me shies away at first, dubious. I cup my fingers around the stone, not letting my magic have an out. The warmth spreads against the backs of my fingertips. This time, my power unfurls itself, tentative curiosity finally making contact.

The sensation reminds me of being at the canyon with my sisters, the hot breath of the earth gurgling up from the depths of the crag in the sea floor, steaming as it comes in contact with the cool waters of our typical depths.

"These may provide guidance as well." Katrine presses a stack of books to her chest and then dumps them onto the bed. "These are the grimoires I've found most helpful."

I've never worked magic from a spell book. We write down our spells, of course we do, but it's simply a matter of record—Father and his ledgers. But as children we don't learn our magic from a list of sentences, rather from intuition and observation. A mermaid feeling out the magic within her is simply another part of growing up. It's organic in a way this is not.

But this is land magic. Unlike mermaids, witches are not made of magic. They must call to the magic in a different way. This is something I need to understand if I am to help them.

Now that I have the stone in my hands, I'm hesitant to part with it. I fold it into my left palm and gently flip open the nearest book, its spine worn. The pages fall open to a well-loved spell, this one called upon more often than any other. The words are faded and the room is dim, and I have to hold the page close to read them.

It's a spell for deboning fish.

My chest falls and I thumb to the next broken line of spine, the next popular spell.

Fermentation.

There's a hand-written notation next to it with chicken-scratch ratios of malt, hops, yeasts.

Hvidtøl. A quick-ferment magic hvidtøl.

This is a magical cookbook. We can't destroy a U-boat operation by magically deboning fish and brewing ale.

"Katrine, can you point me to the more complex spells?" I set the book in my hand far to the side. The cat lays itself out upon it. *All yours, Tandsmør.*

She bends over the bed, running her fingers along the remaining spines. She selects one that is thin but appears disproportionately heavy for all the value in it—a leaf of gold in a shabby binding.

The Spliid Grimoire.

"This one was my grandmother's favorite," Katrine says, rubbing a thumb absently across the bed quilt. "She taught me the few things I know."

"Have you tried anything in it?"

Katrine sighs. "I haven't had a use for these spells in my life."

This sounds exactly like the kind of book I need.

The old witch hands me the book but doesn't look away, her lioness eyes scrolling the features of my face. She's a person from whom it doesn't do to hide—she already knows anyway. "Are you looking for a spell to go home?"

My eyes flash to hers and my mouth drops open, but nothing comes out.

"I don't know if it's possible, Runa. But I do know if it is, I will help you find it in these books. We only have the tale of Annemette and her journey, passed down from a witch known as the Healer of Kings . . . aunt to the woman known as the sea witch. That story is newer than these books, but the magic is as old as time."

I press the leather cover of *The Spliid Grimoire* to my chest.

"You'll help me? Really?"

There's a knock on the door, but before Katrine responds, Sofie comes barreling through, eyes wide and color in her cheeks for the first time since the wedding.

"Agnata has returned!"

In the main room, Agnata has collapsed in a heap at the table. It's been raining again, and she's a dripping, shivering, sniveling mess. Her dark hair is in tatters, cheeks paste white, hands shaking as she accepts a mug of something hot—tea. Not something we drink below.

Sofie presses a rag to the girl's head, sopping up what she can to keep it from running onto the floor. Agnata downs several large gulps of tea, and between the dried hair and the warmth streaming down her throat, the shaking lessens. Sofie tosses the rag over a chair to dry.

Still hugging her hands tightly to the mug, Agnata finally seems willing to accept her audience, glancing up at us, her dark eyes strained and red. She nearly drops her drink when she sees me. "What are you doing here?"

I don't blink. "I was invited."

Agnata checks the validity of my statement with Sofie, Will, and Katrine. They silently vouch for me.

Sofie sits next to her, pulling a chair close. "Tell us what happened."

I pointedly take a seat directly across from Agnata—I know she's been through a lot, but I'm not going to baby her. Katrine, meanwhile, putters over to the stove to warm the remainder of the clam soup and the heel of a loaf of rye. Tandsmør nips at her heels, eager for whatever she might share.

"The king's guard held me and questioned me," she says, turning to Sofie. "Then your father came in and questioned me. And then they questioned me together."

Somehow, with all that buildup, I was expecting something a little more descriptive. Sofie and Will must think so too, as they exchange a look.

"What did you tell them?" Sofie goads gently.

"Nothing about this! And I didn't know what happened in the chambers. Only that the king was dead." She pauses, her voice breaking. "I told them that I saw you covered with blood and relayed your story, Sofie, but then you disappeared and I told them I didn't know a thing about that . . ."

"Good. I was frantic, but I didn't want you to know when I left the castle," Sofie concedes, grappling at her friend's hand. "It was bad enough that you knew where I'd go."

Agnata nods. "I didn't tell them about this place, I swear. I didn't tell them anything."

"And that was enough that they let you go?" I say, slightly incredulous—the guards in the sea kingdom would do no such thing, even the youngest of them. Even Calder. Yet Agnata confirms it.

Wiping his brow, Will interjects. "What about Phillip? Did they question him?"

"He left—went back with his family to Copenhagen. He's out. I don't know any more than that. I took my first chance to leave and then ran."

Will nods. From what he's told me, Phillip isn't a wizard, simply someone with an interest in stopping the war any way he could. He knew there were more players, but not the magical realities of the other members. Though we are one weaker, it's probably best he's gone.

Sofie leans in. "Did they ask after Will? Do they think he's part of this?"

Agnata shakes her head, emphatic. "They didn't ask after you once."

Will frowns. "Really? No one noticed I didn't return

with the guards in my search party?"

Again, she shakes her head, just enough water left in it to pepper the floorboards. "They may have realized it by now, but to be honest, from the cell where they had me, I could see the line of motorcars backed up down the drive. Every guest left as soon as their bags were ready. They don't have the best tally of people right now."

Chaos—exactly what we want to take advantage of.

"So, what *do* they think happened?" I ask.

"They didn't believe Sofie's story—running away didn't help your cause—and now they think you two are working with each other," she says pointing to me and Sofie. "And the other girl, too." Agnata doesn't inspect me for my missing piece like Sofie did hours earlier; instead she simply cocks a brow. "She didn't make it here?"

Will answers for me. "No, she didn't."

Our expressions tell the rest of the story.

"What about Father? He thinks I could be involved?" Sofie shakes her head. "It's just like him to toss me to the wolves as quickly as he was ready to marry me off. Anything to seal that damn deal."

Agnata pipes up. "I'm sorry. It's true. Your father is still going through with the sale. The queen mother approved it from her mourning chambers. He's meeting with the king's head councilman tomorrow morning— Nielsen. They expect the boats to be finished and ready for inspection within two days, and the sale will go through immediately after they're inspected as sound. They'll be in the water within minutes of the money exchanging hands."

At least this confirms it: the deal isn't dead and buried with the king.

Around the table, everyone is silent, still. Pensive.

None of us need to say it. We're all thinking the same thing.

We have two days. We must get to work.

22

Evie

WAR WILL BE COMING IN DAYS, IF NOT HOURS.

The sea king will eulogize his daughter, ingest the very last of his ríkifjor, and gamble the fate of his people to gain the power he needs to sustain himself.

I need to warn Runa. It's a difficult proposition from here but not impossible.

I stir the cauldron, picturing the girl in my mind's eye. *"Líta."*

The liquid within shimmers, steam rising into my pores as my magic searches for her. It doesn't allow me to communicate—it doesn't even allow me to hear a thing, not without an added token like the tentacle the sea king wears. But hopefully, as it was in Niklas's chambers, context will be enough.

The steam parts, and Runa's form appears. She's

changed clothing, into peasant linens. Her hair is clean, the blood washed away, the strawberry blond warm in the glow of candles and firelight.

With her are three women—two young, one old enough to be the mother of any of the others—and a boy no older than the dead king.

Wait. No.

Three witches and a wizard.

The women stand in a line, their profiles patterned in light and dark from a small fire lit in a fireplace. Squinting, I inspect Runa's hands. Nik's ring is still on her thumb. Good. In the same hand is a stone. A wave of familiarity and loss flows over me when she holds it up to the lamp. Its elegant, purple tone glimmers in the light.

An amethyst.

Runa holds the stone, says a command, and her left arm flashes into wildfire.

Arms up, the three repeat the command and . . . fail. The two young girls produce exactly nothing but the command, while a few sparks fly off the older woman's arm.

The wizard participates as a cheering section, while lounging in a rocking chair, spinning what look to be blades of grass into daisy after daisy.

After a second failed attempt in which they all try switching to stones of other sizes, one of the girls rushes over to the boy. Without warning, she tosses the daisies straight from his lap into the fireplace and yanks the boy over to try the spell.

As the girl settles again next to him, her laugh changes her face enough that it's suddenly obvious why she looks familiar.

She's Niklas's bride.

The King of Havnestad, scion of the witch-hunting Øldenburgs, was married for a few short hours to an actual witch.

Now, that's interesting.

Added to my panic over the sea king's move to violence is a sudden pang of envy. In another world, another time, I could've been the witch married to an Øldenburg king. Or, just as plausibly, if Tante Hansa hadn't spent so much time protecting me from how the world saw us, I could've had my own little coven and spent a night practicing spells with our kind. I wouldn't have had to hide my true self.

Or, maybe, in another story, at this same moment, I could be an old lady in another cabin, teaching other witches spells by the light of the fire. Instead, I'm the old lady who has sentient trees instead of cats and spends her days talking mostly to herself.

I turn back to my cauldron. The witches line up again, this time with both arms out in a blocking motion, ready for another spell.

"They could learn so much more from you, Evie. They

don't know what they'll meet when the sea king comes. They're not going to be ready, especially if they can't even pull off a simple wildfire spell. They need you; you can show them."

I nod but say, "The best we can do is warn them." Then, to my cauldron, I say, *"Heitr."*

The fire beneath it shifts from a dusky red to the clear blue of dawn, the pot alive with luscious heat. From safe-keeping in my cave, I retrieve a hair from each of the sea king's remaining water-bound daughters and toss them into the cauldron. As the cauldron trembles in a rolling boil, I give my command to the universe. Exactly as the sea king did from his study.

"Koma, Eydis. Koma, Ola. Koma, Signy."

The girls appear within an hour. They swim three across, all of them with their arms wrapped tightly over their chests. Fear and anger roll off them in alternating waves, and I don't blame them, though I find it misplaced.

"You have some nerve," the oldest, Eydis, spits at me as they come to rest beyond my cauldron. I've silenced Anna yet again, and I face them on my tentacle throne. I meet her fire with a colorless face—we don't have the time to fight.

My nonreaction clearly annoys this girl, her eyebrows gathering sharply, her rosebud lips scrunched as if she's tasted something sour. Though scrubbed clean for sleep, her cheekbones shine with excess diamond dust—there must never be a moment when this girl doesn't glitter.

"Why on earth did you call us here like this? Do you have any idea how dangerous it is for us to leave the castle right now? Since we returned without Runa and were relieved of our hair, Father has us locked within the north tower. Locked in our own home! He's so fearful we'd come to visit you again and all end up on land, chasing our sisters to our own death."

I cock an eyebrow at her. "You came, though, didn't you?"

Eydis sighs. "What choice did we have? I spelled the sense out of a first-year guard sweet on Runa." Her eyes flash, a storm brewing. "Is it true? Is Alia dead? Did Runa fail? And what of her? Will she die too?"

Beside her, the other sisters lean forward, the same questions on their lips, unasked. They stare at me with their own measures of hope flickering in their tired eyes.

"Alia is dead," I confirm, and I have to look down and away from their young faces as I deliver the news. "She failed. Runa's deal, however, is different. She has failed, but death will not take her now."

"What will become of her?" asks Ola, she of the moon eyes and tight curls.

"She will become human."

"Human? *Human?*" Signy screams, the cords in her neck as tense as violin strings. "Alia died because she wanted to be human, but Runa will be a human forever?"

I nod.

Ola's lips tremble and her lash line pinks like Anna's did in her second life. "How can you be so cruel?"

Again, I examine the pewter sands of my cave's sea floor as I answer. I really didn't expect this to be so . . . difficult. My next words are chosen carefully. I'd forgotten what it was like to be gentle.

"Alia made her choice, and I do wish it had ended differently. Runa sought something other than love; therefore, her magical exchange was different." I meet their eyes one by one. "I expect you girls understand magic well enough to recognize this."

The mermaids nod tensely, and I go on.

"Your father will try to return Runa to the sea. He needs the magic within her and her specific talent . . ."

"The flowers," the three of them say at once. I nod and the girls' eyes wander to the mouth of my cave, where Runa planted my ríkifjor.

"He believes I can bring her back. I can't do that. She wasn't able to complete her portion of the exchange either. The magical exchange controls all, not the witch."

"And Father . . . without the flowers . . . he'll . . ." Signy trails off.

"I don't know enough about ríkifjor to know if he will die," I say, "but the complications of withdrawal and his ire during that time may be deadly enough on their own."

Eydis resets her hands tightly across her chest. "So, what do you want? One of us to go up there after Runa? Adding more of us into the mix is not going to repair this disaster."

"You're right: sending another of you up there, even if you wanted to go, would be foolish. That said, I need your help—Runa needs your help."

Eydis laughs. "If you think we're going to help you without getting something in return, you're crazy. We've been *locked in a tower* because of you."

"I understand that, and I will promise you something in return for your help."

"Good," Eydis says. "Give us your remaining ríkifjor and then we'll talk."

"No."

"*Yes,*" Eydis spits back. "That will buy us our freedom and Father's good graces."

"It won't," I tell her. "He'll ask you to grow it, and when none of you is able to, he'll ask where it came from, and you'll have to tell him Runa grew them for me. It'll only prove to him that you can't be trusted, and you'll go to a higher tower with a more intelligent guard."

Signy's eyes flash. "Well, we're not doing your bidding without *something.*"

"I do have something I can give you in good faith that you can explain away to your father."

One by one, each sister cocks a brow.

"Your hair," I tell them.

Ola's dinner-plate eyes narrow. "You can return our hair?"

"Yes. And your father will be pleased, because like with each of you and all his people, he derives a measure of his power from every bit of you, especially your hair."

The girls have an entire wordless conversation between them. Finally, Eydis cocks her head and decrees, "We won't listen to another word until you return it."

And so, I retrieve their hair, setting each skein within a clamshell before the corresponding mermaid.

"*Ávoxtr skor. Ávoxtr skor. Ávoxtr skor.*"

One by one, each girl's hair finds its home, and with a sparkling blue light, each strand becomes just as long and lush as before, the pieces flowing over their shoulders and down their backs. One spun through with golden thread, one tipped with onyx ink, one curly enough even the water can't weigh it straight.

A modicum of relaxation hits the braced cut of each girl's spine. It's not much, but it's a relief.

"Now, before you return to your castle lair, here's what you must do. I cannot leave this place—your father has made sure of that—but you can. I need you to go to Runa. She is in a little cabin built into the country earth five miles from Lille Bjerg Pass in the valley along the southern cut of Havnestad's shore."

The girls nod.

"Call to her in your way, and when she emerges, you must warn her of your father's plans for war. He isn't just coming for humans, he's coming for *all* the remaining magic on land. Meaning, your sister must prepare any witch she can find as fast as possible. Your father will move soon—he needs that land magic like he needs another hit of ríkifjor serum. When the flowers run out, he'll have no choice but to strike."

Again, the girls nod, accepting my terms. They turn to go, but I stop them—because their mission isn't just one of warning but one of retrieval. In a swirl of long, beautiful, magical hair, the three of them face me.

"I have one additional request. As part of her bargain, Runa retrieved a ring from the Øldenburg king. Ask her to give you that ring, and deliver it to me."

23

Runa

My wildfire spell isn't working.

Not at all.

Oh, *I* can call the fire on command over and over again, the distance I was trying to ignore now a gap filled, if not healed and closed. But my comfort has no time to set, completely rattled as I am by the impossible task ahead of me. These witches are practically untrainable.

After running Agnata through the abbreviated version of what we've decided to do, we prioritize our tasks ahead of implementing our plan, and every witch knowing how to call wildfire leaps to the top of list. Useful as offense, defense, and an excellent distraction.

The presence of the amethyst warming my palm and Niklas's ring still circling my thumb, I demonstrate the spell to the three girls—space is scarce, and Will volunteered to sit out until someone got the hang of it and would trade out.

I stand in the center of the room, beside the table, cleared of Agnata's late supper.

"When I call to my magic, it's with authority and a command to action. I don't give it any room to hesitate or disobey."

I point my left arm aloft, fist formed and pointed toward the rafters, though I know I've got a good five feet of overhead to work with. I set my legs in a strong foundation beneath me and call to my magic.

"Villieldr."

Purple flames flicker off my arm, lighting the hopeful faces of the witches across from me.

"Your turn. Command the magic. Ready? One, two, three."

"Villieldr!" the three shout at nearly the same time.

And nothing.

I shake it off. "Again."

"Villieldr!"

Nothing.

"Again."

This time they're even slower. Out of sync. Less enthusiastic. *"Villieldr!"*

It goes on like that for the next hour. Failure after failure. The only success is a handful of sparks that amount to nothing but blacked spots on the floor in front of Katrine. But Sofie, Agnata, and Will all fail to call anything. No matter how forcefully they ask. No matter how hard they concentrate. No matter how many times I try to explain the proper way to do it.

Maybe I'm a horrible teacher.

Sofie presses the heels of her hands to her eyes. "I need a few minutes."

"Me too," says Agnata. I've only watched them interact outside the castle for a few hours now, and I get the feeling Agnata's handmaiden act wasn't really an act. She defers to Sofie on literally everything. Which makes Sofie nothing but happy—and makes me want to vomit.

Yet this time, even with Agnata's agreement, when Sofie's hands come clear of her eyes, all the determination has been stripped from her face. She claims a chair at the table, props up her elbows, and drops her head into her hands.

"I don't feel anything at all," Sofie whines as Tandsmør hops in her lap and sticks his ginger tail in her face. "Is there such a thing as a bystander witch? I feel like a dog on a hunt—I can sniff out the rabbit, but I only get a sniff, never a taste. That's for others."

"Don't be hard on yourself, Sofie. I can feel the magic, but it won't listen to me a lick," Agnata says, slumping into the chair beside her.

Will doesn't chime in, but the way he's squatting by the

fire rubbing a hand through his hair shows me it's been the same for him too.

My legs itch to move, pace, work out the disappointment and irritation mingling in the pit of my stomach. Why aren't they getting it? I go through the motions, breaking down to the basics of how I form a spell. I close my eyes and take a deep breath. In my hand, the magic of the land beats like a pulse from the stone, and inside, the magic of the sea swirls like a whirlpool in my veins, calling the wildfire forth.

I stop and open my eyes before the spell has left my lips, shaking my head in disbelief. How blind I've been. This spell, this wildfire spell, is from the sea. No wonder they can't do it. A mermaid's sea magic comes from within, but these land witches must somehow summon it. Perhaps there is a way.

"Katrine," I call, though I'm already entering her room. She's in the rocking chair in the corner, paging through a reedy old book with a crooked spine, searching for something to help me go home. I gesture to the chest next to her, thrown open and full of gemstones, dusty bottles, and any books she's already paged through and discarded. "Do any of these bottles contain octopus ink?"

"Sure, and squid too. Why?"

"I have an idea."

I hug as many of the little bottles to my chest as possible, the inks within sloshing merrily with each step. I ask

Katrine to take the rest and goad Will up from his spot by the fire to grab enough gemstones for everyone.

Sofie perks up as we plunk the goods on the table.

"What's this?" Clearly these items have never been a part of her lessons with Katrine.

"An idea," I answer again.

The other girls' gowns are exactly like mine. Rough-spun and long sleeved, with buttons around the wrists. But Will—he's got his sleeves rolled up, forearms filled with the requested gemstones. Their unpolished edges mince the light into flickering pieces—lavender, sea green, fire-kissed reds. He sets them gently on the table, transferring them one by one to the corner closest to his cousin.

When the gemstones are accounted for and his arms are empty, I snag his wrist without preamble. His lips drop in surprise, ruddiness returning to the hollows of his cheeks.

I haven't laid a finger on him since our dance at the wedding reception, when we were both pretending to be something we weren't. My eyes rise to his. The blue in them rages near black in this light and heat immediately creeps up my cheeks. I lift his wrist up a little, gesturing with it, and ask his permission a moment too late. I hold up the bottle too, suddenly a little flabbergasted. "May I?"

He accepts without question.

I draw his arm down in front of me, uncork the bottle,

and dip my forefinger inside. The ink adheres easily, half soaking in, half sitting atop. I paint the near-onyx ink from the thick band of his wrist up the farm-strong muscles of his forearm to the crook of his elbow. The process would feel something close to intimate if it weren't for our audience, taking in each stroke with confused stares. Will watches me work, too, cheeks pinking deeper, but body completely still. When I'm finished, I hesitate to drop his arm. So I don't. Instead, I work my fingers through his and thread them together. I lift our arms as one and give him a confident smile.

"Okay, we're going to do this together," I tell him. "On three, let's tell the magic exactly what we want."

A smile quirks up at the corners of Will's mouth, self-effacing. "I suppose we'll find out if my flowers are flammable."

"Only if you say the wrong spell and have grass hidden in your fingers." The smile on my own lips drops, and I spear him with all the concentration I have left. "On three."

"One." We count together, eyes locked. "Two. Three. *Villieldr.*"

My arm lights as it always does, despite my amethyst hanging low in my pocket—Will's connection to the earth spinning through the power within me, tethering me to this place, an anchor in the deep.

In the moment after my arm goes alight, my stomach

quivers with the mistake I've made. I'll burn him like I did those castle guards. Melt his skin into something scarred, scabbed, boiling red.

But Will doesn't rip himself away. Instead, he stays, fingers hugging the backs of my flaming knuckles. And, finally, his inked skin begins to glow, fuzzy and lavender. The disturbance grows, along with a smile on his face, and within the space of two blinks, that slow burn becomes deep purple flame as defined as my own.

In our periphery, the girls' chairs scrape back as they stand.

"Will!" Sofie exclaims. "You did it! You did it!"

"He did," I say. And then, holding his eyes with mine, I ask, "You ready?"

"Yes."

I peel my fingers one by one from his until he's standing there on his own, a torch alight. Finally, hours later, proof that the magic of the sea can meet the land when the spell is just right.

~

We coat each witch's chosen arm in octopus ink, and within minutes, all of them save for Sofie have successfully called forth flames.

She's tried several times but still finds the spell's power frustratingly out of her reach. She's threatened to retire for the night, Katrine's copy of *Grimms' Fairy Tales* calling her name as all the magic she needs. But I won't let her give up. Not yet.

Maybe the distance she's described isn't so different from what I've been feeling, though my magic hasn't yet completely failed. Perhaps she needs grounding in the same way I do. Not just connection with the sea through the ink, but maybe with her own land too.

I pull her aside, into the corner of the kitchen with the washbasin. "I have an idea for you. But only for you."

Her face seems to fall farther, as if this isn't an opportunity but yet another strike against her. "Let's face it, I really am a dog on the hunt. Woof."

"Stop."

She rolls her eyes but says no more.

I hold up my left hand. Niklas's ring shimmers there, red as the center of the earth. "I want you to try with this ring."

Her lips drop open and she hesitates for once. "That's his."

"It was."

I tell her of its origins—a gem heaved from the belly of the earth to the crust. And though she might have reservations about wearing it given the past twenty-four hours, it might be exactly what she needs. "Please try it."

Sofie stares at the ring, sitting at the ready in my palm. "I . . . I don't know. He's worn that ring since his grandfather passed. It seems too . . . close." Pain flashes in her beautiful green eyes, the hurt she had planned for Niklas never physical. Never so permanent as what I've done.

It's then that I notice her wedding rings are gone. They didn't make the journey from the castle with her. I wonder if they would have if she'd slept in them, or if she would've ripped them off the second she was free of her father's arranged marriage, the plan she'd developed underneath those circumstances dead along with the king.

I take her hand and press Niklas's ring into her palm. "If it doesn't work, you don't have to keep it. Give it back and that will be that."

I close her fingers around it.

Sofie sucks in a deep breath and places the ring on the thumb of her ink-black arm. Her hands are so petite it slides on a little too easily. "May I?" I ask, my hand hovering over hers.

"What are you going to do?"

"Just tighten it so it isn't a flaming projectile when the spell works for you."

There's nearly another eye roll from her, but she extends her hand anyway. I place a single finger on the ring. *"Smár."*

The red stones shimmer just a touch, that specific burnished red of sunset. Sofie holds her hand out in front of her, as she must once have admired the ring Niklas gave her in the beach ceremony. It fits perfectly; the distant candlelight dances off each facet. She tears her eyes away long enough to glance over to where the others are trying to race each other in calling the spell, seeing whose arm lights first.

"Let's give it a go right here," I say.

"Now?"

"Sure."

In response, Sofie raises the arm, ready. She squeezes her eyes shut, a grounding breath filling her lungs.

"Feel the magic," I whisper as she takes a few more deep breaths, visualizing success. "Reach for it. Tell it what you want."

There's a long moment where I think she might chicken out.

Then . . .

"Villieldr." Her voice is so quiet it's almost as if she didn't say it at all, her eyes closed.

It starts with the shimmer of the high summer, just barely. Sofie's eyes fly open as the sensation runs from her mind's eye to the actual flesh of her skin.

"Hold it. Concentrate. You've got it . . ." I say just under my breath.

The shimmer shifts into a haze. And then, blessedly, her arm becomes hot, unequivocal purple wildfire.

24

Runa

BY MIDNIGHT, WE'RE FLUSH WITH SATISFACTION AND completely drained. Not only has each witch successfully pinned down the wildfire magic—both restricted to a single torch-like arm and allowing it to take over one's whole body—but they've also learned the shield spell I used in my fight with the castle guards.

In the morning, I plan to teach them how to put a man to sleep. And then, when night falls again and it's relatively safe to be out in plain view, I plan to teach them more uses for the wildfire spell, including how to blow the flames onto a specific target with magic-made wind. But for now, we can call this a triumph.

Everyone begins making motions to bed down for the night, Sofie and Agnata heaping quilts by the fire, Katrine carefully stowing away her little library collection in her trunk. Tandsmør is already out, a poof of orange fur curled next to the hearthstones.

Exhaustion hangs off my bones—I haven't slept since the night before the wedding, and even then, I was playing catch-up. That lack of sleep piles upon my shoulders, adding to the weight of what has happened since I last slept—the wedding, the murder, the failure, Alia's death, and my own uncertain fate. Focusing on the U-boat plot and our magical breakthrough has kept it all from dragging me down. Yet deep in those same weary bones, I know I can't sleep. Not yet.

I stand on stiff legs and accidentally make eye contact with Will, who whispers, without missing a beat, "Would you like to get some air?"

"Yes, please."

We step out the door and into the sweet heart of midnight. The sky is clear of storms, but there's a restless wind kicking up from the water, bringing the sea to me. Closing my eyes, I inhale deeply, letting the scent fill my nose, throat, lungs.

For the first time, I feel like an outsider to the sea. Though I'm standing in a field and not on the beach, it's as if I've got the tide lapping at my heels and the waves at my back, my toes gripping the dry land as I straddle these worlds.

The moon sits low over our shoulders, fat and silver. The light of it bathes Will's hair in a fuzzy halo, and highlights the hair sparkling on his cheeks like individual grains of sand.

"Can I ask you something?" he says after a few steps into the cooling night. It's going to rain again, and that promise sits in the air between us.

When I don't say no, he looks me right in the eye so there's no escaping. "Do you want to go back?"

I'm not sure if he's asking because he wants me to teach him more, or because he doesn't think they can pull off our plan without me, or even because of the way he couldn't stop the color from rising in his cheeks when my hand touched his. Whatever the reason, I tell him the truth.

"It doesn't matter if I want to," I say. "I broke my promise to the magic. It won't be kind."

"From what I've seen of you, I firmly believe you can do anything."

He says it with a sort of openness that makes me blush, and I hope he can't tell under the moon. I dodge, looking at the grass smashed flat beneath our feet. "You've been talking to Katrine."

A smile kicks up on his mouth. "She may have told me the story of Annemette and her four days. And that you're hoping for inspiration in those old magic books."

"It's home. At this coming dawn, I'll have a day, or I'm here forever. I have to try." He nods, and a shock of realization nails me right between the eyes. "You can go home, can't you? To your chickens in Aarhus?"

Will's nose scrunches a bit as he frowns. "I'm afraid

home is a dicey prospect once they realize I didn't go there after Niklas's murder. And considering what we have planned with the U-boats, it will be an impossibility."

"What we're doing or how we're doing it? It's magic, yes, but . . . but the magic is in your blood. Someone has to be a witch in your family. They'd understand, wouldn't they—"

Will twines his fingers in mine and the surprise of it cuts me off cold.

"We don't discuss our abilities any more than we discuss what we've already lost with this war. If I go home, and my family chooses to protect me, it'll mean them sending me off to be conscripted by the German army." His eyes lift from our twined hands to mine. "If they call me a traitor on the spot, I'll be turned in to the Havnestad crown without so much as a good-bye."

"Your family would do that to you?"

His lips tip up, but there's something sad in it. "There's nothing quite as dangerous as a child who thinks he knows better than his parents and acts on those instincts."

He's so serious, but I nearly laugh because he's summed up exactly what Alia and I have done. Instead, I look him in the eye. "It won't make you feel better, but I think your instincts are right. Rebellious or not."

The grief in the dark blue of his eyes shifts, that sad little smile curving into something real. We're standing inches apart, his hand still tangled around mine, and yet somehow, though I'm not sure I've physically moved, we're closer.

He brushes my hair back behind my ears and brings his mouth a breath away. I lean in, but before I can meet his lips, something catches my ear.

Singing.

The wind carries a song I know as well as any in my heart. Will hears it, too, as I pull away. "What—"

"Stay here—please. I'll be right back. Just stay."

Heart in my throat, I sprint toward the sound. The wind off the Øresund Strait beats against my progress, pressing back on each step. My legs creak like a rusted door, but I dip my head and push through, feet aching with the stretch and contact of each step.

I crest the top of a low hill, and there it is—the shore, sand twinkling in the moonlight. The surf whips and breaks heavily, agitated in the coming storm. Between the whitecaps and waves are three bobbing heads, the song they sing undeniable.

My sisters.

I sprint toward them, joy and shock working together as a balm for my exhaustion, the pain in my legs, the cooling of my skin where Will's hand once was. I hit the shoreline and keep going, my legs not stopping until the sand beneath my feet is far enough away that only my head remains above. I don't know how to swim, but I can't stay away. I have to be as close as I can.

Eydis, Ola, and Signy greet me with open arms, and I collapse into them.

My sisters, oh my sisters.

"Alia's dead. I'm so sorry. I failed. I tried and I failed and I'm sorry," I sputter into the crook of Eydis's neck. My legs nearly give out, too, but my sisters hold me up. "I should've told you what I was going to do. I'm sorry. I knew Alia wouldn't go through with it on her own, and I had to try. I had to."

"We know, Ru, we know," my oldest sister assures me. "You've always been so very stubborn."

"And unable to accept reality," Signy says, droll as usual.

"And a know-it-all," Ola adds.

I laugh sadly. "And look where it got me." I glance down, and though my legs are barely visible under the roiling tide, the meaning is clear. Still, I hug them closer. "I missed you girls. Hey, wait, your hair—"

"The witch returned it on the condition that we deliver a message," Signy says.

"Wha . . . what does she want?"

"She knows what happened to Alia, and that you failed your mission too."

I nod. "Alia lost the knife in a tussle with the king's

bride. Who's a witch, actually—go figure."

"Does the bride have it?" Ola asks, hopeful.

I shake my head. "No, it fell off the balcony . . ." And then I realize where it would've ended up. "Into the sea."

Eydis's eyes light up with understanding. "Wait. If it's in the sea, we could get it. Or she could retrieve it maybe, with some magic. Either way, if it came back to her, and we brought her the ring, do you think that would be enough to satisfy the spell and bring you back?"

"I don't know. . . . It all went wrong. The Øldenburg king is dead, but I killed him, not Alia."

"That's still a sacrifice," Eydis says. "Maybe Urda will oblige."

It's just like my eldest sister to give me hope. "Well, I have the ring, and if the knife makes its way back to the sea witch, the only thing missing from the spell is the Øldenburg blood on my feet."

"I suppose there's no way to get our hands on that," sighs Ola.

Wait. My mind pages back to those early minutes in Katrine's home, when Sofie stepped out of the shadows in her nightgown.

"I actually might have access to some."

"Øldenburg blood?" clarifies Signy, brow arched.

"Yes!"

"This could work!" Eydis says.

I want to agree with her but it can't be that simple. It won't be.

"But quick, bring us the ring. The witch asked us to retrieve it," Ola squeals, releasing my arm and half shoving me in the direction of the shore.

"Wait!" Eydis snaps, drawing me back. "The witch had a message as well."

"Oh, yeah," Ola says, shrugging. Signy is appalled and frowning at such a blasé reaction, which means this must have been important.

I look to Eydis, and her expression is dire. She's dreaded sharing this, whatever it is.

"Since you left, your garden . . . it's dying. Without your magic, the ríkifjor can't seem to survive. More than half the crop died right away. Now it's almost all black and wilted."

My heart catches in my throat. "And Father . . ."

"Father is panicked. He blamed Alia's death and your disappearance on the humans, saying you've been maimed in a mine explosion."

My lips drop open as I process this. I hadn't thought at all about how Father would explain away my absence or Alia's—I thought the truth would be enough. Everyone knows the truth of Annemette. . . . I hadn't thought this would be any different.

The wind kicks up, and the tide comes with it. Suddenly

my mouth is full of salt water. I gag and cough, spitting it back out as my sisters pat me hard on the back, my lungs choking and gasping in a way I'm totally unused to.

When I can talk again, my voice is fuzzy and weak with another coming cough. "What . . . why . . . what's the point?"

Eydis tugs back a lock of hair matted into my eyes after my hacking fit. "Without the flower, and with the people's anger and permission, he's planning to wage war on the humans."

"But that goes against everything we've done for survival. I don't—"

"Without the ríkifjor, Father needs more power to sustain himself. He already possesses all the power in the ocean. The only thing he doesn't have a finger on is the remaining magic on land." Eydis clutches at my wrist. "Runa, he's telling our people we must attack the humans for revenge, but the sea witch believes he'll attack the witches and claim whatever magic he can get on land."

"But . . . no . . . we're trying to stop the war already raging here—there is something much worse than the mines, called U-boats, and we're seeing them destroyed."

"It doesn't matter what you—*they* are trying to do here," Eydis says. "He doesn't care. He only wants the magic. His anger has spun to madness."

It can't be. This can't happen. Yet, I believe my sisters. I believe the sea witch.

"What if I come back? Then would he hold off? I'll grow him a thousand flowers. A million. I'll eat and sleep in the garden, and make them every waking breath. I . . ." My voice trails off, high and unwieldy. "He can't attack the witches here. They're so few . . . and they're so weak. They barely know how to spell more than warm soup."

"Soup? What's that?" Ola asks.

But I continue, "And they're doing what they can to halt the great war that's already arrived here. They're good people, and they're trying to make a difference and save lives."

Eydis spears me with a look. "If you come back, it could make the difference, Ru."

Yes. This might work. The ring, the knife, the stains on Sofie's nightgown. I'd have a day to complete the exchange. And a day to finish training the witches for their mission.

It could work.

"I'll get the ring. Stay here."

My steps are heavy, but I run back to Katrine's as fast as I can. I'm much better at running now but still not as fast as I wish to be. Will is waiting for me outside, sitting cross-legged under the shuttered window. I run past him.

"Runa, what is it?" he says, tailing me as I wrench open the door and quickstep across the room to where Sofie sleeps facing the fire, Agnata curled head-to-toe in the opposite direction next to her, Tandsmør between them.

I maneuver around Agnata's arm, propped out like a

pillow, and around Sofie's stocking feet, and touch her shoulder. Her hands are pressed together beneath her cheeks. "Sofie," I whisper louder than I mean to.

The girl stirs, confusion puddling in the fine features on her face. "Wha . . ."

"The ring, I need it." Still working at half speed, she lets me take her hand, and I wrench off the king's ring, scraping her thumb knuckle as I go, the magic doing its job of keeping it snug.

"Wait. No, you gave that to me. It's mine. I—"

She pushes herself up, but I'm already hopping over her and Agnata and running for the door.

"Runa—" Will says, trying to catch my arm.

"It's important," is all I say to the room before sprinting out the door and back into the night, the ring tight in my palm.

I've almost made it to the hill where I first saw them, lungs working hard against the resistance of the wind, when I hear it.

The unforgettable boom-and-spray of an explosion at sea.

"No, no, no . . ." I drop my chin and dig deeper, cresting the hill.

White foam shoots for the moon in a huge starburst, right where my sisters would've been waiting.

A mine. A floating mine where they were.

"No!" I scream, and thunder down the hill.

The water roils and rolls, whitecaps as tall as I am pulsing and shaking, dipping and cresting.

This time, I keep my distance, toes barely in the tide.

"Eydis! Ola! Signy!"

I scream their names, but there's nothing. My sisters are gone.

Escaped, injured, or murdered. I know not which.

And then, far in the distance, under the fat moon, I see the outline of a tail fin.

At least one survivor. I'm relieved, though I know with the same certainty that I can sense a storm, that I will likely never see her, or any of them, again.

25

Evie

AS I WAIT FOR THE SISTERS TO RETURN WITH THE RING, a new crop of flowers appears in my lair. Right outside my cave, the red flowers Alia brought me from her garden take root.

Without a body, Alia's polypus will be unusual. Though Anna expected her, I wasn't sure the magic would agree. The polypi surrounding me were made from humans—not just Anna but the king's guards who died during my last stand. Their bone-lined branches are the work of real bones, their structure created from what they were.

Alia wasn't a real human, and she didn't die here. But there she is—flowers like blood, taking root and growing fast. Their blooms are already misshapen, once-supple petals gone knobby, rigid, graying in this new existence beyond life.

"I told you she'd come," Anna says, an edge of satisfaction in her voice.

I'm reminded again that I don't know this Anna at all—the one who delights in being right even if it means a life is gone.

Bile churns within me at the finality of it all. Those little flowers represent a life I'd tried to improve, only to lead to its end.

My voice wavers when I speak again, and in her glee, I hope Anna won't notice. "You did. You were right."

"I always am."

We sit in silence with that statement for a few moments more before the clear *swish, swish, swish* of tail fins announces the arrival of the princesses.

They enter in a heap, blackened with sand embedded in their skin like soot—Ola is worst off, the length of her right side a full rash of pits and protrusions.

"What happened to you?"

"A mine. Stupid humans. Some bull fish got too close and it went off not feet from us."

I swim up to Ola, hands out. "May I?"

"May you what?"

"Heal you."

The girls exchange a look. I press. "My aunt was called the Healer of Kings for a reason. Let me try. It won't hurt, and your father won't be able to tell when he visits you in your captivity."

In response, Ola turns her head away, the sand-blasted portion of her body edged toward my hands. I press my palms lightly on the curve of her neck up to her ear, where the grains of sand first appear embedded in her skin.

"Forsjá, afli, fullting, lið."

Ola braces and then melts under the press of magic. Her quick breath slows; her heartbeat normalizes. In a shimmering shower, the sand dislodges itself, falling to the sea floor below. The micro-pits in her flesh smooth over until there's nothing left but unblemished skin.

I remove my hands and face the other girls. "Who's next?"

Once they're clean and whole again—a simple matter of minutes later—I can't hold my questions back anymore. "Did you make contact with Runa?"

"Yes," Eydis confirms. "But we don't have your ring."

"Runa went to fetch it right before the blast," Signy explains.

"Fetch it? No retrieval spell?"

They shake their heads. "We got the sense that even being in the open was dangerous for her, let alone doing that sort of magic."

Of course it would be. The palace must be on the lookout for both her and Alia after the incident.

"But we did learn your knife is safe!" chimes in Ola, rubbing a hand over her newly healed arm.

Eydis explains. "Runa says the knife slipped from Alia's

hand on the balcony and went into the waves beneath the king's window. There was a little cove she was always yammering about to Runa late at night, something that butts up to the kingdom."

I know exactly where that inlet is. I could look down on it from the cliff where my home sat under the watchful eye of the castle. Father would bring particularly unwieldy catch—a full whale and the like—straight up to the castle through that inlet rather than carting it through the streets. The kitchen maids would meet him, and they'd carry the thing on a shoulder apiece like pallbearers at a funeral.

"Thank you," I say.

"She seemed to think if you were able to get the knife, plus the ring, she might be able to satisfy the magic . . . all she'd need is the king's blood."

"Which she might have!" Ola pipes in.

This is news to me. I saw that boy dead in his bed myself, his lifeblood wasted. Still, the hope in the sisters' voices is so tangible, I wish I could tell them that with the king's blood, Runa would return to the sea—to them. But I can't. Not with any confidence. Alia didn't kill Niklas— Runa did, and their deals were linked.

I shift my tentacles beneath me. Is it possible? A sacrifice *was* made to Urda, but no, I can't give these girls false hope. If Urda accepts this boy's life for Runa's, we'll know for sure in one day's time.

"I'm afraid she's mistaken," I tell Eydis, and I'm truly

sorry to do so. "But were you able to warn her about your father's plans?"

"Yes," the eldest confirms, her eyes far away. "She says the remaining witches are weak and in no state to fight him. They're barely holding it together in trying to undermine the human war already raging."

"They're going to destroy something . . . U-boats?" Signy adds.

The fire spell, failing repeatedly in my view, comes to mind.

"But we don't know how. She says they can barely spell soup, whatever that is," Ola says, lips pinched. "And that's exactly when she started talking about trying to come back. She believes if she can grow Father more ríkifjor, it'll prevent an attack."

What's left of my heart trembles for this girl. Runa, always trying to fix and heal things. Unafraid to sacrifice her needs and wants or even herself for another.

I'd say it reminds me of the girl I used to be, but that would be too generous. I was only interested in saving Nik—and when I wasn't saving him, I was saving myself from the plague I'd caused.

There's not much to say after that. The mermaids turn without a good-bye, dread trailing in their wake as they return to their captivity and to a guard who hopefully kept their secret.

"You're kind to help them," Anna says when we're alone.

"I wish they were the only ones who needed help. So many are in danger—Runa and the witches, the merpeople—literally all magical creatures above and below are at risk." I gesture to my surroundings. Uneaten catch litters the pewter sands; everything I own is either tucked away in my cave or strewn about, my life for the last fifty years dumped into this place. This prison. "I can't just stay here eating shrimp while the world is at war."

"Go up, then! You don't need him to release you—you've had fifty years. Surely you can break the magic that keeps you. You've just made two mermaids human, one permanently. If anyone is talented enough to crack these magical bonds, it's you." Her voice grows more frantic and emphatic with each word. "You've got to go up and help them."

It's too much, I think. "You're quite insistent about getting rid of me for someone who just days ago thought for sure if I died the sea king would, and I quote, 'vaporize this whole place and those of us literally rooted to it.'"

"Evie, he's coming for you anyway. Once Runa's changed for good, he won't need you anymore."

She's right. I don't respond because we both know it.

After a time, Anna speaks again. "It's probably better for all of us if you leave."

My vision skips to Alia's fledgling body. My cross to bear. My mistake.

I close my eyes and twist my tentacles to face the approximate direction of the little inlet cove my father would navigate with a whale heavy enough to sink a lesser ship and a lesser man.

"*Koma minn knífr.*"

A thread of the magic from within me shoots through the murk, past the bubbling mire, through the forest of polypi, and into the cool blue of the open ocean.

Reaching, reaching, my magic scrapes for the knife. And then I feel it coming like a shot blast from a rifle, big and bold and unstoppable. A few seconds more and the distinct whiz and whisper of an object rocketing through the water echoes through my lair. Then it's slicing right past the spindly arms of Anna's tree, smacking into my hand hilt-first.

The knife. It's chipped. But its magic held—Ølden-burg blood still clinging to the blade despite the ocean waters' relentless churn and pull over the last day and more. Exactly as I'd hoped.

I turn my back to Anna and clean my cauldron for the most important spell of my life.

26

Runa

I STAY ON THE BEACH LONGER THAN I SHOULD, STARING down the waves and praying to Urda to spare the lives of my remaining sisters. It's early morning but still dark when I return, sodden.

I creep in quietly, the ring safely in my pocket, and bed down in the kitchen, away from the fire, away from all their unsleeping eyes. I don't even change into anything dry—wanting to rest with the comfort of the sea's embrace, even as the salt scratches at my skin.

When we rise I let their unanswered questions hang. Let them pile up one by one onto each other like rays of the sun until they're blinding and only shining on me. But even if they ask again, I'm not sure I will answer. Or how. What happened last night just feels too close, too important to trust someone else with.

Without a word among us, we gather 'round Katrine's table for bread and butter served with a pot of steaming tea. Sofie and Agnata glower at me across the long end of the table, frowning into their tea, eyes untrusting. Will sits closer, but there's still a distance between us, as if he's put up the shield spell he's recently mastered.

Katrine silently refills my tea, Tandsmør snaking around her ankles.

Though it's daylight now, the night's fire is still going, and even the shutters are pulled back. The rain has returned, slanting down in an utter pour, surely flooding the unpaved country roads. No one is likely to be out in this weather looking for us.

I would thank Urda for this, but I have doubts that this weather is her doing. Ever since the night Niklas died, each storm has been stranger than the last, the clouds coming from the Øresund Strait, a weather pattern moving in the opposite direction of what is typical for this time of year. I've tried to ignore it, but today's angry gale has Father's fingerprints all over it. I want to believe it's his sadness or his grief, but more likely, it's part of the plan my sisters relayed. The first step is testing his ability to call upon the weather to do his bidding.

The sea gives life in the Kingdom of Havnestad as easily as it can steal it away. When Father wages war here, it won't be with soldiers, bombs, or shotguns. No, he'll use the fury of the sea first. Turning everyday life on its head, making his opponent weak while using his strengths.

I have to tell the coven. They have to know Father's plans so they can prepare. So *we* can prepare. It's my duty. My fault. My responsibility to help. And once I do, I must try my best to go home and stop Father from coming at all.

Another impossible task. My sisters' optimism, so reassuring last night, is beginning to wane inside me, but I need to hold tight to what's left. Niklas's ring sits heavily in the pocket of my ruined dress, right next to the remaining twenty or so ríkifjor seeds I removed from Alia's garden. Somewhere in this house is Sofie's nightgown from her wedding night, and unlike my feet, it was splattered in Niklas's blood. It's dried now, but if I'm able to draw the liquid out and onto my toes before dawn, along with the right spell, I might be able to regain my tail fin and stave off a war. Yet this task and any preparations for Father's surge must wait. We have a mission to complete. It's the one thing we can control.

After the plates are put away and the mugs of tea cold, Will's eyes find mine. It's time to begin. I stand and he follows. The girls stay put, pretending to ignore me. Katrine tamps down the fire. The rain has finally calmed—perhaps Father is tired—and the sun is peeking through the clouds. The smoke will make us too conspicuous.

"We have approximately twenty-four hours," I say as a start, though no one really needs a reminder. "Let's finalize our plan and run through it."

"Who put you in charge?" Sofie's eyes flash though the rest of her is still, hunched back in her chair, her knees pulled to her chest.

"Yeah, who?" Agnata parrots, as expected.

"Lest you forget, it was Runa's idea to expand our mission and destroy not just the U-boats but the whole operation," Will says, from over by the rocking chair. He pulls a roll of paper out from behind it and returns to the table, eyes pinned on his cousin. "There's no time to be petty about this, so let's start."

"It's not pettiness, it's about trust," Sofie spits, not looking his way, only at me. "I want my ring back." Her voice catches on the last syllable. Tears spark in a rush in her green eyes, and she lets them come as her words strike out, each one cutting. "You gave it to me like it was the least you could do, and then you stole it away like it was never mine. What is there to trust about that?" Her eyes narrow. "What do you need it for, Runa? What? So you can wear it around like some sick memento of the life *you* took?"

She wants to hurt me, but there's nothing she can say that I don't already feel. Her dagger stabs a wound that will never heal. I'm a murderer. Despite my intentions to save my sister, a man died. Good, bad, I don't know. I don't deny it. But she can't have the ring. It could save more lives than she will ever know.

"I need it for a spell," I say finally, so we can move on. We don't have time for this.

"What spell?" Sofie pushes.

"She answered your question, Sofie. Drop it," Will snaps, a vein I've never seen flickering down the middle of his forehead. He frowns it away, rolling the scroll of paper across the table—a map of the kingdom's port city.

"I will not." She sniffs like the komtesse she is, or at least was until suspicion fell at her feet.

"Sofie, the second those boats go up in a fireball, I will gladly buy you any damn ring you please. Now, let's focus," Will says calmly, more himself, but still with an air of authority that commands both respect and action. Determination solidifies in his eyes as he pins them on her handmaiden. "Agnata, where is the sale going to take place?"

Agnata glances at Sofie, who nods her okay. "A warehouse where they are fabricating and sheltering the boats."

Will nods and glances my way. "They must assume the spies who infiltrated the castle are also looking for the U-boats."

"They're not wrong," I deadpan. That earns me a smirk from Will.

"No, they're not," he agrees. "Agnata, the warehouse is located here, correct?" He points to a spot on the map not far from the docks.

Pencil in hand, Will circles the warehouse. It sits fat and heavy on a dead-end street shaped like a mushroom. Katrine draws a finger around the wide portion, telling us that her oma had a house on that street long ago. There'd been three cottages there, all bulldozed in the name of industrial progress under the reign of Niklas's father, who had the same name as his son and his father but had been colloquially referred to as King Bryn.

"What are the entrances and exits of this warehouse like? Is there more than one? Will they be guarded? What can we expect?" I ask, looking from the map to Agnata.

Her face is blank and unsure as she tugs at the ends of last night's braid.

Will is drawing in a breath to ask the question in his own way when Sofie cuts him off with the first truly helpful thing she's had to say all morning.

"I toured the warehouse with Father—it's where they housed the prototype for him to inspect when we confirmed our engagement."

Oh—oh.

Will shuffles the map on the table, pulling out a notebook, from which he rips a blank page. "Do you think you can draw it?"

Sofie takes the pencil, tentative. Then the paper. "Yes."

As she draws, Will turns his attention back to the map and dots a meandering course from the building through the streets, picking the ones with the fewest shops before winding his way up to Lille Bjerg Pass.

"What about a water route?" I lean in and cut a course with my index finger from our likely position, through the

Øresund Strait and up to the beach just beyond the public one. "The mines are an obstacle, yes, but with the right magic, we might be able to navigate them and hit land while saving time and without being spotted overland."

Will's eyes light up. "Oh, how the world opens up when a mermaid teaches you the right spells."

Sofie rolls her eyes. "Will, stop flattering her. Her head's already big enough to float a zeppelin after teaching us how to burst into flames."

A flush climbs Will's cheeks. He still hasn't shaved, and the combination is striking enough that I really need to stop looking.

~

We work until what's left of the sun begins to settle again, the light shifting from slate to smoke. The rain returns, pattering against the windows, not as harsh as before, but still there. Maybe this time Father's grown hungry, letting the magic cease long enough for a few bites of shark fin and a pull of hvidtøl from his secret stash.

As much as I fear what he may do, I don't let myself think that the weather's change is a sign that he's growing weak, his ríkifjor serum rationed. Because of me. Will's words from the night before snake through my mind.

There's nothing quite as dangerous as a child who thinks he knows better than his parents and acts on those instincts.

No, there's not.

Sofie and Agnata declare they need some air, braving

the rain in hoods Katrine fetches them. Once they're gone, Katrine turns to her supper tasks in the kitchen, asking Will as she chops potatoes for yet another stew—labskovs—to fetch and dry more kindling for the fire.

As they both get to work, I have my chance. I lock eyes with Katrine so she knows where I'll be and then retire to her bedroom, *The Spliid Grimoire* tucked under my arm. I set the book on the bed—one piece of the puzzle at hand. Next, I tiptoe to the wall perpendicular to the door, where three trunks sit, stuffed to the gills with clothing of various types. Katrine has been collecting for safe-house life for some time now.

In the corner, wedged at the end of the row of trunks, is a basket containing our laundry. I kneel and begin to rummage through it, carefully piling dresses, trousers, and socks on the floor.

Finally, at the bottom, is Sofie's nightgown.

It's cut lace and new—meant to be white as snow. And it would be, save for the gaping red-black smudge of Niklas's blood down the front.

"Blood magic?" I startle, and there's Katrine at the doorway, watching as I hold the nightgown up to the light. "Will it work to get you home?"

"Yes. I think."

Katrine nods, and when she moves to return to her stew, Will is standing there. Staring at me, at the bloody dress in my hands, now clutched to my chest as if it's the most precious thing in all the world.

And maybe it is.

"Will, let's leave Runa be," Katrine calls. "Come help me refresh the fire."

"It's all right, Katrine," I say. Then, to him, "Please stay."

"You've found a way," he says once she's shut the door behind her. It isn't a question. His nose does its handsome little scrunch for a moment before he lifts his eyes to mine. "I knew you could do it. Literally anything, including repairing a broken spell." He grimace-smiles and continues. "I knew it, and yet I still had this little glimmer of hope that you would be there with us tomorrow. That you'd see through the plan you made happen."

I weave my fingers through his, and it shocks me though his skin is so much more familiar than it was yesterday. His hands are stained from wet wood bark and octopus ink.

"Will, I want to help. You know I do. You also know I want to try to go home. But things have changed, and now I need to be there."

"We need you too." He cups a knuckle under my chin, tilting my face up to his.

I squeeze my eyes shut, seeking just the right words to explain without saying too much. "And I need to protect you."

Will hesitates. "Protect me from what, Runa?"

I open my eyes, and he's looking right at me, trying to read the thoughts flashing behind my features. Searching for answers as directly as I search for what I can say.

No. He deserves to know. I've kept it from him, from everyone all day; though I didn't want to disrupt our plans, the timing may never be right before dawn.

"Will, I need you to sit down." I pull him across the room and dump him in the rocking chair.

He sits accordingly, watching me, waiting—the listener that he is.

My legs itch to move, and I begin to pace between the laundry basket and the bed.

"Remember when you guessed that I knew a thing or two about royalty?"

He nods.

"Well . . ." I squeeze my eyes shut again and stop pacing for a moment—walking blind is not yet in my skill set. "My father is called the sea king. He presides over every mermaid and merman, and he has for more than a hundred years."

My eyes flash open, and Will nods, face still locked up tight without reaction. Good.

"As you can imagine, he's very angry about what happened to Alia. He's angry that she left our world for this one, using magic banned long ago. He's angry that I went after her. He's angry that we failed to save her from the consequences of the magic. And he's even more unhappy that if I don't change back by dawn tomorrow, I'll be a human forever."

"Why is he unhappy about that? He should be pleased that you won't . . . *return* like Alia," he says, by way of being respectful. I suppose she did return; all water goes to the sea eventually.

"He's very happy I'm alive, I'm sure. He'd rather not have a dead daughter. But he's also very upset that it's me in particular who is staying here." I meet his eyes. "Because I'm the only one who can give him what he needs."

Will steadies his elbows on his knees and looks up at me, face and voice calm. "And what does he need?"

I take a deep breath. "Power."

"Power? And you can give that to him?" he asks.

"Yes."

My answer works across his face and the roll of his broad shoulders. "And the alternative is why I need protection."

"Yes. You, Katrine, Sofie, Agnata, and any other witch to be had will be in danger if I don't go back."

"Not power then, magic? He needs magic."

"Yes. And unless I can help him in my way, he'll do anything to get it. I have to stop him, Will."

He nods, understanding. He gets to his feet, and in one step he's right in front of me, smelling of the earth and wood and fresh cotton. I let him draw me in, his hands cupping my elbows, as I place my palms on his chest.

The nightgown hangs off my arm between our bodies, a reminder.

He looks deep into my eyes and again presses a finger under my chin, tipping it up. "You'll stop him. I know you will."

I kiss him on the cheek. He still hasn't shaved, but I like that he's rough with stubble—the burn on my lips will last longer, the memory forming as clear as the scratch I feel at this moment.

27

Runa

AFTER SUPPER, IT'S IMMEDIATELY OBVIOUS THAT nerves are setting in.

A copy of *Frau Jenny Treibel* untouched in her lap, Sofie stares into the fire like she's watching the day unfold within the dancing shadows and flashes of light. She'd been carrying books around the castle to pass notes to the team, but it turns out she likes to read in her spare moments. Now, the orange tabby snores softly against her feet as the book goes unread. Predictably, Agnata is by her side, trying very much to do the same thing, but she's restless—legs crossing and uncrossing, and crossing again.

Katrine is cleaning, scrubbing, straightening. As if we won't return to this place and she can't stand the idea of it being a mess when the inspectors arrive to arrest her.

And Will, he's in the rocking chair, eyes closed, running

through the plan, the blocking, the sequence, over and over. His lips move, but he makes no sound. His hands flash up occasionally in little movements as he runs through his spells—sleep, shield, wildfire.

I'm bent next to a low-burning candle, paging through *The Spliid Grimoire*. This book's power is undeniable. It's a solid collection, rife with information in a scribe's never-ending looping scrawl—it's very easy to see why it was the one Katrine picked right away.

Still, I've yet to find an overt spell that will help me go home, but my hair stands on end when I find a passage where my plight is described, nice and tidy, the balance laid plain.

The sea is forever defined by its tide, give and take the measure of its barter. In magic, as in life, the sea does not give its subjects lightly—payment is required, the value equivalent, no matter the ask. A shell, a fish, a pearl of the greatest brilliance—none can be taken without debt to be paid.

The directness of it all makes me grin, but the magic behind it is so much more complex. Eydis would say that my sacrifice of the king should be payment enough, but I know it's not, no matter how much I want to believe it is. Niklas was to be Alia's payment, his blood only useful to either of us if she completed her end of the bargain.

Still, Urda is a fickle witch, and a sacrifice *was* made. Perhaps she can be convinced. She must be. I have no choice. After all, intent should matter. My deed was *for* Alia, to absolve *Alia*. I took her burden onto me. Now I just need the magic to see this and accept the exchange.

I page through the grimoire for what feels like the hundredth time, searching for something, anything that would transfer her debt. And then the answer is so clear. It's a transaction *like any other*.

I have to buy Alia's debt. *Skipta*. Exchange. The most basic of spells.

A devastating realization punches me hard in the gut. If only I had thought of this before, Alia might still be alive. The transfer now won't bring her back no matter what, but it may help me. If I assume her obligation, I will have fulfilled her deal, having murdered Niklas, rendering his blood usable again. I can only hope what I have to offer will be enough to cover the price of such an unfathomable deficit. In my pocket, my fingers grip a handful of ríkifjor. Seeds that blossom with magic—magic my father has been hoarding. Alia was trying to stop him. It's time Urda is repaid.

I shoot from the chair to standing, the blanket across my lap spilling from my legs. Will looks up from his spot on the rocking chair, trance broken, concern in the slant of his eyes. I run to Katrine's room for a cloak. It's not raining, but the cloak is necessary to allow me to leave the house with the nightgown but without questions. I drop a small cobalt bottle and stopper from one of Katrine's chests in the cloak's pocket, fingers shaking with excitement. I know exactly what to do.

Will is on his feet as I exit Katrine's room. The fire reflecting softly on their sharp expressions, Sofie and Agnata whisper between each other, drawing into themselves—suspicious that I've gone moon-crazy like last night.

When I step to the door, their eyes follow, and Will physically does. "Can I come with you?"

My heart stumbles inside my chest at the meaning behind that simple question. He knows he's not asking for an invitation to stroll under the stars. And yet he still wants to come.

"Of course," I say.

Will doesn't grab a cloak, a jacket, or anything else— only my hand. We step into a night much like the last one, the day's sun a distant memory as clouds hover low in the sky, the air damp enough to collect in the hollows under our eyes. Like the morning that Alia died, we walk in silence. This time, I lead him, tugging him along by the crook of his fingers. The wind whips the hair off my face with each step closer to the beach.

At the water's edge, the waves are furious. Frothing. Wicked. They toss themselves against the sands, against the rocks dotting the shore as a warning call. The bugle through the forest before the attack.

The breeze whips color into our cheeks, chins, and noses as we walk along—brisker than it should be for September, but Will doesn't hesitate, doesn't let go of my hand. He just keeps walking.

The sea witch might have been right when she assumed I didn't believe in love. I'm not sure I believe in it now. But what I do believe is that I have a connection with this boy that won't die in this world or the one I'm from. No matter what's to come.

After a long while, we come upon two sturdy rocks on the dry beach, flat like tables and paired together as if they're meant for us.

I take a seat on the nearest one, its surface slick with sea spray and dew that soaks into my cloak on contact. Will squats on the other, his long legs coming up at a sharp angle in front of him, knees to the shrouded sky.

"What needs to be done for you to go home?"

I squeeze his hand and then disentangle our fingers, immediately sorry that I must.

Will cups his hands together and blows warm breath into them, eyes on me as I draw the nightgown out of my cloak, the tiny glass bottle too.

"The spell that made me human was uttered by the famed sea witch—the one who saved Niklas's grandfather from death." Will nods, knowing the story like everyone else. "The spell required four items from me for my return:

Niklas's ring, his life, his dying blood on my feet, and the knife that killed him."

I can't believe I'm telling him this any more than I can believe I shared my true identity as a merprincess, but Will listens calmly, his chin propped on his knuckles, his blue eyes watching silently as though nothing can surprise him.

"I have the ring, and the knife has hopefully gone back to the sea witch, so now I have to retrieve the blood," I say, holding up the nightgown. I don't want to tell him about the spell I must offer. The uncertainty of Urda's response is too much to explain right now. He believes that I and my magic can do anything. And he'll need that confidence in magic if he's to have any chance at destroying the U-boats.

"What did Alia need?" he asks. "Was she here to kill him? That whole time? I mean, I really believed she was in love with him."

"She did love him," I say immediately. It's important to me that much is understood. "She never intended to kill him—she saved him this summer when he nearly drowned with his brothers and father. Alia was sure he'd recognize her in an instant and marry her on the spot when she came ashore as human, that the love in his heart would be enough to satisfy the spell that would have kept her alive. He adored her, but he didn't love her, and so . . ."

Will's voice drops. "And so the only way for her to survive was to kill him, like the legend of Annemette."

"Yes. Stabbed through with a specific knife, his blood

dripping upon our toes, but we never got to that part."

Will eyes the nightgown. "And that's his blood, then?"

I nod. "And if it doesn't work, you'll be human forever?"

Inhaling a deep breath of the thick salt air, I nod again. "Those were the terms of my exchange."

I spread the nightgown across my knees, the red-black smear angry as it faces the moon. The amethyst I've used so successfully sits heavy in my palm, the little bottle in the other, shining like midnight. I pop the cork and hand it to Will for safekeeping.

Then I drive my feet into the sand, the earth fast to my soles, meeting my magic, holding tight to the amethyst and my intentions.

"*Slita sasí blóð.*" Rend this blood.

Shimmer and shine, the stain quivers deep within the ruined fabric.

"*Slita sasí blóð,*" I command again.

The massive smear is no longer a monolith. It separates and shifts.

"*Slita sasí blóð.*"

Finally, finally, the droplets pull and lift, evaporating into the air in a red mist.

"*Hálmr, lœkr.*"

The mist clings to itself, creating a stream thinner than the pencil tip Will used to mark our plan on the map.

"*Efna.*"

I hold the bottle straight under the tip of the stream,

—269

and it goes right in, filling it straight to the top. Will hands me the cork, and I stop the vial.

The nightgown is again perfectly snow white, the lace as delicate as a butterfly wing, though I doubt Sofie will want it.

"Runa . . . you're not going to go and do it now, are you?" Will asks, panicked.

"Oh! No. No. Will, of course not." I stand, grip tight on the bottle, my other hand reaching for his. "But I would like some time to think, if you'll leave me a moment."

Will stands with me, a reluctance in the speed. His eyes narrow. "You'll say good-bye?"

"I promise I'll wake you." I slip the bottle into my pocket and press both hands to his chest. Strong and rich, his heartbeat thumps into my palms.

He takes my hands in his. Warm and rough, his skin is there and then it's gone, the nightgown in his hand, rustling in the wind off the sea as he walks away.

I sit again on the rock and watch the waves. They break and burst, curl and sweep, churning, turning, agitated.

"Hello, Father."

I wish if I could concentrate enough, my sisters would just appear. Pop above the surf, something between us telling them exactly where I am at this very moment. And what I must decide. I suppose a summoning spell might do that, even at this distance. But love them as I may, Eydis, Ola, and Signy are not Alia. We don't have the same connection, and we never will.

My thumb grazes the bottle cork. I should just do it. Spare myself what will surely be more than the dull pain in my gut that's festered since I realized I could return to the sea, leaving this all behind. How is it possible to miss something you barely know? Or someone?

I can tell myself that this pain is a residual effect of Alia's absence. That I haven't had time to process what happened. To truly accept it. But that's not true. The pain I feel for Alia is different. I meant it when I told the sea witch that it felt like an arm had been ripped from my body with Alia gone. And I accept that I may never feel whole again, living with the phantom pain of her holding fast to whatever body I'm in for the remainder of my days.

"Oh, Alia," I say to the waves. I stand and walk straight to them, careful to remove Katrine's shoes this time.

Then I dip my toes into the water. I pretend Alia's there in the gurgling bubbles. Soaking into my skin with a chill of truth.

Though she didn't say them aloud, Alia's words rumble through my mind in the voice that was once here.

There's no more balance.

But by working with the few remaining witches on land, I can help. I can make a difference. I can restore the balance— restore Father to the amount of power he can handle.

There really is so much I can do here.

And what will happen if I make it home?

After I make my offer of ríkifjor seeds to Urda, there will only be a handful left. Enough to sustain him for a day.

A day.

And I'll need to save a few to get another crop going if the rest of the plants have died. He won't be pleased, and his impatience—and the physical toll that goes along with it—won't be good for anyone.

If I survive that first planting, it's very easy to see the remainder of my life in service to the crown. Chained to the tower, not to be trusted with any hint of freedom. Or maybe, chained in plain sight to the ríkifjor crop—sleeping among their ghost-white blooms.

No adventure. No life beyond duty.

And who does it help besides him?

My people? Only if his threats of war cease. Only if the serum staves off his anger, entitlement, thirst. But even then, maybe not. If the U-boats appear en masse, we'll be in even greater danger. We can destroy these, destroy the program, but the Germans already have these boats. They're in the water, and these aren't the only boats being made. They're just the ones closest to the sea kingdom. To home.

There's no telling how long they'll be a threat.

The mines too.

Or how long Father will use the humans' actions to sow the seeds of his war as he grows stronger on my ríkifjor.

So strong that there's nothing left for him to do but attack. Out of boredom, or greed, or recklessness. No matter what choice I make, there are no guarantees.

"Good night, Alia," I tell the water kissing my toes.

Then I turn and walk back toward the safe house, Katrine's shoes and stockings in one hand, the other holding tight to the bottle in my pocket.

As I come to the little hill that leads down to the beach, voices whisper across the wind. Intuition bends my spine and crouches my legs, until I'm pressed to the dune, listening over the *thump thump thump* of my heart pounding in my ears.

"When do you strike?" asks a man or boy, it's hard to tell. He speaks in an accent that reminds me of Sofie's father.

"Broad daylight," I hear a girl's voice or maybe a woman's say, low enough I don't recognize it. "The warehouse will be up in flames before supper."

I press my face to the damp sand to stifle a gasp.

Our plan is out.

28

Runa

I STAY ON THE BEACH UNTIL THE VOICES AND FOOTSTEPS are long gone. Betrayal lays a thick track in my lungs, like an oil slick atop the sea surface, suffocating everything in its reach, as I stay motionless, tucked against the sand.

I slip into the safe house at midnight, the firelight dying, as a traitor sleeps within.

Though the door is tightly shut, Katrine's snores echo from her bedroom. In the main room there's just enough of a glow from the last embers to see the outline of the girls asleep on the floor. They lie side by side as they've done before, only Sofie's books between them, the nightgown folded on top of her latest read.

Will attempts to sleep, shoved up next to the door, waiting for my return. He shifts as I walk in, exhausted eyes following my movements across the room. The quilt I claimed as my bedroll last night is draped over a chair at the table. Throwing it around my shoulders, I go to him, sliding down the wall to the floor.

There's no surprise in Will's eyes. He's been expecting my good-bye. He thinks he knows what I'm going to say before the words are out—some excuse of being from other worlds, not belonging, *it's better this way*.

What I say instead is, "We need to talk."

~

Sleep does not come easily. It barely comes at all. Yet I wake before dawn, the sky still smoky with clouds but the light changing just enough beyond the shutters to prove the time.

I put the kettle on, as Katrine has taught me to do, brewing water for tea. Mug hot and fragrant in my hands, I crack the shutters just enough to watch the sky change. Charcoal to iron to ash. It shifts like the tide, slowly, slowly, until suddenly it's undeniably closer. In moments, the sea witch's spell will no longer rule me.

Tea finished and fingers shaking, I set the mug on the sill and fish a hand into the folds of my dress. Niklas's ring, the ríkifjor seeds, and the glass bottle are mingled together in the same pocket, the amethyst lonesome on the other side. Fingers wrapped tightly around the cool glass, I draw it out.

Even in the low light, it's easy to see the line that delineates blood from air. Where one life ends and another begins. Or—where one journey ends and the old life returns.

I stand there, sure in my legs, watching the sky change

further. It's now or never.

I could run for it. Use these legs while I have them. Over the pasture, down the dunes, offer my spell and spill blood onto my feet with my toes in the sand. Testing Urda's forgiveness, I could go home. Sow seeds. Do my part in making Father the most powerful being on the planet, hopes high that I alone could stave off a war.

Or I could stay here. Make my own decisions. Do my part in another fight with people who need me for more than just what I can do for them—working together to end one war and halt another before it even begins.

The ivory promise of day slips into a candlelight glow, breaking through the clouds, reaching for me. Calling me home.

Across the room, Will stands.

If I look at him now, my heart will rip right down the center and fall to the wayside, defunct. I don't know how Alia made this choice so easily. How she could see her future clearly enough to leave us, knowing she could never return? Knowing what she was risking.

Sunlight streams into my eyes, brilliant and blinding. I close them, letting it wash over me in painted lines through the shutters. The fire and fury I felt when drinking the witch's brew returns. It blazes a scorched path through my skin, cauterizing every cell, the magic that once built me seared shut. Scar tissue collecting. Each inch of progress hollows me out, scrapes me clean, reforms what and who I am.

When I open my eyes, I am a mermaid no more. A human made of blood and bones, no magic. But I can still wield it. Of that I am sure.

"Runa?" Will takes a step toward me, tone unbelieving.

I steel my heart, willing it to hold together. And then I look him right in the eyes and slip the bottle of blood back into my pocket.

He comes to me, wraps me in close, and draws me into a cocoon of strong arms, soft cotton, a beating heart.

"Thank you," he whispers.

As I press my face to the warmth of his chest, my first ever tears begin to fall.

An hour later, our arms are coated in octopus ink.

We're dressed alike, in breeches and button-ups that I've spelled to be black as midnight, just as I did our dresses the night of Niklas's murder. On top, we wear the sea-worn coats popular at the docks, pilfered and doctored from what Katrine had available in her trunks. With any luck, they'll give us the ability to hide in plain sight.

Our rucksacks are packed with more ink and gem-stones, plus weapons of a more traditional kind—knives, matches, guns, and ammunition.

Will has taught me how to load the pistol I took from the guard, though the risk was too great to show me how to shoot it. I don't plan on using it, but if I have to, I hope it works.

We say our good-byes to Katrine, and then it's time. As a team, we exit the safe house into the denim light, clouds hanging low.

"Meet you at the checkpoint," Sofie says, green eyes lit with determination and certainty as Agnata stands at her side, much less talented at hiding the nerves within her.

Will and I nod, and then Sofie and Agnata turn for Lille Bjerg Pass. Shoulders brushing, Will and I turn for the sea.

When the other girls are gone, I slip Niklas's ring out of my pocket and onto my right hand. Sofie may not like it, but even though it's no longer needed to return to the sea, I need this ring as a reminder of the past. Of Alia. Her sacrifices. Why I'm still here. And what I'm about to do. I'll take the risk of being a target of guards for all that.

The miles pass quickly as we walk along where the pasture meets the shoreline, up and up until there's a drop as tall as the spires of Øldenburg Castle between us and the ocean below. Our route is longer and less direct than the one Sofie and Agnata are taking through the mountains, but we should arrive at the same time, their path more technical with the changing terrain, while we skirt the edge of the mountain range.

When I confirmed I would participate, we'd decided to hedge our bets and split up, as the four of us together would be much easier to detect. Slipping through the waking town and down to the docks in pairs would be safer.

The miles pass quickly. Will and I are able to walk in silence together without it stretching the space between us into something awkward. I like the quiet moments with him, where we can be in our own heads, existing but together. Like the night before, his eyes drift into the middle distance. Practicing the script, the moves, the spells. It makes me smile more than it should.

"Don't fret, William Jensen. Your rebellion is perfectly choreographed."

His eyes come back to the here and now. "Choreography is one thing. Execution is quite another."

My vision snags on Niklas's ring. *Don't I know it.*

For the first time this trip, Will's fingers find mine as he cuts in front of me to lead us to a set of grown-over switchbacks trailing down the cliff to the beach below. As he traces our path along the spine of the shore, I realize this slip of beach will take us past the channel into the Øldenburg Castle cove, with its marble balcony and memories.

We're not to go in there, of course. No, we need to hop from one rock face with its hairline beach to the other, and then work our way around to the little lagoon where I first changed. Then up the switchbacks, through the woods, past the tiny vacant house and onto the sea lane with a direct shot to the docks and, by proximity, the warehouse.

When we've hit solid beach again, Will squeezes my fingers and drops my hand. And it's a funny thing, because I know if we survive this, it'll be mine to hold again. The silence and steps return, until we're past the castle, marble balcony skeletal in the low light. Past the sheer rock faces. And sloshing through the little shallow lagoon.

When we get to the beach, I force Will to pause long enough that I can dry us both. *"Purr klædi."*

Finished, I straighten the buttons on Will's coat. "Wet footprints are a dead giveaway."

We push up the switchbacks, top the cliff, and put our heads down as we enter the woods, the eyes of Øldenburg Castle looming down. They can't see us. I know they can't. But my stomach twists under their watch, Niklas's ring tight on my finger. I slip my sleeve down over my hand.

Yes. I'm the one who buried your king and ended your line. Get a good look, because I'm not finished yet.

I stop him on the edge of the woods, just in sight of the abandoned cabin. "Will, whatever happens today . . . don't lose faith in your abilities and start sprouting flowers."

Will laughs. "Good pep talk."

"I'm serious, and I'm saying this now. Just hear me—you're strong, William Jensen, and whatever comes—remember that."

He'll need that strength if we survive long enough to see Father come. If we have a war on two fronts and no end in sight.

Will's eyes don't break from mine. "I will, Runa."

Satisfied, I draw in a deep breath and drop his hand to raise my hood over my too-short hair.

The streets are alive with the weekday buzz. A few brave ships ready for a day on the water, the promise of catch as lucrative as the idea of sea mines is prohibitive. We wade through, chins to our chests, trying very hard to blend in to the ebb and flow. Our disguises are good, fitting right in, but as the warehouse looms into view over the top of a row of shops, each lingering set of eyes sends my heart hammering helter-skelter against my ribs.

Almost there.

We're to meet the girls in the alley behind a dockyard pub, Vœrtshus Havnestad. But when we cut around the building and into the alley that beelines to the back of the warehouse, only Agnata stands there.

She gasps at the sight of us and rushes forward. Her face shines with tears, her dark eyes shot through with red.

"What's happened?" Will whispers, tugging her into the shadows of the building, against a rubbish barrel brimming with molded bread. "Where's Sofie?"

"I—I don't know." She sniffs into his shoulder.

Will pries her off so that she can face us. We're huddled together in the shadows, our rucksacks providing necessary cover, our backs to both the warehouse and the rest of the alley.

She presses on, careful not to use names—this is something we discussed. "We were together on the mountain when she said her stomach hurt. Nerves, you know— she didn't eat any of her bread this morning. And then,

I waited. And waited. And when I checked on her, she wasn't there. I thought maybe she got lost and had found another trail. I thought she'd be here waiting for me and she wasn't."

Agnata begins crying again, and I nearly press a hand to her mouth to keep the noise down, but I fear it might make her even louder. "What if someone caught her? What if they've taken her to the castle to interrogate her about the murder? Or this plot or something else?"

She finishes in a near shriek, and I try to counter that by keeping my voice calm and near a whisper. "Or she could simply be working her way here, as you said." I glance to Will. "Should we wait?"

Will immediately shakes his head. "There's no time. We have a very small window. We'll have to go on without her."

Agnata's eyes grow big, those nerves we saw earlier nearly shooting fireworks straight out her eye sockets and into the dank of the alley. Her lips drop open, and I dig deep in my brain for a spell to silence her, but it's too late because she's already screaming. "Watch ou—"

Blunt and unforgiving, something metallic comes crashing into my skull. The blow is nasty enough to knock me forward into Agnata, the surprise and the weight of the rucksack on my back ruining my balance. My hands are slow to react and protect Agnata or myself. But then she's gone; the plaster of the tavern wall scrapes against my cheek, and I slide into a sandbag heap, half prone, half curved against the building.

The head wound I suffered in Niklas's royal chambers, scabbed over the last two days, is busted and liquid again, blood seeping from my wound into my hair and down my neck as I scream at this new body of mine *to move*.

But it won't.

Next to me there's a giant *whoosh*, and Will's body hits the cobblestones, blood slinking across his hairline. Somewhere behind me, Agnata is screaming until there's a metallic whomp and she's quiet.

My hands finally react, and I try to push myself off the wall. But as soon as I shift an inch, my vision swells and then contracts, all the blood seemingly rushing out of my body through the newest hole in my head.

I'm banked in the shallows, beached, and fading fast.

As the color slips away from my eyes and the world goes dark, I hear my name come from Sofie's tongue. "Runa's the most dangerous. Don't let her out of your sight."

29

Runa

I WAKE TO THE SOUND OF LAUGHTER AT MY EXPENSE.

"She's a witch. Maybe we should burn her. Who's got a stake?"

More laughter. Close by, maybe even close enough to spit on, though I can't see them.

I'm somewhere dark and small. There's room enough for just me and the chair I'm tied to with the types of rope sailors prefer. There's a gag at my mouth, and it tastes vaguely like iron, the blood from my head wound leeching into the fabric. I've been relieved of my rucksack and Niklas's ring, and even worse, of my friends—Will and Agnata are somewhere else altogether.

"Hold your horses. No one is burning anything. Open flames near my father's boats before he inspects them is definitely not going to earn anyone brownie points."

Sofie.

The men laugh again. Throaty. German. Yes, clearly German.

Great.

Sofie's speaking again, and the men's laughter dies off as they listen. "Let's record her confession of King Niklas's murder first. After that, burn at will—away from the U-boats."

Footsteps head my way, and then there's suddenly light, streaming in on my face, a door unlocked and thrown open.

Two burly men in green uniforms pick up the chair I'm sitting on and plop me into a room twice the size of any I've seen on land, even in the castle. One rips the gag off my mouth, my hair caught in it, a fresh prickle of blood tinkling down the scoop of my neck and into the collar of the coat still sitting on top of my blouse and breeches.

Dull pain drubs against the backs of my eyes as they adjust to my surroundings. The lights first. Sodium lamps blaze overhead, as blinding as the new day. Then the U-boats, lined up and ready for inspection—six altogether, the five Phillip warned Will about, plus the prototype Sofie described back at Katrine's.

Then the people. I count ten men all clad in the green uniforms, which bear the seal of Holsten—though the German pronunciation *Holstein* is scrawled beneath its red-and-white jags. Sofie stands before them, holding the mouthpiece of some sort of machine.

"Runa,   darling,   aren't   you   bright-eyed   and

bushy-tailed?" she says with a smile.

I scowl at her. "Sofie. How could you?"

"What? Did you think I'd run forever for a crime I didn't commit? Leave my family, title, and all the money that goes with it behind?" Her smile is brilliant, even in the sallow light. "Of course not."

She laughs, and the men laugh, and dear Urda, it's annoying. Though it does nothing for my headache, I roll my eyes.

Sofie continues. "And you're going to give me back my life with the truth."

Smile on her face, she saunters up to me, puts the mouthpiece to her lips, and presses a few buttons. "My name is Komtesse Sofie of Holsten, Queen Consort of the Sovereign Kingdom of Havnestad. In the early hours of the twentieth of September, 1914, I watched as a girl named Runa murdered King Niklas of Havnestad in my wedding bed. The next voice you'll hear is that of this girl, whose family and home are unknown."

With a tilt of her head, she comes closer, setting the mouthpiece right under my chin.

I grind my teeth together. I won't do it. I won't. I won't be recorded on that thing.

Sofie leans in, her breath close enough that I can feel the heat of it on my scraped-up cheek.

"You will speak your truth, Runa. I'll get it out of you one way or another, and hear me now, if you're difficult, your confession will be the very last thing you do."

I look her dead in those beautiful green eyes of hers. "Not going to happen." Then I smile at her, fury in it. *"Fœra."*

Bloodred beams blast from the closed fist behind my back and straight up into the light above. The glass shatters, and I kick Sofie square in the stomach as everyone scatters away from the raining shards.

Sofie's training kicks in, and at the same time as I do, she yells, *"Skjoldr!"*

Glass fragments bounce off our shields, tinkling like music as they hit the floor. From where they've scattered, the men watch, bent in posture with their arms thrown over their heads.

One by one, the guards' mouths fall agape as they stare at their commander's only living daughter.

"The komtesse is a witch!" a guard yells, a mixture of fear and righteousness frothing at his lips.

Sofie stumbles to her feet. "What? No!" Her voice is high and pleading with them to unsee it. "No, I'm not."

"You are! Just like that dead sister of yours!" shouts a particularly brave guard. "Hung herself for being a witch, she did. Everybody knows it."

The surprise falls from Sofie's face, anger in its place. And then she smiles at the man. "You're right. I'm just like her."

She catches my eye, and again we say our spells at the same time. *"Villieldr!"*

As we practiced, Sofie's right arm goes up in violet flame, right before their eyes. It's still weak, but it's impressive, and the men's confusion melts into strict, undeniable panic.

Their eyes swing away from her only because my whole body has burst into purple flame. The rope, the chair, everything searing off into a stream of smoking, instant ash.

Free from my bonds, I walk toward them.

Sofie is advancing too. The men take in the flaming, witchy pair of us and stumble back. We're everything they've been told witches could be. Powerful, unpredictable, logic-defying.

"Burn us at the stake, will you?" I say. "What if we don't burn?"

Still, the braver ones draw their pistols with fumbling, shaking hands. But we're ready for this.

Sofie angles both arms out, protecting herself and the majority of my flaming form. "*Skjoldr!*"

Shield up and safe, I close in. Again, I use Oma Ragn's favorite fighting technique. Smite.

"*Fœra!*" I scream, sweeping both arms out and away, encompassing the men. The red line of magic stuns them hard and, as dominos, they fall one by one into a heap on the floor. Prone. Disarmed. Useless for at least the next twelve hours. Still, to be safe, I add an extra layer of protection. "*Ómegin. Rata.*"

Sofie helps me deliver the spell to each of the men.

"You're going to destroy that recording, aren't you?" I ask, finally allowing myself to smile, while checking the back of my head for yet another goose egg and a never-healing cut.

"Yes. Wouldn't want a little thing like that hanging around for the wrong person to find."

"Good—it *was* a really nice touch."

She waggles her eyebrows. "I thought so too." Then, she tips her head to another closet—this one larger than my little holding pen—something meant for actual storage.

Sofie pulls a key from her belt, and the lock releases with a quick tug. And there, inside, gagged and bound in just the way I was, are Will and Agnata. Their eyes are huge at the sight of us. I pull up Will right away, slipping him off the chair, releasing his gag, then his hands.

Agnata waits patiently for her turn, smiling beyond her gag, clearly expecting Sofie to begin untying her any moment.

Instead, after Will is free of his binds, the three of us simply turn to Agnata and watch the realization creep across the angles of her face. Sofie cocks her head and shoots us a satisfied smirk. "Now, what should we do with her?"

30

Runa

WILL PULLS THE GAG DOWN, PLACES HIS HANDS ON HIS knees, and sinks to eye level with Agnata. "What the hell were you thinking, selling us out?"

Sofie doesn't give her a chance to answer. "She was thinking she'd get a pretty penny, that's what. How much was it?"

Agnata's lips snap shut.

"Worth more than all our years together, then?" Sofie spits, eyes flashing. "More than my life?"

Agnata's desperation grows as we drag her and her chair out of the closet and into the warehouse proper. The girl's eyes bounce from the guards piled on the floor to the ashes, to the glass littered and sparkling in the remaining sodium lamps.

There, massive, looming, and flammable, are the U-boats, lined up as Will put it, "like pigs for slaughter."

"I—Sofie, you've got this all wrong. Please. Please, listen!"

Sofie doesn't respond except to disarm Agnata of her gemstone.

"I met with them, yes, but it was only to help get information for our plan. It was—"

"Agnata, save it," I say, temper flaring enough that I might as well be spelling purple flames straight from my nostrils. "We know they let you go from the castle only so that you could supply specific details about our plan. We heard you talking to the guard last night outside the safe house."

I say "we," and this was part of what Will, Sofie, and I discussed in the middle of the night, once we spelled Agnata to make sure she was in a very deep sleep. "You were planning to let them attack as penance for your role in the plot against the U-boats. They'd get Sofie and myself for the king's murder, they'd get Will on the U-boats, and you'd get your freedom and a cut of the sale."

All the color in her face drains. "I did say all that. I did. But it was just because they needed to hear it." She turns to Sofie. "You know how they are—they're relentless. And they escorted me to Katrine's, so I couldn't get out of reporting back."

Will rubs his brow, and even my head falls to my hands. We've been compromised. Our safe house is no longer safe. And neither is Katrine. How could we have missed it? Yes, we've been focused on the spells, but last night? Last night a guard was mere feet from our haven. I raise my face and stare at this traitor. We were so fixated on countering her efforts, the guard became a distant memory.

Sofie looks as if she's swallowed glass. The komtesse moves like a woman possessed, busting open a retrieved rucksack and cocking a pistol sitting on top. My pistol, to be exact.

"I—I . . ." Agnata tries to fight against her binds, the meat at her wrists bulging against her restraints.

"Tell me now, are they going after Katrine? Do they have her? Yes or no?"

Agnata bursts into tears, her head shaking. "No, no, no! They don't know about her! Please! You have to believe me! Don't shoot."

Sofie's eyes swing to Will's and then to mine, but she doesn't stow the gun. It stays pointed at the girl—her friend, her handmaiden—as she looks to us to tell her what to do.

"We don't have time for any more of this," Will says calmly. "Your father will be here to inspect the boats in less than an hour. We can't risk talking about this anymore."

Sofie's hand begins to tremble, the gun barrel with it. In one step, I've gently swept her arm down and to the side.

As she disarms the hammer, I squat down on eye level with Agnata. The girl sobs harder as I raise my hands in front of her face, amethyst peeking out of my palm. And then I use all the mercy I have left.

"*Ómegin. Rata.*"

~

If only there were a spell to pause time.

With the Agnata affair, our window to execute our plan has shrunk. But at least knowing it was going to happen got us in the door and able to turn the tables, thanks to Sofie's commendable acting skills. Yet there's no calling this a success until it's finished.

Looming over us is Sofie's father's famous punctuality, because he's not just on time, he's early, especially if a deal is involved and he might finagle himself a better price with the element of surprise. Arrive early; find things imperfect, unfinished, or otherwise at fault; win a discount for disarray. That was how Baron Gerhard of Holsten ran—like clockwork, but ten minutes ahead of schedule. There's absolutely no time to lose.

We move the bodies first—Sofie and I working together to carry men one by one, head to foot. Will puts his back in it, throwing a man over his shoulder one at a time. He carries out Agnata next, slipping her off the chair and into one of the motorcars the guards drove down from the castle.

We line them up in the overgrown summer grass behind the warehouse, and then each pick our man and get to work. Stripping away everything but their undergarments—boots, pants, button-ups, weapons. Then, we pile the boots into the car with Agnata, dress ourselves in the remainder, and run back into the warehouse for the final piece of our plan.

We stand three abreast, spaced evenly before the six ships.

"Ready?" I look to the cousins, on my left and my right. They nod.

"Set?" They raise their inked arms in a double-fisted salute, gemstones set in their palms.

"Light!"

Will and Sofie scream out the wildfire command as one. They ignite as if they've done this their entire lives— luscious purple flame leaping toward the rafters.

Now it's my turn. *"Vindr!"* I direct my hands toward their flames, and a gust of wind kicks up and guides the flames to each boat.

One and two. Three and four. Five and six. They go up, two by two, steel taking the flame with a twist and a sigh, the heat of it bending, curling, buckling. Within the space of a minute, they're nothing but molten lava.

Almost finished.

"Vaxa!" I scream, and with the wind's help, the flames leap to the rafters, which catch fire in an instant.

"Run!" I say, and they do, each extinguishing their flaming arms.

We push out into the noontime glare, smoke chasing us out of the building, but it's just starting on the roof. If we hurry, we can be out of here before anyone notices.

Maybe.

Sofie jumps over the car door and into the back seat of the open-top motorcar, tucking her long hair up into a bun and pulling a guard's hat over the mess of it all. I have a much easier time, but I know I'll look suspect up close. It'll have to do.

Will gets the motor going, and the car rumbles to life. He shifts a few cranks and gears, and we jolt back and then forward as he edges around the other car and the sleeping stunned men.

"What are you smiling about?" I whisper, because he is indeed smiling and it's completely ridiculous that he should have this expression on his face while driving a getaway car.

"I can't believe they've got a Vauxhall," he says. I have no idea what this means. When he sees me frown at his glee, he adds, "It's British."

Ah. Made by the same country that produced the ship they destroyed with the first of their U-boat fleet. Now, I grin back. "Traitors."

As we come around the corner of the warehouse, I hold my breath. A few dock workers have noticed the flames, but they've yet to notice us fleeing the scene.

Will turns onto the sea lane, and there's an identical

car rumbling down the narrow road, coming from the direction of the castle. Inside is a single driver with two men in back—one in the blue of Havnestad, the other in a coat as green as ours.

Will tenses, and I know it's exactly who I suspect. The baron and the councilor working to make a sale in the dead king's place.

I immediately find something very interesting to look out my window, which faces town and away from the vehicle about to pass within inches of us. Will props his elbow up on the door, his knuckles to his temple as if this is the most boring drive ever. In the back, Sofie slumps in her seat, head down. I can nearly hear her praying.

We're close enough that her father could reach over and remove her hat without much trouble at all.

Will obscures his profile with a quick salute and I hold my breath, waiting for Baron Gerhard to recognize his nephew despite the hat pulled down low. The baron doesn't linger and neither does the driver—though the vehicle slows through the pinch point to avoid scraping the paint of either motorcar.

When the pass is complete, all three of us exhale deeply, the other car gaining speed as it chugs down the hill toward the docks, pointed toward the prize that's cost everyone far too much.

Will hits the gas, and we lurch forward up the hill. As we take a hard right off the sea lane and into town, a rumble begins. Soft, so soft, until it's suddenly a volcanic and undeniable BOOM—ripping toward the sky as the clouds gather again over the Øresund Strait.

I glance in the side mirror. A fireball the size of Ølden-burg Castle lights the noontime sky—the warehouse and the U-boats inside it now nothing but memories and ash.

31

Evie

THERE IT IS.

I feel it like the earth quaking. Like a volcano erupting. Like the flood of waters that cannot be stopped.

Like I did when Alia died. Or when Runa's transformation from mermaid to human was complete and permanent.

The magic around me and in me has shifted again—the balance tilting a little to the left, to land, to the place in the shadows. Those shadows spent centuries growing. Since before the tragedy of Maren Spliid and Christian IV, the witch-hunter king. Before families, covens, and the magic itself was split and divided and cut and ripped into minute slivers of a whole and tossed into the blowing wind.

And, oh, it feels good.

Runa and her little coven have produced the most powerful magic on land in a generation.

Since the day Nik lived, Anna succumbed, and I was made.

Real, true, strong land magic, depleted for generations, driven into hiding, and then, weak and tired, sleeping for so long, is now awake. Eyes open, yawn shaking, raising its head. It's here.

And it just killed Havnestad's fledgling U-boat program. I know it.

My cauldron's in use, bubbling with a spell that might change my world for the better, too. So, though I cannot see Runa in action, I lift my eyes to the surface and smile up to the clouds blanketing the sky.

"Look at you, little witch," I say to no one at all but the bubbling turfmoor and waving polypi. "Not yet human a day and you've already done more magic than the land has seen in fifty years."

I allow myself a smile for Runa, the little gardener, planting magic and immediately bearing fruit.

"She's talented indeed, but she needs your help," Anna answers.

I nod, my back to her. "Yes, and she'll get it soon."
She must.

If I feel the magnitude of what just happened on land, I know the sea king does too. He will be coming. He might already be on his way. And before he arrives, I must be ready.

The glee for Runa fades, replaced by the concentration

I must have in its place. The potion in my cauldron simmers happily, steam rising to the surface in an endless drifting current. It must boil longer than Tante Hansa's pea soup ever did—or at least that's what I think it'll take—I've never performed this spell before.

I lean over my cauldron, giving the contents a stir with my swordfish spear. It's been a day since I first put the potion on, and the color is good—the bright yellow of sunshine. Fitting for the freedom it provides.

But it's not ready. It has all the aspects necessary—land, sea, lifeblood—save for one.

Love.

All I need is the ring.

Just that word bouncing through my mind's eye brings me back to childhood. Back to the time when we were ten and Nik bashed his leg on a rock during a climb of Lille Bjerg Pass. It wasn't a deep cut, but it was right on his shin and bled like his entire life was going to flow right through it and into the dirt as Anna and I carried him down.

Nik passed out for a moment, and we had all his weight on our shoulders, which wasn't as much of a problem as his size—tall and gangly, the angles of him made him nearly impossible to drag down without scraping up his shins and boots worse than they were. So, when Anna's mother appeared from inside a shop right near the trailhead, we decided it would be best if I stayed back with Nik, and together they went to fetch the royal physician.

Nik came to as soon as they rounded the corner, confused and then slightly embarrassed, his ears blushing hard as I relayed what had happened. "Mother will have something to say about this." Nik's eyes were on his hands, long fingers playing in the grass. "'Niklas, a king shouldn't be scarred—the eyes of the people are always watching,'" he said, trying very hard to mimic his mother's particular affected speech pattern. Then he smiled, dark eyes flashing. "Yes, as if the kingdom will crumble when I roll up my pant leg, flash a scar, and prove that I am indeed human."

"Blame me," I said, knowing his mother already disliked me. "She'll have the comfort in knowing that your disfigurement was all my fault." Trying very hard to be self-effacing, I shrugged.

A tight smile crossed Nik's face. He tossed a few blades of grass and then plucked out a tuft of lady's cushion, its tiny pink leaves dwarfed after a dry summer. His eyes flashed up to mine. "Evie, you know I don't care what my mother, my father, or anyone else thinks about you."

"I know," I said, because I did. Though I was young enough to think that the opinions of one boy didn't matter against a sea of opposition.

I know better now.

And I think Nik knew better then. Because he was quiet for a moment, messing with the flowers, and just when I thought we were done talking, my eyes focused out in front of me, looking for the telltale stovepipe hat of the royal physician, Nik nudged my arm. When I turned his way to respond, he held up a little circlet of flowers. Then he took my hand and placed the ring on my fourth finger.

"Thanks for staying with me," he said, his eyes meeting mine, blush reddening at his ears.

I glanced down at the ring of wildflowers, mostly because looking at his face was too much. "Always."

Oh, Nik. What we could've had.

What we should've had.

I need that ring.

Closing my eyes, I reach up through the onyx waters of my prison cell, into the open ocean, round the mines the sea king so fears, and into the warm exhale of late summer air.

I picture my toes in the sand and running along the beach. My magic pumping, churning, streaming—as unstoppable as life itself—straight from the earth through me and out my fingertips with the right words and sayings.

I run past Greta's Lagoon and my first lair, filled with long-rotted clams spilling their pearls, a library of spells, and rows of bottles left to time.

I run past the inlet leading to Øldenburg Castle. The marble balcony added after Nik's death looms white and arching. If I squint, I can see where my father once docked his fishing boat, kitchen staff waiting and eager to get their hands on fresh whale meat for tvøst og spik.

Magic swirls around me, renewed with what has just occurred on land.

And still, I reach.

I reach for the origin of this magic.

A register. A signal. A mark of where it started from.

Reaching, reaching, reaching.

Until I find it. A ghost of an impression. The sandy footprint dying in the tide.

The place where the witches honed their magic using Runa's knowledge. There is living magic in this place, coiled and ready, though locked away, key dangling.

I push into that dark room and feel around.

Put my hands on something familiar.

The Spliid Grimoire.

The same book I borrowed from Tante Hansa in the middle of the night when she saw me so clearly though I was invisible. That old woman always saw through me and into me in a way no one else could. In a way no one else ever will.

This book is another version—a copy with different binding and a calf-skin cover that's seen better days. But it's perfect. I dig in my nails and grab hold.

That's enough to put me there. Anchor me. Give me time and space that allows me to reach into a fire gone long cold.

"*Kveykva.*" I whisper into the kindling. Sparks answer back, claiming the kindling.

A fire roars to life.

And then, I grab the smoke by the throat, and I write my message, whispering *"Dveljask"* when it's complete so that it will stay until Runa's eyes are upon it.

And then I prepare for both her father and the ring.

32

Runa

THEY SAY EVERY DROP OF WATER FLOWS TOWARD THE sea, but in Havnestad, at this very moment, every person flows toward the sea in a never-ending stream.

Our motorcar is headed against the tide, up the crooked streets as men, women, children, donkeys, goats, and dogs course out of every home and shop and yard in town, ambling down the cobblestones with stunned looks on their faces, running toward the harbor. Toward flames licking the clouds just singed by a fireball.

I tell myself what we just did will save lives, like the ones streaming past us, just somewhere else.

Maybe it will save them too. Will was right when he said war doesn't know its bounds—neutrality isn't a shield. It's simply a statement that can be easy to ignore.

Only when the people stop coming and we're alone

with the rumble of the car and the open road over Lille Bjerg Pass ahead do I let myself relax.

"Hey," I say to Will. His arms are braced against the steering wheel now, doing what they can to keep moving in the direction of the road as the wheels navigate the bump and skid of cobblestones meant for boot soles and horse hooves. I hang a hand on the ridge of his upper arm and lean in. When his eyes flit my way, I toss him a full grin. "We did it, William Jensen."

He smiles back. "We did."

A quick blush creeps across his cheeks as he checks the road, but then his eyes come back. I want them to always come back.

I lean in farther, drawn to him—warm and true, and flush with the thrill of success.

He's close enough to kiss. For real. Not just his cheek.

Above the scruff he's left, his lips are the same pink as his cheeks, and the combination makes his eyes even more blue, like shallow water on summer days and—

"Stop the car, Will! I want to watch. Are you guys seeing this? We have such a great view!"

I yank myself away, and there's Sofie, wrenching around from where she's clearly been watching the flames.

"I don't think that's a great idea, Sof." Will's voice is soft but stern. "Agnata hosed us—the second those men wake up, the one who met her by the safe house is going to lead them straight there. We have to beat them."

He's right, though we deserve to watch. I can't argue with that logic and neither can Sofie, apparently.

"Okay, fine. You're right. I just want to revel," Sofie pouts.

"You're reveling fine from the back seat, I'd say," Will notes. "How about you be on the lookout for anyone tailing us while you're at it."

"Fine, but if you guys kiss, I'm still going to see it even if I'm turned around. I have eyes in the back of my head."

Cobblestones drop off the road and make way for hard-packed dirt. The wheels churn smoother underneath us. Motorcar-related glee returns to Will's face and his lips kick up. "Let's see just how fast this baby can go."

A few gear shifts and movement of his legs and suddenly we're going twice as fast, barreling down the hill, wind whipping at our faces. Sofie spins back around, holding on to the sleeping Agnata in her lap as we barrel down the hill and into the valley, green pasture streaming past under the gray sky.

My hand flies to my head, holding my hat in place. Too late, I realize Will's isn't safe either, and the wind claims it for its own. Sofie tries to catch it, losing her own in the process, the hats gliding into a pasture dotted with sleeping cows.

We decide to stash the car in a small cave carved by the sea into a cliffside on the beach. Will secures the soft top to the frame and backs away, unhappy.

"Salt water will be hell on her engine."

"Oh, heavens, Will"—Sofie groans—"tell me you haven't named the car."

His cheeks pink and he pulls a frown to cover. "Freyja deserves better than this cave."

Sofie rolls her eyes. "Where would you like to park *Freyja* instead? On the beach, where someone could easily snag her? Or maybe right in front of Katrine's house, to give the guards a big, fat Freyja-shaped tip?"

Will frowns, and I grab Sofie's arm to stop her from responding further. We don't have time to waste. Sofie obliges, and she and I shoulder the rucksacks and the extra sets of boots for Katrine's collection, while Will folds Agnata over his farmer's shoulders. She's still bound, and we've returned her gag, just in case she wakes up and starts screaming.

Freyja's cave is about a mile from the safe house. Not far at all, but not ideal, considering we still have to drag Agnata around. We go in silence as the clouds seem to drop closer to the earth, lightning from a coming storm snagging the water across the Øresund Strait. It's enough that we pick up the pace without exchanging a word.

I watch Will's boots ahead of me as we press forward, almost there, trying very hard not to think of what comes next. Surely, more time spent running, the safe house compromised. None of us can go home, we can only go forward. To the next safe house. The next mission.

Almost by reflex, my focus strays to the waves beside us. The water sluices through the sand, making its mark with each inhale and exhale of the tide. Its energy sparks into the air we breathe, and though I haven't eaten in hours or truly slept in days, it's invigorating and cleansing. It puts a smile on my face because I suddenly feel I made the right choice. But then something taps my foot. I look down and stifle a scream.

A fish stares up at me, blood black as night clotting where its eyes should be.

The sight of it stops me dead in my tracks. Sofie bumps straight into my back with an audible *umph* and a "Hey, what—oh my God, what is that?"

"I—I don't know."

Ahead, Will stops and turns as quickly as Agnata's weight will allow. "Guys . . . ," he says, and my eyes immediately jump farther out into the waves.

And there, coating the surface, are hundreds—thousands—of fish belly up, their eyes oozing rotting blood into the water.

Oh, Father, what have you done?

I glance to Will. "We need to get back right now. Can you run with her?"

He doesn't answer, he just starts running. Sofie is

scared enough that she simply does, too, though I feel the questions building in her throat.

We race down the beach and veer up the little hill where I'd first heard Agnata selling us out. Over the hill and then it's just a few steps more and—oh.

The little bushes disguising the windows and door are gone.

There's nothing but another sloping hill, cloaked and green.

"What?" Will pants. "I've been here a hundred times. It's always right—"

"Magic," I whisper with a smile. Clever Katrine. "I can smell it. A cloaking spell of some kind."

"Well, how do you uncloak it?" Sofie asks, thumping her rucksack to the ground. "Katrine! Are you in there? It's us!"

Will grabs her arm to try to silence her, nearly dropping Agnata in the process. "It could be a trap."

"Wait, look!" I say, and they both quit fussing.

The hillside before us shimmers, and then a hole appears, door-shaped and yawning wide. Katrine's wild hair blows into the wind, almost a vision. She looks both pleased and horrified to see us.

"Come inside, quick! Runa, there's something you must see."

She leads me into the room first, almost herding me

inside. As my eyes adjust, my lips fall open. There, hovering above the fireplace in words as clear as any inked on paper, is a very succinct set of instructions.

Your father's war is here.
I cannot fight by your side without the ring.
Return it to me as soon as you can.

The ring.

I look to my hand but know it's not there.

It wasn't there the moment I came to inside the warehouse.

As this realization washes over me, Sofie is in my ear asking all the questions she didn't whisper-scream on the beach.

"What's this about, Runa? What is it about that ring that's so special, and who the hell is writing words in the air with smoke like some third-rate ghost from my fairy tales, huh?"

I swallow and catch eyes with Will. He's the only one who knows, and it's very clear he's kept my confidence. Behind him, Katrine watches calmly.

I take a deep breath and turn to Sofie, who's mowing me down with that unflinching glare of hers. "The sea witch who changed me into a human needs the ring to stave off war from my father, the sea king. Happy?"

Shock blinks across her features and then morphs into something closer to camaraderie. "And I thought *my* father was an ass for aiding a war. Your father is going to *start* one? Doesn't he know we're already busy enough with our own up here?"

"That's exactly why he's doing it, Sof," Will says, as he sets Agnata more gently than she deserves onto a dining chair. "Strike 'em while they're down. Works in world domination just as well as it does in boxing."

I nod. "For reasons that are partially my fault, Father is in a position where he needs more magic. He has a monopoly on the sea's lot of it, so he's coming to claim the only magic that isn't his—ours."

Sofie accepts that news by dropping into the closest dining chair, her bones heavy. "I did not renounce my family, become a witch, and destroy royal property to be assassinated by some magical merking."

I draw in a deep breath. "Sofie, this wasn't exactly my plan either, but it's what we've got. At this point, the only way we—and any other witches within our general proximity—are going to survive this attack is with the sea witch's help. We need to get her Niklas's ring, and we can't wait. Those dead fish? They're just the start."

"Well, we all know *I* don't have the ring," Sofie sniffs, crossing her arms over her chest.

"No," I say, before tipping my chin to our captive. "But she might."

Sofie and I search Agnata's pockets, Will watching and waiting with a frown. We all know it won't be there, but it's still a disappointment when we find exactly nothing of the sort. Though we do find a small drawstring bag of krone.

Agnata indeed sold us out for more than just her freedom.

Will pockets the coins as I crouch down in front of the girl and remove her gag. Her head lolls to the side, dark hair fallen out of her braid.

"Vakti."

The moment the spell is out, the girl's eyes fly open and she inhales a deep breath as if she's been underwater for the last couple of hours, not asleep. Her eyes snap from my face to Will's before finally settling on Sofie's. Katrine ignores her altogether as she puts on the kettle.

"Am I still . . . here?" Agnata's eyes narrow on mine. "I thought you were going to murder me. Like you did those guards. Those poor men were doing their—"

"Save your righteousness. They're not dead, dummy." Sofie shoots to her feet. "You're lucky you're not, though, so I'd save your critiques for someone else."

"Where's the ring?" I ask, because we really don't have time for this.

"The ring . . ."

"Agnata, seriously, I'm ready to singe your eyebrows off, and Sofie would do worse. *Niklas's ring*," I snap. "I had it on

—313

before I was knocked out and dragged into the warehouse. Where did it go? None of the guards we frisked had it."

"I—I," Agnata stumbles.

Sofie takes four long strides and lights her inked arm in wildfire like it's nothing. I feel a pang of pride. "How do I aim this stuff at her eyebrows, Runa? Still learning."

"No! I'll tell you," Agnata screeches, her eyes squeezed shut as if that can protect them. Her voice comes quieter this time. "Just please put that away."

Sofie kills the fire, glaring hard at her former friend. "It's easy to see why you didn't last long under castle guard interrogation."

"Go on, Agnata," Will says.

"After you were knocked out, I sold it to the man you heard the night before—the messenger. He's a member of the king's guard, not the Holsten contingent, so he wasn't at the warehouse . . . but he was waiting in the vœrtshus. And then I joined you as a captive in the warehouse."

Oh, Urda. We can't go into the castle looking for a random guard with the ring.

"Where is he now?"

Sofie waves her arm in front of Agnata's face. "Before you say 'I don't know,' I want you to again consider your eyebrows."

Agnata scrunches her whole face into a ball before answering. "This man, called Møller, he said he had a buyer for it. Promised me another ten percent once it sold."

Her eyes flash open. "He planned to meet this person at the vœrtshus tonight. Eight o'clock. He told me to be there by nine to collect my cut."

I glance to Will and Sofie. "Time to brew another plan. And quick."

~

We lock Agnata away in Katrine's bedroom, and then proceed to work away at the table with mugs of piping tea and open-faced sandwiches that Katrine has prepared. We huddle over the map we used this morning, but a plan is slow to form.

To get the ring, we have to go back to Havnestad, into a tightly packed tavern, with Agnata, who's already sold us out once. Worse, the man we're meeting is a king's guard who will most likely recognize us on the spot. As will literally anyone else in town. A disguise will be essential but tricky—we must blend in long enough to get the ring and get out.

We drag Agnata back into the main room and take turns changing clothes in Katrine's bedroom, each finding something suitable for a night out. I spell them clean and make them dark so that they look fancier than they are.

Then, I get to work spelling Will's hair darker and Sofie's to be much redder.

I reach for a bottle of squid ink Katrine has deemed inert and expired to do my own, when Sofie grabs my hand.

"Why don't you just do to yourself what you did to me?" she asks, sweeping her hand around her head in a little loop. The dark red looks lovely on her.

"I've tried since I came ashore, and it won't work. The sea witch took my hair as part of our deal, and nothing seems to change it."

"But have you tried since you became human?"

I blink. "No . . . I haven't."

Sofie arches a brow. "Worth a shot, don't you think?"

Okay. Yes.

She holds up a small looking glass. "Go ahead."

My hair hangs just past my chin. I've come to like not being bothered by long hair in the past few days, but it is very noticeable.

I close my eyes, take a deep breath, and feel my magic, amethyst pressed against my palm. *"Vaxa."*

It starts as a tingle on my scalp, then a burn. When I open my eyes, the girl I was is staring back at me, different but the same, with hair past my shoulders.

"Lovely, Runa," Sofie says softly.

She means it as a compliment, but suddenly there's pressure behind my eyes, and a tear slides down my cheek.

"Runa? I—it was lovely before."

I wave my hand at my long hair, searching hard for words to explain the grief sitting on my chest. "It's her. It reminds me of Alia."

Sofie snags my fluttering hand and tucks it into her

warm palm. "You don't have to explain." Her words catch and she glances down. The guard's words about her own departed sister hang between us, a truth.

I draw in a shaky breath. "Can you help me braid it?"

Her rosebud lips press together in something of an actual smile. "Yes."

33

Runa

THIS MISSION MIGHT BE MORE DANGEROUS THAN SET-
ting the warehouse afire. It's strange to think of what we've
accomplished, and yet this last piece could undo it all.

"Now we're wanted for two crimes," Will says as he
secures his cufflinks. He's wearing a suit that makes him
look very important and expensive, but not regal. "Regi-
cide and destruction of kingdom property." It sounds so
official and stark as he lays it out. "Probably robbery too,
considering we still have Freyja in our possession and I'm
not planning to give her back."

"Four crimes," I correct. "Let's not forget witchcraft.
That's part of how you sold it to me."

He grins. "I did."

Sofie rolls her eyes. "I'm glad you two found each
other, but could you just stop making me want to vomit?
Because if I vomit, we don't have time to clean it off this

silk, magically or otherwise."

I've come to learn Sofie's mechanism for survival is to deflect actual feelings as forcefully as possible. That, or bury them. Which is what she's done with Niklas—we haven't spoken his name while planning to snatch the ring, and we won't.

"All right, everyone. Good luck. Tandsmør and I'll be waiting for you here." Katrine doles out hugs to each of us, even Agnata, and sends us on our way.

The storm started an hour ago, and I feel Father inside it like a heartbeat. The sky won't quit. The rain is sheeting like it aims to dump all of Havnestad into the sea. And maybe it does. I keep this to myself. The weather is making everyone nervous enough without an additional explanation from me.

We load into the car as we did before—I'm next to Will, and Sofie sits in the back, minding Agnata. Agnata is dressed just like us but disarmed, her forearms clean and bare, no stone in her possession. We tied her hands as precaution for our travel, though the binds will have to come off the second we exit Freyja.

The road winds through the valleys, past grass overwhelmed by the rain, the earth unable to soak up any more. Water sits atop the pastures, glistening when the moon finds a sliver in the clouds, as we repeat nearly the same route we took earlier today. Urda—or maybe Freyja—is on our side, and the road is smooth and the wheels don't stall, though the headlamps do very little to light the way as we crest Lille Bjerg Pass.

"There they are," Will says, under his breath, as the headlamps key back down toward town. "But what is that?"

The lights illuminate a line of guards standing in the road, gas lamps in hand.

"It's a checkpoint," Sofie says, leaning forward into the front seat.

My stomach tightens. We were lucky that we didn't pass by one earlier in the day, but now, the guards of Holsten and Havnestad are working together, both on the lookout for the same traitors.

Luckily, they think what has been stolen is a green motorcar. Freyja is now a sleek black.

Will pulls into the checkpoint and shifts his features to put on the same show he so often performed at the castle. He's affable, a real man's man, and, here, he's out for a night on the town with not one but three ladies, all dressed to the nines to hang off his well-appointed arms.

A guard in a rain-drenched coat and hat of Øldenburg blue leans into the driver's side window, flashing a gas lamp across the faces in the back. As he does this, two other men begin to search the perimeter of our car.

"Name and destination, sir?"

"Remy Johansson, and these are Frigg, Fulla, and Hela. We're headed anywhere with a sturdy roof and hvidtøl on tap." He smiles at the man. "Do you have any recommendations for me and my gals?"

The guard's sternness cracks just a bit. I'm not surprised. Men can always bond over the objectification of women.

Behind me, Sofie is coiled tight, her hand digging into the top of my seat, ready to bat Will across the ears if he says something worse, even if it means we can drive away.

The guard cocks a brow at Will. "I do have a recommendation, Herr Johansson, but only if you have one in there for me."

Will laughs and, oh, Urda, he winks. "A man doesn't share his greatest treasures, my friend."

The men checking our car for the marks of the missing one are finished and give the guard at our window a signal. But then the man's smile dies on his lips.

"That's understood, but can you tell me, are all these women able to speak?"

"Of course, sir."

The guard smiles briefly and then his stern face returns. "Please have each woman say her name so that they can prove it."

Will's smile is stretched so thin it's almost a grimace. "Why, sir?"

"We happen to be on the lookout for three women wanted in a plot to kill King Niklas of Havnestad. Surely you heard the news."

"I . . . wasn't aware it was a woman's doing."

"It was," the guard says before spearing each of us with his dark eyes. "Now, ladies, one by one, please say your name loud and clear for me. Let's start with you."

The guard looks to me, in the front of the car. The one who looks most like Alia's description, no doubt. I smile brightly and repeat the Norse goddess's name I've adopted. "Frigg."

Sofie goes next, her name nearly trampling over the end of mine. "Fulla, sir."

Heart crawling into my throat, I let my eyes swing to Agnata, sitting in the back, her bound hands covered by a blanket over her dress. I bite down hard on the inside of my mouth and stare at her, not knowing what I'll do if she outs us. Our firearms are hidden under the carpet at our feet. Would we have time to grab them before the shooting started? Or would they force us out of the car? How many guards can't we see? Is it just these four?

Agnata seems to calculate this too, glancing at the sliver of space between her and Sofie. Will forms a tight smile at the guard. "Hela's a bit shy." He turns around to lock eyes with her, kindness in the set of his features. "Come on, my dear, tell the man your name. The night awaits."

Agnata's mouth drops open and my hand slides into my pocket, fingers wrapping around the amethyst there. Sofie is smiling at Agnata like her face might crack in two.

"Sir, my name is Hela."

I exhale slowly out of my nose.

"There we go," Will says. "I hope that will suffice. I'm sure your job isn't easy in a downpour like this."

The guard doesn't comment. "Have a safe night, Herr Johansson."

~

With the checkpoint behind us, Will finally exhales. "Good job, ladies." The way he says that, I know he really means "Agnata."

"I wasn't going to out you," Agnata pouts.

"You were thinking about it. I know you were," Sofie accuses, not looking at her.

"I made one bad decision and now there's no trust between us? At all?"

"You made two bad decisions, actually," Will says, eyes flashing up to the mirror. "Sharing our plan and selling the king's ring."

Sofie turns the knife. "And it wasn't a bad decision for you; it was a bad decision for the rest of us, and that's the problem."

"What would you have had me do? Rot in the castle cells?"

Sofie cocks a brow. "Yes, actually."

"Can we save this argument for after we get the ring back?" Will asks. "Driving in this weather isn't exactly the easiest."

"What—oh," Sofie says, finally looking out into the streets.

Water streams down the cobblestones at least two inches deep under our tires. The wheels struggle to hold fast to the road, and we list from side to side down the narrow streets.

As we turn onto the sea lane that runs parallel to the shoreline, the Øresund Strait looms ahead. Lightning spider-webs across the sky, and I gasp. The water is a living mass. Frothing, festering, churning, boiling. Whitecaps crest into waves that slam into the shore with enough force to swallow the beach whole. There's not a grain of sand to be seen, except in the little cove, cordoned off by rope and respect—the sea witch's lair.

Cluttering the storm tide are the bodies of more fish, all bleeding black from their eyes, deposited and then shuffled again with each new wave, unable to rest. Freyja's wheels skid and thump over a few of the dead fish.

"It might be best to park the car here," Will says when a school practically washes beneath the wheels.

"You want us to walk in that?" Agnata asks, eyeing the streaming water outside her window—high enough to soak the hem of her dress right along with her boots.

"Do you have a better idea?" Sofie says. "Get out."

Will hops out first and helps Agnata from her bindings. Sofie and I grab the pistols from under the carpet at our feet. We each hand them to Will, who is the only one whose clothes can cover their bulk. If it comes to it, Sofie and I have our gemstones—we're already wanted for horrible things, and those guards suspect we're both witches, so there's no real point to hiding our magic if we're under fire.

We slosh through the water, our boots bumping the bloating carcasses of fish along the way.

"Why are their eyes like that?" Agnata asks, looking to me, for obvious reasons.

"Magic," I say. "No more questions, please."

We haven't told her of Father's plans. Nor have we told her why we want the ring. Despite an afternoon of her pestering questions, there's no way we're spelling anything else out to her.

The air smells of rain, rot, and smoke, as the ashen remains of the warehouse settle behind the steep roofline of a row of shops catering to dockworkers. The Vœrtshus Havnestad is at the end of the row, its shingles white-washed and dingy. It doesn't help that sandbags line the foundation and are piled two deep at the door, keeping the water at bay.

For a moment I worry that Møller won't be out in this weather—maybe nobody will. But Havnestaders are hardier than most and, despite the relentless rain, the tavern's windowpanes glow warm with firelight on either side of the single entrance. I think back to the alley—one exit there, likely from the kitchen. These are good things to know.

At the red-lacquered door, I run a quickly whispered

round of *"Purr klædi"* to dry us. Then, we lock arms as planned—myself on Will's left, Agnata on his right, Sofie bracketing her on the outside.

When we enter the værtshus, music is playing, a trio of stringed instruments going from the corner. Laughter cloaks the room, people pleased to be dry, warm, and slightly drunk. I've never been in a place like this before. Luckily, though, Will either has or is really good at pretending.

We grab a table that has an excellent view of both the entrance and the doors to the kitchen, which we know lead to the alley. Will deposits the three of us at the table before calling the serving girl without much more than a kind look her way. "The last of your summer wine for the table please, Fru . . ."

"Caren," she says, smiling prettily, dropping napkins on our table. "Will that be it for now?"

Will nods with a grin that makes both the girl and me blush, and Caren leaves, flying over to the bar.

When she's gone, Will's pocket watch comes out. Ten until eight. "See him, Hela?"

Agnata is slow on the uptake, but finally begins to carefully sweep the tavern. Her lips flatten into a line as she concentrates, running her eyes over faces in profile and full-front view, the backs of heads, the cut and hunch of shoulders.

"Well?" Sofie demands as Agnata's eyes bounce around

the room for the third time.

I have to admit, I'm impatient too—we have to identify him before the buyer does. Or before anyone recognizes us. The longer we sit here, the more likely someone is to spot us despite the changes we made to our hair and clothing.

"I—I'm not sure."

"Well, what does he look like?"

"Brown hair, blue eyes, stocky build."

Sofie sighs. "That describes literally half the bar, *Hela*."

"How did you find him so quickly earlier in the day?" I whisper. "Your turnaround time to give it to him after Will and I were knocked out couldn't have been much."

"Frigg has a point," Will says.

"I can't believe I let you out of my sight," Sofie mumbles.

"I'm sorry, okay? I thought we were on the same side, Sofie. But look, it was empty in here this morning, and he was in his guard's uniform. No one in here is wearing one," Agnata whispers.

A minute more ticks by as we search around the room for someone in the blue of Øldenburg Castle, or with brown hair and blue eyes and a particularly expectant look on his face.

"Ah, Caren, excellent service!" Will chirps, and we all automatically smile as the server returns, depositing four glasses of summer wine garnished with slivers of orange.

Pressing a lock of hair behind her ear, she whispers

close enough to him that I nearly lean back, her grinning profile looming right in front of mine. "So kind of you, sir. My regulars aren't so complimentary anymore."

Will smiles tightly. "Well, they should be. Are there many regulars here?"

"Oh, of course. The wedding crowd is gone, and it's back to just the locals squatting on their stools like they own them. And then there's you—though you look familiar."

Will's smile doesn't waver. "I'm afraid I've never been here before."

"Hey, girl!" a man calls from near the door, and Caren's head whips around. Four men hard with ocean life gape at her, the cups on their table empty and ready for more.

As she runs off, Will takes a deep sip of his wine. "Hela, what seat was Møller in this afternoon?"

Agnata's eyes skip over to the bar. "Second from the right."

There is indeed a man with brown hair of stocky build sitting there. "Frigg," he says to me. "Why don't you and Hela inquire at the bar about the loo?"

I stand and take Agnata's hand, leaving Will and Sofie behind. We skirt through the crowd, steering our way to the bar. Caren is there. I face her, smile up and ready, as Agnata looks around, supposedly for a sign, but she's really inspecting the man's face.

"Caren, I should've asked earlier, but where is—"

"Agnata, you're too early!"

Oh no.

The man in the second seat is red-faced, and hvidtøl sloshes over his cup as he turns his whole body toward us. That's when I see the ring on his hand. His knuckles are bulbous from work, and with the smaller size made for Sofie's fingers, it only fits on his pinkie, above the second knuckle.

"I haven't sold the damn thing yet, kœreste. Greedy, girl, aren't you?" He laughs far too loud, and despite the music and merriment, I feel half the eyes in the room turn to us.

In my periphery, Will stands, hand reaching for the pistol in his pocket.

No, we can't do this here. Not with the ring still on the man's finger.

Møller finishes laughing, and that's when he sees my face. "The mute!" He stumbles off the stool. Alia and I were not identical, but with my hair long again and in the low light, the resemblance is close enough for his mistake. "The entire kingdom's been looking for you."

The girth of him spills into the space between us— this man is the kind who could reel in a baby whale all by himself, and then drink his weight in hvidtøl to celebrate. "Why don't you come with me, right up to the castle. My buyer can wait."

He places a hand on my wrist.

"Excuse me," Will says, appearing next to Møller. "Unhand my friend, sir."

The tavern is now completely silent, every eye on our little circle. Møller with his hand wrapped around my wrist. Will with his hand on the hidden pistol. Sofie and Agnata both standing with their eyes the size of dinner plates, now completely recognizable as the komtesse bride and her hofdame.

My eyes swing to Will's. His swing to Sofie's. In a blink, we're all in motion.

Will's other arm rockets forward, punching Møller in the face. The man stumbles back but doesn't let go of me.

"*Frijøsa.*" I whisper, making my wrist go cold enough to burn.

Møller reels back, frostbite already blackening his fingers. Sofie takes the opportunity and lunges, yanking the ring off his other hand. She stabs it onto her thumb and grabs Agnata's wrist to run. Will takes my hand, and the four of us are now sprinting, triumphant, toward the door.

But it's already open, and twenty guards in shades of Øldenburg blue and Holsten green are streaming over the sandbags and into the room.

34

Evie

THE RAIN HAS BEEN GOING NONSTOP FOR HOURS, THE sea king's anger now unrelenting.

It's enough that the water crests yards above my polypi branches, sloshing up and over the cove's boundaries. This teacup of mine is already spilt, the contents running up the pewter shores, lapping the fence of boulders surrounding the place.

And worse, the ring isn't here.

I asked for it before the rain began, but it has yet to come. I'm a powerful witch, but this magic I need will not work without it.

"Evie!" Ragn's voice carries across the length of my lair. She rushes past the polypi and the bubbling mire. Her long hair streams behind her in a straight line. "It's happening!"

I move to meet her, but she's going so fast, I barely get

away from my cauldron before she collapses in my arms, her heart a hummingbird beating against my breast.

The old woman draws in a few heaving breaths—and I wait. There's no point in peppering her with stupid questions. I know what's coming. I just need her to confirm it.

"It's happening," she repeats, ice-blue eyes wild. "The ríkifjor is tapped out; the magical balance has tipped closer to level. It's happening tonight. He's already flooding the shores and claiming land so he and his army can make a move. But there's more. . . ." She takes in another few breaths. "He blamed mines for Alia's death and Runa's disappearance . . . whipped everyone into a frenzy over them. But *he's* been detonating them!"

This last part I didn't know.

"The humans laid them first for their war, yes, but he took that technology and made it his own," she says, a sob coming. "I had my suspicions, but it wasn't until after he lied to everyone about the twins that I was able to find the truth."

"It's not just fear; it's propaganda."

Ragn shakes her head, disgusted. "If we were humans, we'd be lighting torches and carrying pitchforks."

"What if you talk to the merpeople? Maybe you can calm them? Keep them from blindly following?"

"I don't—"

"Runa joined with the witches on land and blew up the entire Havnestad U-boat program," I say, cutting her off before she can fully tell me no. "She's using her magic to protect the sea kingdom and strengthening the land's hold on magic in the process."

"She did? Oh, Ru." The old woman smiles. "She can grow anything from nothing, even witches."

I bring the woman to arm's length. "Ragn, understand that if the sea king brings war to the humans, he'll be battling Runa. Your people will be discovered, they will be outmatched, and they will be directed to harm one of their own."

She takes a deep breath. But before she answers me, I ask for more. As long as I'm chained here, this is the best I can do. "What if you tell them the truth? That the king has been detonating his own mines? That Runa is safe, and that Alia died going to land?" I won't spell my friend, but I wish I could send her straight back to do all of this. To use her power as queen mother to plant enough seeds of doubt to prevent the worst. "If you did that, if you told them, would they still follow the sea king?"

"Of course they will," another voice adds in. "And she will do no such thing."

We startle at Alia's voice, coming from Anna's polypus.

We weren't careful. I didn't silence Anna, nor did either of us seek our privacy from her presence.

Ragn turns to Anna, a sneer on her face, and for once I feel a hint of betrayal at giving Anna the voice that belonged to Alia.

"And what will you do, *polypus*?" Ragn spits, not daring to use her name.

"She'll report back to me, Mother."

The sea king is there, head proud and swimming straight for us, dressed for battle. Gilded helmet over his long hair, muscles cuffed at the biceps and forearms, a chest plate shining deeply, my tentacle hanging low around his neck. Atop his head, even his crown of eel skulls appears to be bathed in gold.

My stomach drops and twists. The sea king's magic holds me here—of course he'd have a connection to every living thing within my confines. As the realization crosses my face, the sea king smiles. "Witch, there's nothing I don't know, but it never hurts to have more minnows."

"Aegir." Ragn uses his first name—something only she would ever dare use. Not even that wife of his would attempt it. "Listen. Please. This is suicide. You are sending your people to their deaths."

Her son smiles at her, blood in it. Suddenly his face both resembles hers and eclipses it, relative youth and the last of the ríkifjor serum in his veins making him bright as the moon. "I am not forcing them to do anything. They know humans are our biggest threat. And we are nothing if not a brave civilization."

"Brave? Brave? We've been hiding under these waters for millennia because we know it's best to hide. Our ancestors knew it, our parents knew it, and you knew it too until you filled that hole in your heart with power, magic, and greed." Ragn gains strength, pulling away from me and daring to face him, unbidden, chin high. "There's nothing brave in asking your people to sacrifice themselves and their future for you and your ambition."

At the last syllable, without hesitation, Ragn casts both arms out before her and shouts a spell, quick as a lightning strike. *"Færa!"*

But the sea king is quicker.

He deflects easily with the golden cuffs at his wrists, shooting the spell right back at her, striking her in the chest and stomach, and sending her falling back.

"No, please!" I scream, lunging for Ragn.

"Morna, herfiligr kvennalið!"

The same spell he used on me slams into his mother. It takes her out like a cannonball the size of the moon, barreling into her slight frame. I'm still coming for her, and the spell hurls her body into mine with enough force to drive us both deep into the sand.

I try to sit up to check her, but before I can right myself, the sea king looms over us both.

"Now you'll do what I say, Sea Witch, or your friend dies."

35

Evie

"DON'T HELP HIM, EVIE." RAGN SAYS IT TO HER SON MORE than to me, defiant even as her heartbeat slows to an occasional hiccup against my skin where her chicken-wire spine is pressed to my sternum. "Whatever he wants from you . . . it will be at the risk of our people."

"Mother, wake up," the sea king says with a sort of disdain. "The world is so different from before. The Havnestad U-boat program? It's a drop in the bucket. Every great nation on earth has the same technology. And that technology grows by the day—in my lifetime, humans will sprout steel gills and live in the sea. I would rather reveal ourselves for the good of our cause than wait for someone to do it for us."

"But our people . . ."

The sea king's hand shoots out, his patience gone. *"Prífa ørindi."*

Ragn seizes, her capacity to breathe left in his hands. Her body shudders and squirms in my arms, thin lips gagging open as she reaches for any oxygen in the surrounding waters. Her chest falls concave, her veins shriveling, capillaries drying. Her face tinges blue and her eyes bulge. That heart against my own quiets.

"Stop! You'll kill her!" I scream at him.

"Despite what my mother may think of me, I'm not foolish enough to put my people on the front lines. I'd rather have *you* do it."

Me? What can I do that he can't?

Impossibly, the sea king smiles. "Want her to live? Turn your polypi into merpeople."

My polypi were formed from those who died that night I was made—castle guards, Anna. Alia is the only one added by the magic in fifty years. I've never questioned what they could be other than creatures subsisting here with me. Anna's spying is painful enough, but turn her into a mermaid? Turn them all into mermaids?

"I'm not sure that's possible. I—"

"You better make it possible or that will be a corpse in your arms."

I look to his mother, thrashing out for oxygen. *Stay with me, Ragn.*

I take a deep breath and reach for the polypus farthest from me, the lions that lurk at the natural entrance to my lair. *"Frjáls líf innan haf, minn polypi."*

I repeat the spell two dozen times over, as fast as I can.

With each repetition, there's a flash of blinding light—and a soldier who fell during that final battle rises up, peeling off the largest branch of his polypus tree. And a new merman is formed—blank-faced and gray as an Øldenburg statue, but he's undeniably beautiful, smooth and shiny as a bark-bald tree under the light of a full moon.

Each spell takes something out of me until my words are beginning to slur. Around us, the new mermaids are testing their bodies, moving in a spinning school around the dark waters of my cave, hurtling snatches of silver under the storm-filled sky.

Drawing what little strength I have left, I finish with the polypi closest to me and most important to the sea king—Alia and Anna.

Anna's polypus is nearly vibrating with excitement, and as I get the words out and tip my fingers up to her branches, she peels off the tree and whirls around, yelling even during the blinding light of her transition, "I'm free!"

She dances around in a little circle, stretching her arms and tail, as I draw a deep breath and turn my attention to Alia, my little cluster of spindly flowers in the shadow of Anna's tree.

"Frjáls líf innan haf, minn polypi."

Alia appears in a final flash of brilliant diamond white.

She's instantly recognizable, a marble-and-moon version of herself.

The sea king's hardened face goes slack with surprise. The magical hold he has on Ragn collapses, and I check her pulse—still alive, barley. Thank Urda.

He drops his hands and swims over to Alia, approaching as if he's seeing a ghost. "Alia? Is it really you?" He takes her hands. "I thought I'd lost you forever."

She doesn't answer, but he doesn't care. With a wave of his hand, he produces a tiara from seemingly nothing, placing it in her long, flowing hair. A gift, for a daughter who only wanted the one thing she couldn't have.

Anna's mouth drops open, jealousy set into her stunning features—unlike myself and my silver hair, she looks not a day older than when I last saw her in human form. When she speaks, it's again in Alia's voice. "I'm your daughter too. I was loyal to you. I helped you."

"Gefa!" He snaps, eyes flashing her way, omitting the name he once gave her.

Before another word of protest, Anna's voice is no longer her own. The weight of it sits in the sea king's palm as he passes it to Alia, touching her cheek so gently I'm surprised he's capable of it. This man as he is now is the kind who only leaves bruises. And he is, but on Anna.

"You've done your duty, distracting the witch with thoughts of land, goading her to think she could become human again, but you are no daughter of mine."

He sneers in my direction, where I clutch his failing mother to my chest. "Fifty years later, and you still don't know your boundaries, do you, girl?"

The sea king's eyes flick to his mother. "Not that I should be surprised: more than two hundred years old, and she never learned her boundaries either." He raises a hand.

"No!" I scream, and try to cover Ragn, turning her pale face into my chest.

"Ykkarr dauðadar, móðir—morðvig!" The spell blasts out of him with the force of a meteor on impact, engulfing Ragn in a haze as dark as a starless night.

Around us, the new merpeople swirl, spinning in a ghastly churn, sharks smelling new blood. The sea king's eyes are pinned on the shadowy mass.

Love and pain for her oma Ragn is etched plainly in the sadness of Alia's eyes. Her hands flutter out, as if trying to stop what's already been done. Sadness envelops Anna too. She was once close with Ragn, but behind the grief in her eyes, I know that fear is brewing. If the sea king will do that to his own mother, what will he do to her?

When the darkness fades, Ragn's body appears encased in ash, fragile as an eggshell. Gone are her fierce eyes and wild hair. Her heartbeat is silent against my own.

"I didn't need my mother," the sea king says, as if he really was born the god of the sea. "She's been a traitor to me as long as the sea witch has been in this place." His lips quirk up with righteousness. "Oh, I know about your little notes, *Evie*. Your visits. How she admired you for what you did to protect us—her words, never mine."

He tosses around what I did with sweeping hands. "Repair the plague you created. Kill Annemette when she threatened to take us down with the young prince. But it was never about us; it was always about you, and it was wrongheaded for Mother to think otherwise, let alone admire you for it." His teeth flash in disgust. "Still, I kept her around because every little note and visit got me closer to the root of your magic."

Magic—his voice lowers in disgust as he says the word. But it's tinged with something else: jealousy. His fingers trail along the rim of my cauldron, the potion all but finished.

He doesn't know what it is. He can't. But there's a sharp tilt to his shoulders, and I see it happen before he completes the movement—my cauldron toppled over, the most important spell I've created in fifty years spilling, golden and promising into the dead water of my cove.

My last chance, diluted. Gone.

My life is the next to go.

"I needed you to bring Runa back—surely you know that was the only reason you survived this long." Yes. I know. "But now, there is no return for her. So, you must take her place. Grow me ríkifjor and spare your life."

"No."

"No hesitation?" He nearly laughs, mirth flashing in the blue depths of his eyes. "Has your life been so horrible here? Do you miss home that much that you'd gamble with Urda's graces on the afterlife to see all those you've left in your wake? Your mother, dead because of you. Your father, dead because of you. Your aunt, your Øldenburg loves, suffering under the weight of that day until they left this earth."

Gently, I place Ragn's body in the sand, laying her down for a final rest until I can properly bury her, do my best to honor her as she deserves. Then, I square my shoulders and reveal myself to him fully, defiantly. Every inch of my years, my power, my penance, stated in the tip of my chin and the smooth presence of my tentacles, black, shining, regal.

"Me?" I spit. "You would question me? The man who just murdered his own mother?"

This seems to take his shoulders down a tick. I smile, gaining steam. "The man who feels so betrayed by the two humans he saved that he's willing to risk literally his entire species and the lives of thousands of humans to satisfy his own greed?"

He seems to shrink and shrivel a bit more. Good. I inch closer to him, not letting him escape my stare. My wrath.

"Trust me, Your Highness: revenge doesn't mend a broken heart."

The sea king doesn't let his gaze stray. Doesn't look to his mother, or to his girls, horrified over his shoulder.

"Oh, but it does feel good," he tells himself. His jaw hardens and he regains every lost inch, chest puffed out. Chin out. Decision made. I just need him to say it. "Goodbye, Sea Witch."

36

Runa

A DOZEN MORE GUARDS ARRIVE THROUGH THE KITCHEN door.

We're surrounded.

Both exits are blocked.

"Hell and high water," Will curses under his breath. Then he drops my hand and steps in front of me. In front of Sofie and Agnata too. He moves with his hands up, slowly presenting himself to the guards.

"Will, what are you doing?" Sofie whisper-screams.

He doesn't answer. Instead, he again slaps on the grin he used while dressed in his castle finery, title to his name, the king's newest cousin. He projects his voice, loud and clear and ready to play. "Let's not get into it here, boys. We can talk up at the castle, eh?"

The guards respond by drawing their pistols.

"This isn't a negotiation," their leader says. "I'll take

all four of you for destruction of kingdom property, witchcraft, and the murder of our beloved king. Have I missed anything, Herr Jensen?"

The ring in Sofie's hand and the car outside—theft. But our crimes are not my concern. We'll surely break a few more laws by sunrise. If they're going to take us, let it be quick. The sooner we're outside, the sooner we can use our magic. Our spells are utterly useless here. Fire and wind are too dangerous in close quarters. If the bullets start flying and we draw shields, we're likely to kill a bystander with the ricochet. Even the sleeping spell is no good, because when the guards go down, at least a few of their pistols could discharge.

"Ah, I didn't think so," the leader goes on. "Binds, then we march."

They start with Will. Three men rough him up as they remove his coat, pistols, and clean out his pockets of our extra amethysts and inks.

"Make it as embarrassing as possible, gents. Baron Jensen would be most approving," Will says as the guards do their best to wrench his shoulders nearly out of their sockets while stringing his arms together behind his back at a barbaric angle.

The guards approach the three of us next. Agnata whimpers the whole time that she's done nothing wrong, but they search her anyway. From the folds in our skirts they retrieve the amethysts Sofie and I had tucked away for safekeeping, and my little pouch of the remaining ríkifjor seeds too. Each item is tossed into a burlap sack. We are utterly disarmed. All except Sofie, who has managed to slide Niklas's ring to the tip of her thumb, burying it so deep in her fist, the guards have yet to notice.

Though Will works hard to keep his chin up, even in my periphery, his face falls as they double-knot our weapons away. I catch Will's eye, trying to convey that he's ready. That he can call magic without his stone. I firmly believe both Will and Sofie can be a vessel without aid or a crutch. Agnata, maybe not yet, thanks to her deception, but I'll protect her anyway.

Finished, they line us up for the door. Some guards holster their pistols, but not all. The patrons begin mumbling again, glasses scraping against tables. The shock and danger seemingly worn off—they can go back to discussing the show my father is putting on outside. Some shoulder on hoods, deciding it might be time to close up the tab and slosh home.

"Wait, that møgkœlling took my ring." Møller holds up his frostbitten hand, a spiderweb of blackened decay, and points a finger at Sofie.

The leader of the Øldenburg guards seems to recognize Møller. "Retrieve it, but make it quick."

Møller stumbles forward toward Sofie. She fights him, but his strength pries her palms open.

"Ah—there it is."

I make a whispered decision. We must act now. *"Fri-jøsa."*

I reach for the magic, now at the tips of my fingers, giving it no room for error. My shackles freeze and shatter. I hold still, hoping the guard at my side notices nothing amiss.

Møller goes to yank it off, but Sofie whirls on him, the guard slow to stop her. She clenches her fist tightly again, keeping the ring safe. Møller reaches for it again, his eyes now a bloody shade of red. His forearms bracket her waist, blindly reaching for her fists held behind her back.

"Don't touch me." Sofie wrenches away and spits in his face, chin held komtesse high and dignified.

Møller wipes a forearm across his chin before lunging for the closest guard's pistol. He steals it with his good hand, and in a blink, he's got it pressed to her sternum.

I dive for the man's arm, pushing it up and away. As the bullet bursts out of the barrel, I scream, *"Skjoldr!"* My shield bursts out, covering the length of my body as I try my very best to protect Sofie and anyone else in its trajectory.

The bullet bounces off the shield, and with the range so close, it has nowhere to go but straight back at Møller, connecting with that puffed-out chest.

The man stumbles backward, just as Sofie and Will call their wildfire. Their arms flare, and a thrill moves up my spine as I get to my feet. Their shackles melt off and their hands come out front and free. Agnata sinks into a crouch. Without ink or stones, she's still stuck in her binds, her wildfire not as practiced or strong.

For one stunning moment, the room is silent again—every face agape at the flames dancing purple across Sofie's and Will's arms. Jaws drop open; glasses drop, too, with a clink and crash. The guards are stunned still.

"Run!" I screech. I grab Agnata by her bindings, freezing them off with a single word, and we make a beeline for the back door, Will and Sofie ahead of us.

We follow them down the alley, past the backs of the other shops in the row. The water is knee-deep here and running river strong, climbing inch by inch. Father will have it rise to crest Lille Bjerg Pass before the night is out.

"What's the plan?" Sofie screams at me as we thunder toward the end of the row.

"We have to get the ring to the sea witch!" Will answers over the pounding rain.

"The sea witch?" Agnata screeches. "She's real? You have to be kidding me!"

"Shut up, Agnata!" Sofie yanks the ring off her thumb and hands it to me as we reach the end of the alley.

Behind us, a set of guards bursts from the vœrtshus's back door, spotting us. Their pistols are already out, and the shooting starts as soon as our heads snap in their direction. Agnata decides that's the time to run—she'll take her chances away from us, declaring her innocence to anyone who will listen.

We don't stop her. Instead, we send our shields up and sprint around the corner as best we can through the streaming water. Dead fish have collected against the side of the building in a silt pile, and the ground beneath our feet is growing less solid by the moment, the grass giving way to the dirt below as it turns to mud.

Ahead, Agnata speeds into what used to be the street, shouting at the guards that she did nothing wrong. Reminding them that she worked with them after her release from the castle. Arguing that she's unarmed.

They bind her anyway. Two guards rush forth with new lengths of rope as she thrashes against them, kicking water and words at them.

If only she had stayed with us.

"I've got her," Sofie says, and I'm pretty sure there's an eye roll in it.

We follow Sofie into the street, arms raised and shields out. There's immediate fire, nervous fingers jumpy on ready triggers.

The sheeting rain, howling wind, and cloud-soaked moon make it impossible to tell which guards are which. Øldenburg or Holsten, it matters not. All wish us dead for what they assume and what they've seen. Such is a witch's life.

Sofie tackles the two guards handling Agnata, wild-fire igniting instantly as she plows a palm into each of their faces, leaving her handprint burned into the writhing men's features. They fall back and away, and she grabs Agnata, setting her burning hands to her new binds. They fall off in a burst of ash.

Although a few other guards are also down, their own bullets finding them after hitting our shields, they still outnumber us by many.

I make eye contact with Will. "Take my lead."

Holding our shields with our left hands, we squat and dip our right hands into the rushing stream. "*Slyngva fiskr!*" I shout, and Will follows.

Within seconds, the black-eyed carcasses of a thousand rotting fish fly through the air. Pelting, swatting, smacking the guards—cutting them off at the knees, cannonballing them in the chest, tossing them back into the water with a flying splash.

"To your left!" Will calls as the guards who chased us down the alley appear around the side of the building, barreling straight at us with knives.

"*Frijøsa!*" I scream, hands still in the water.

A vein of ice hardens immediately where my hands have contact, spidering down the tide into the men sloshing directly at me. Their feet stop on a dime, frozen in blocks of ice.

"Yes!" Sofie yells before casting the spell herself at two more men coming her way. They try to jump, only to slip and fall facedown into the street.

"Let me try," Agnata says.

The three of us line up, placing our hands six across, and yell the spell together; it sends several more men sliding. Over my shoulder, Will has sent two guards burning, and three more are facedown in the water with other various injuries.

"Runa! Go! We've got this!" he yells.

I believe him, but I won't leave until I check the numbers—the guards have dwindled to just a handful. With Agnata's confidence back, we've added another fighter and she and Sofie are working side by side to bring down those remaining in the street, while Will works the side yard.

He's right: it's time.

Shields up, I let a crack of lightning orient me to the beach and the sea witch's cove just beyond. I begin to run but get only a few steps before a pinch of anxiety stops me cold. My eyes immediately find Will—who's face-to-face with a guard, fighting hand-to-hand, rolling on the ground, through the water. Slash, punch, splash.

And though he's fought several times before, both this night and others, there's something in my heart that makes me hesitate and watch, every sense trained on the altercation below. The rolling stops, and the guard has Will stumbling up, his hands pressing into the siding of the shop row.

"Show me your hands, Witch!" the guard screams at Will, pistol trained straight at his chest.

Will smiles, straightens—and presents the man with a

daisy made from thin air. "Wizard, actually."

The man gasps and overreacts, batting at Will's hands with his pistol. Will tosses the daisy in the man's face and gets a hand on the barrel of the gun.

But then it goes off.

This time, the blast doesn't ricochet. There's no shield.

Will stumbles backward into the building and falls in a heap in the water.

"No!" The wind steals my voice as I scream. I change course and sprint straight for him.

The guard gets to his feet and cocks the hammer again. Aiming at Will as his back is turned and he struggles to his feet.

Oh no you don't.

"Fœra!" With laser focus, light bursts forth from my hands and plows the man backward, stunned and landing hard on the cobblestones, the gun sliding away as water splashes around him.

Will's on his side when I get to him, face in the water. He's trying to get up, but one arm isn't working and he's inhaling water. I wrap my arms around him and get him sitting up. "Will, I'm here. I'm here. I've got you."

"You need . . . to be . . . over . . . there . . ."

"I know, but I can't. . . . Hold still." The bullet didn't pass through. It's in his shoulder, and the damn thing needs to come out as soon as possible or he'll get lead poisoning. The sea kingdom has seen this a million times with what hooks and harpoons can do to merpeople who come too close to the surface.

Face blanched, Will tries to smile. "*Still*. No problem."

His body shivers and so does mine. With shaking fingers, I tear open the remains of his shirt, exposing his shoulder, stained with blood that not even this water can fade. I place my hand over his wound as lightly as possible. "*Slita*."

Will immediately cries out, his legs sloshing and kicking in the water as pain wrenches through him. His head slams back against my shoulder, every cord, tendon, and vein in his neck tense.

But the bullet and all its fragments come out, dropping right into my hand.

Will breathes hard, trying to gather enough force in his lungs to say something. Before he does, Sofie sloshes through the water toward us, blood rolling down her cheek from a cut above her eye.

"I've got him," she says, sucking in air. Behind her is Agnata, looming over three dispatched guards who are tied in their own rope, propped up together so as not to fall over and drown. Their feet are blocks of ice. "Go, Runa! Go!"

"Not yet. Hold him."

"But you have to get to her, the whole harbor is going to wash away in—"

"*I know!*" I scream. Sofie drops to her knees, and without another hint of protest, takes my place at Will's back, and I scoot in front of him.

I toss the pieces of his bullet into the water and place both hands gently over every inch of ruptured skin. Then I meet his eyes, holding the blue there, trying to calm him. *"Leyðra. Sauma."*

Will's gasping slows as my palms warm, the magic sterilizing his wound before sealing it right up. Only when the skin is smooth and beginning to cool do I move my hand.

And then I take the last moment I need.

I cup his face with my hands and bend down to give him the kiss I've been aching to share with him for more than a day now. This boy who picked me up at my very lowest and trusted me with his life and his fight. Will's body melts, all the tension flooding with the water rushing against where we are, solid against the tide.

His eyes flit open, stark blue in the low light as color returns to his cheeks. "Runa . . . ," he whispers.

"I need to go, I know," I say, standing. I glance to Sofie. "Keep him safe."

And then I run.

I haul my dress above my knees and sprint into the coming tide. The stream and punch of the full force of the sea resists me at every sloshy step. The wind whips my hair into my face, sodden ropes slapping across my cheeks, forehead, and into my eyes. Hail drives into my shoulders, eating holes into the tatters of my dress.

The beach is no more. All the boats in the harbor have come loose from their moorings, piling up in a tangle of metal and broken glass. Some are capsized farther into the harbor and the Øresund Strait, their bows pointed up to the sky like drowning men reaching for air before falling under.

Very soon, all of them, large and small, will tumble past the dockyards into the streets, and then climb the sea lane into town. If even one large boat makes it into the frontage, it could mean the end of all those people in the pub, any guards left breathing in the lane, and my friends, if they're not out of the way.

As I run, I raise a hand to the boats, calling on what I can to keep them from moving farther inland. I don't know if it'll work against the force of Father's storms, but I have to try.

"*Dveljask!*"

Up ahead are the very tops of two large boulders, sitting sentry on the sea witch's cove. There's a historical marker that's barely reaching over the tide now, too, the wooden pole and the plaque atop bending with the rush of the water.

Almost there.

Beyond the cove entrance, my feet are lifted off the ground, and I automatically begin to move my arms in a swimming stroke, trying to get farther out. But I've not swum in this body, and my legs are a sorry excuse for a tail.

I'm barely moving forward, and I'm not sure I can make it into the boundaries of the cove. I look around for another way.

In the middle of the cove is a massive wall of stone. I can climb.

Better yet, looking at the wall now, it must be aligned with where the sea witch's cave is. Outside her cave is her cauldron—the wall is my best shot.

Each breath I take is half air, half water now. Waves rush up from below where the sea is surging, and from above, where rain still floods down in sheets.

The sky cracks through with lightning, and I take a look back and up at the town. Every light is on. Windows gape open, little faces peering into the night. They're watching the world end.

Not if I can help it.

I push forward and get a hand on the wall. It's slick as ice, rainwater a finger thick buffering the stone from the air.

"Purr bjarg," I say, and the water flees from the patch of rock covered by my hand.

It's suddenly completely dry, affording me a handhold. Yes, this will work. I repeat the spell over and over with each new grip, each step on any finger of a ledge with my boots. My body is heavy with the water my clothes can hold, and it takes all my strength to pull myself over the side and onto the summit of the rock wall. Hail pits welts into every exposed inch of skin—my face, my neck, my hands stinging. But when my feet touch, I get to my knees and then I stand, wind gusting in big-mouthed threats to send me over the other side.

But I hold strong. I push myself to the point that reaches farthest into the sea witch's cove and well into the swirling storm. With all the magic inside me and all the fight I have to give, I yell out, "*Sœkja*, Sea Witch!" and fling the ring into the wicked, churning deep.

37

Evie

I AM NOT TO BE OBLITERATED. NO, THE SEA KING WANTS my magic as much as my life.

That means he'll take his time. Draining. Absorbing. Cleaving. Until every last bit of power is leeched from my skin. Starved from my muscles. Carving marks left on my bones as he ensures whatever magic I have in me is properly added to his account.

"Skafa fróðleikr."

"Drjúpa fróðleikr."

"Réna fróðleikr."

"Samna fróðleikr."

The sea king doesn't wait for what went into his ghost soldiers to renew. That piece of me within them is already coursing through the sinew that forms his kingly body. I feel it like blood loss—a fuzziness in my mind, a lightness about my limbs.

Each sip of light that he steals sends me lower, until I'm pressed to the sea floor and sinking in. Left staring up at his looming form, watching him grow stronger before my very eyes.

The mass of him seems to burn beneath his golden armor, the sun rising beneath the swirling clouded ghosts of his polypi generals. Yes, generals—there aren't enough of them to be called an army—two dozen, maybe. But the collection of them is enough that, if he leaves this place with them at his disposal, they can easily set off the mines, then unflinchingly lead any of the brave merpeople into battle.

It's exactly what he wanted.

I watch them swoop and spin, ready to go, to move, to charge, and I feel something else within me fading. Not my magic—that has dwindled enough that I'm hollowed out, skin and structure and vacant space—but what is left of my soul.

Anna told me once that mermaids don't have a soul. Not like what inhabits humans. I'm not a human anymore, and I haven't been for a long time, but I'm not a mermaid either. And for as long as I've known myself in this body, I've recognized that there's a shadow of my soul left. Residue of the spirit I once was.

Evie. *That girl.*

It's the last I have of who I once was, of Nik and his heart and what could never be. Of my mother's sacrifice, and my father's tragedy. Of Tante Hansa's good intentions and wisdom. It's fading, that last bit of the true *being*.

The sea king can feel it. Of course he can. He closes his eyes and revels in it, arms above his head—his crown—in triumph.

My eyesight is failing with my soul, with my magic, with the rest of me. My cheek is pressed into the pewter sands of my lair, and I sink in, ready to become one with it in the days after my last breath. Until I'm bones and nothing more.

But then something floats into my vision. Small, fire-red, round.

In this state, I nearly think it's an illusion. My mind's gift of peace. What I want and what I need appearing in front of me before my eyes close forever. I reach out to it, expecting to feel nothing but the end. But then my fingers dust across something real. Hard. Flecks of gemstone fastened in a perfectly round circle.

Runa, my brave little witch.

I slip the ring straight onto my ring finger, and it fits perfectly. The stone warms to my skin, merging with it. Becoming the epicenter of a thousand memories of my time on earth. Of Nik, of his love, of the magic both between us and in the lies I wove to hide my true self. I haven't set foot on dry sand, in the salt air, under the full strength of the sun for fifty years, but somehow, I'm suddenly of the earth in a way I never realized I was when I was above. All that's drained out of me has returned tenfold.

From my deathbed, I lift my head and shoot my body upright, each of my tentacles flaring as I spin in wondrous, joyous movement. The sea king watches, jaw wired shut, fighting mightily not to reveal his surprise, but I glimpse the panic in his eyes.

I'm not dead. I'm thriving with power. Sucking up all that's around us. I've opened a vein straight to what the sea king has left. And he knows it.

"Soldiers, line up!" he orders, ripping his eyes from me.

The polypi generals do as he commands—they have no other choice. They're marionettes without strings. Even Alia. Even Anna—who visibly struggles against his directions. Her eyes wild, confused, betrayed. She really did believe she'd earned her freedom.

I feel the tiniest pang for her. Everything Anna did to get to this point was in the name of independence, having her own agency, being the mistress of her own destiny. It didn't work the way she hoped, betrayal not paying what it promised.

The sea king beckons his girls up front. Alia is first, her crown a sparkling second to her father's. Anna follows because she must.

"This isn't over, Sea Witch." His voice lifts up at me as he rushes out of my lair, his soldiers in tow. The opening cannon fire of a war unlike any other just minutes away.

When he's gone and all is quiet except for the storm

he's created above, I answer him.

"No, it isn't."

～

I swim to my cauldron, still toppled flat on its side. I return it to its base and inspect the contents. Most of my serum spilled into the sea, but some clung to the pot's curves.

Dear Urda, please let it be enough.

I get the fire going below, and the contents begin to boil, steam lifting to my face.

When it's good and hot, I again pierce the skin of my breast, this time right above my heart. The blood drips into the cauldron in fat rivulets. After a dozen good drops, I reach down with my left hand, Nik's ring shining on my finger.

The contents should burn but they don't. Instead, the warmth of a summer afternoon streams up my arm, swaddling my heart in the sweet, luscious memory of true freedom. Of stick princesses and sand castles, and days defined by the tide rather than titles, duty, and secrets.

There's no blinding light. Shock of smoke. Searing, freeing, just-get-through-it pain. No. It's more like the turn of a key. I'm not changed. My tentacles still coil beneath me. My lungs still find enough oxygen in the water to sustain me. My heart beats and buckles for what has happened and what is to come.

But I am free.

I sprint for the limits of my lair, no hesitation. This

time it won't be as if I've smashed into an unbreakable wall of glass when I reach where the gray of my home bleeds into the azure of open waters. For the first time in half a century, I can leave.

Into the open sea and moving fast, seeking the sea king and his generals before it's too late.

The sea is choppy, the winds above ravaging more than the surface. The water is clogged with black-eyed fish, stunned belly-up by whatever magic the sea king has already used. He may not only send his people on a suicide mission, he may kill all the creatures below in his quest for power as well.

I swim faster until the taste of blood settles in the back of my throat. My heart pounds and lungs clench. My muscles burn, but the path ahead is clear. I follow their magic building, like it's the strongest current in the ocean.

Up ahead, the noon-sky iridescence of the sea kingdom shimmers in the distance. The castle rises in spires and strokes of coral and sand, every glittering thing under the sea affixed to its walls. Homes cluster at the foot of the castle, separated from nobility by acres of gardens, pinned together in plots by orderly paths of sandstone and pearls. At midnight on the sundial layout is a fat swath of vines, shriveled and black.

Runa's garden—the ríkifjor. All dead.

And that is where the polypi generals have congregated. Above them, a string of mines. Long enough to take out a good portion of the castle, the rubble barreling full-force onto the dwellings below.

He's mad. Completely mad.

I swim faster.

"Don't do it, Your Highness!" I yell, as much for him as for his generals, and for the people sleeping below. They need to know the truth apart from what he's sold them. I will scream at the top of my lungs until he is revealed for the urchin he is.

His golden head whips around; true surprise again rings his features. Below, windows spark with light, the citizens waking. Yes, please wake. Please see your king.

"Don't set off those mines! Your people will suffer!"

Groggy faces begin to appear in each window and balcony, eyes trained on us above.

I won't just let them see. I'll tell them. Loudly.

"Your king—"

An explosion rips through my words and the sea, water shooting in every direction.

"*Tjald!*" I scream. A leaf-green light shoots from my fingertips, running straight toward the massive cloud of debris. In a blink, a canopy of light stretches and curves with the weight of the explosion, catching the massive disturbance and holding the weight until the force of the bomb dissipates.

I assume one of the polypi generals not only armed the thing as told but also accidentally set it off by brushing up against it. No matter how it happened, the sea king has realized two can play at my game.

"The sea witch's magic set off the mine! Look at it! The traces are still there!" he yells, as if he's not wearing his golden armor and his crown, as if he rolled out of bed and heroically ran to save the day. "I'm disarming them!"

It's a feeble string of lies, but when you're as practiced as he, it sticks. I won't answer to it. Instead, I make sure there's no way he can hurt his people for real this time.

"*Gœðalauss!*" I shout, stripping each mine of its explosive power. Making them barren.

"Stop!" the sea king yells, and rather than shout a spell, he orders the two closet soldiers after me. "*Sœkja!*"

The men do as they're told, their eyes blank with blind determination. Warriors in their first life, they are relieved of their weapons, but not of their skill.

But I have skills too. "*Sjoða!*"

A thick current of water rushes forth to meet the soldiers as they descend, seething, streaming, boiling. It hits their marble-white bodies with a certain fury, immediately singeing their exposed skin. I was unsure when the spell left my lips whether the ghost soldiers would feel pain, and now I have my answer. The pair of them arch back, trees bowing to a summer storm. They don't make a sound as the smooth tone of their skin erupts into a mottled mess of boils and blisters.

"*Gœðalauss!*" I scream three more times, disarming the

last of the mines. Then, I turn to the crowd below. "Good people, *your king* had plans tonight to detonate a string of mines *he set*, to win your favor for a war against your best interests. All he cares about is power and revenge—to him, your lives are pawns to be spent."

The sea king's voice grows louder. "Says the witch who brought us the black death and the famine of abundance! You're an evil monster."

"My reputation is all of those things, and yet I'm fighting against you for the lives of your people. What does that say about you, Your Highness?"

He explodes, a mutilation spell on his lips. *"Meizi!"*

But I'm ready. *"Skjoldr!"*

His spell ricochets off my shield. Two soldiers swim into the line of fire, hurtling toward the sand the second they're hit.

The sea king gathers himself from a lower position, hair singed by magic, crown tumbling straight off his head, itself taking the brunt of the spell. I could stun him now, but I want these people to see the desperation on his face. The cruelty. I don't want them to miss a second of who their king really is.

From below, he tries again, his mother's favorite spell shooting from his fingertips. *"Fœra!"*

I twist and dodge, red laser lights shooting past me, taking out an ear on the statue of Niklas in Alia's garden. The merpeople crowding the paths of the garden dive into beds of rainbow flowers, hands over their heads as they scatter.

"The sea witch speaks the truth!"

My heart leaps—Eydis.

The sea king's second set of daughters lines up next to me, their faces defiant, daring once again to leave their tower. The three of them facing off against their father is more powerful than anything I could ever say.

Eydis catches the eyes of the merpeople congregating below. She addresses them.

"Our sisters were not maimed by human-made mines. Alia sought freedom to love a human by asking the sea witch to help her go above. Runa went up to bring Alia home once she knew the mission was doomed to fail." Audible gasps rise from the streets, windows, and cracked doorways. "We lost our sisters to love, not hate."

More gasps. More eyes.

"Ask Alia yourself. Her ghost swims before you," Eydis says.

Yes, ask her.

I push my magic through the waters between us. Reaching only for Alia. Reaching for the bonds that tether her will to her father's. In my mind's eye, I gather them up, bunching them, and rip them clean. *"Bresta! Sjálfvili!"*

The bond breaks, and Alia's eyes go wide. As the cord is cut and her free will is renewed, the sea king flinches hard, his body convulsing in actual, physical pain.

I haven't just freed her—I've severed a thread of his power.

The polypi generals swim around me. I have two dozen more strings, tied straight to the strength he has left.

As her father writhes in pain, Alia finds the voice he's been stifling. "I am Alia! I am! Eydis speaks the truth!" she says to the people below, arms wide. "Runa did not die—the magic binds her to the earth now. She's working with human witches to take back what our king has stolen from the earth and from you."

There's a loud gasp—both at Alia's admission and the sea king visibly suffering. I see now that Queen Bodil and the older princesses and their families are out of bed, pressed against the exterior walls of the castle. Though they are silent and shadowed, the sea king's eyes stray to them, desperation sinking the corners of his mouth.

"She left us for humans! She betrayed our kind!" he screams, desperate.

"I left for myself!" Alia snaps. "And Runa left for me." She looks from him to the crowd. Her people. "Runa will continue to make the world safe from *you*, Father, restoring the balance of power that *you* tipped toward the sea. Power you keep for *yourself*, Father, stabilized by the ríkifjor."

With each word, the sea king winces. It's as if she's ripping what was left of his control grain by grain from his skin.

He shakes clear of the pain and zooms over the crowd. "What you are seeing isn't the truth; it's a lie twisted into the light."

"I'm not lying. I'm dead, Father. I have nothing left to lose. You have so much to lose that you just murdered your own mother before my very eyes."

There's a commotion as heads swing around in the crowd, eyes searching for Ragn. The remaining eight princesses all react in mirrored shock, clinging to each other's hands, shoulders, waists.

"No, it's not true!" the sea king screams, and shoves Alia away, knocking her into a polypus general. "The sea witch's magic controls this *imitation* of Alia and the rest of the ghost soldiers! She doesn't know what she's saying."

He wheels on me, a powerful spell coming within him, rumbling and at the ready.

"She knows exactly what she's saying." I grit my teeth. "You were minutes away from bringing your people to war. I intend to stop you."

I call to Anna. "Anna! *Bresta! Sjálfviki!*"

Anna's body jerks, her lips dropping open. She pauses right where she's been hovering around a mine, prepared for the order to detonate. She glances at her palms—free to move on their own. And then her white-marble tail sweeps in a flowing arc, moving away from the mines, toward us.

The sea king reels back again, eyes squeezed shut.

—369

"No!" He wrenches his eyes open, looking only to me. "Stop!"

I point my hands to the nearest guard. *"Bresta! Sjálfviki!"*

At the same time, the sea king unleashes a spell on my unprotected side. *"Villieldr!"*

The magical wildfire hits my side straight on, a blistering burn immediately clustering on my skin. My tentacles aren't spared—three of them singed, immediately curling and misshapen.

My vision goes black with white-hot pain. But I'm successful and I know it—another cord cut. I blindly aim for other polpyi generals as my vision spirals back from total darkness to gray tones. *"Bresta! Sjálfviki!"*

Several more bonds break, and with each one, the king thrashes more violently.

As my vision returns completely, he gathers all the breath he has left and erupts with the spell that murdered his mother. *"Morðvig, sea witch!"*

I throw a shield, and with everything I have in me, I yank the remaining cords of his magic from the polypi at once, ripping them from the root.

"Bresta! Sjálfviki! Allr minn polypi!"

Magic bursts out of me in a sonic wave. The soldiers jerk back, stunned. They slip and freeze and shake their heads—each reaction as different as when they were men in Øldenburg blue, not marionettes of one mind.

With each and every bond severed, the sea king

writhes as if struck by a bullet. One, and then another, and then another, until, finally, he is all too still. His eyes are wedged open in pain, his mouth hanging agape.

"*Morna . . . herfiligr . . . kvennalið . . . ,*" he slurs, but there's no magic in it.

Agony haunts the last of his voice as it peters out. Then he falls. Tumbling, hurtling, barreling, with the brutish grace of a cannonball, straight toward the sea floor.

And as he goes, Alia ascends to me and grabs my hand—Eydis, Ola, and Signy clutching at her other hand, joined together in a wreath—and watches, free as a bird with a song on her lips.

"Come away, come away—"

38

Runa

I WAIT FOR MY FATHER ON THAT WALL OF STONE, STAND-ing tall against the beating wind, the hail, the downpour. Staring out at the teeming waters, I can't see below the surface, but I feel every inch of what he's created.

Hysteria from Alia's death.

The desire for revenge.

A belief that there's no other way.

If I had never come here, I would believe it too. If I hadn't seen for myself what Alia had tried to do, and if Father had sold me that story, I would be down there, learning to fight. Ready to get revenge. I'd probably triple our stash of ríkifjor, fortifying Father. Driven by blind faith and misunderstanding, but mostly by fear.

And now, as I look out over these waters, I'm not afraid. I did my best to honor my sister. To honor myself. To restore the balance. If Father comes with an army of my people, I will not fear him. I will not. There is so much to fear in this life that you cannot live at all if you let it rule you.

As dawn comes, blue fingers in the black of night across the strait, I hear it. My name, shouted above the howling mess Father has made.

"Runa!"

I turn from the sea. Will and Sofie are wading through the muck side by side, about to reach a depth where they will need to swim. Above the water, I see his exposed shoulder, pitted and bruised but working as it should as he propels himself forward and helps his cousin along.

Up the hill, the city is under threat. The ships I spelled are holding fast for now—battering ram after battering ram still where I left them—but the tide has crawled up the sea lane, spilling onto the first of the town's shops. I'm sure the Vœrtshus Havnestad and the ashes of the U-boat warehouse are underwater now too. I just hope the towns-people made it to higher ground.

Beyond, the waters are lapping at the gates of Ølden-burg Castle. An inch more and they'll dump into the rose garden before crawling up the steps. I'm more concerned about people's homes. Even the little abandoned house in the castle's shadow—it meant too much to someone once to be swept away.

"Did it work? Is she coming? Will she fight with us?" Sofie asks, reaching the rock wall. She's already trying to gain purchase to pull herself up to me, her hands slipping.

"I don't know." And I don't. I wait for that spark of certainty. The way I felt watching the sun rise on my last day and my first.

But there's nothing. Not yet.

I place my hands over the edge and dry the face of the rock wall, helping them up. Sofie first, then Will. I squeeze her into an embrace. And then she gives way to Will. Once my arms wrap around him, I don't want to let go—as warm and grounding as he is, a sliver of sun in the cold, pounding rain.

"What can we do?" Will asks in my ear. Then a spark comes to him, and he brings me to arm's length. "Is there something we can do together?"

I think then of Oma Ragn, singing in the dark. Of Alia and her beautiful voice, gone now and forever, singing "The Mermaid's Vengeance." Speaking of the power of mermaids and what we can do.

We cannot forget what humans think of us. Or what we can do to them.

Of my answer, after Alia's death, with new perspective.

Or what we can do to ourselves, Oma.

But there's a third piece that I didn't find until I met these people.

We cannot forget what we can do *for* ourselves. We cannot forget our strengths. The bonds we've made. The things we've done.

I grab Will's hand and hold mine out to Sofie. "Will you join hands with me?"

Sofie doesn't hesitate. She's about to join with Will on the other side when we hear a little cry. "Can I join too? Please?"

Agnata.

Sofie squeezes her eyes shut. "Of course." Then, she reaches down and helps Agnata up to the top. When she's there and ready, panting, we join hands again. The four of us, in a little circle, on the slim plateau of rock.

We don't need special inks or amethysts. What we need is each other. To stand up against this storm and the next, in this war and the next.

"Repeat after me and then let's chant in a round," I say. They nod. Sofie and Agnata shut their eyes, but Will meets my gaze and I hold it.

"*Logn ægir. Long haf. Logn harr. Logn sær. Logn spór. Logn ver. Logn víðir.*"

We ask for calm. We demand calm.

"*Logn ægir. Long haf. Logn harr. Logn sær. Logn spór. Logn ver. Logn víðir.*"

"*Logn ægir. Long haf. Logn harr. Logn sær. Logn spór. Logn ver. Logn víðir.*"

We repeat it over and over, the sky and the sea crying around us.

As we hit the fifth repetition, another voice joins ours, carrying another tune.

It's a voice I know as well as my own. Will can hear it too, his brows pulling together, unsure of where it is coming from. Sofie's eyes spring open. Agnata's too.

"Who . . . ?" Sofie asks, her voice a trailing whisper despite the raging storm.

"Alia. That's Alia's voice." I look to them. "Will you sing with me? Please?"

Come away, come away—
The tempest loud
Weaves the shroud
For him who did betray.

As we sing along, something almost tangible seems to spread warm and true over my back, down my arms, and into the hands of Will and Sofie, connecting us. Bonding us. Will draws in a quick breath at the touch of it, his grip tightening on my fingers. Sofie lets it flow over her—Sofie who lost her sister, too, who knows this pain. She breathes it in, lets it flow. Agnata's eyes pop open, and for the first time in a day, she's not protesting or lying or running. She's with us.

Come away, come away—
Beneath the wave
Lieth the grave
Of him we slay, him we slay.

Alia is with us as we finish the final stanza with one voice.

There's a lilt in the wind then. A temperature drop. And the four of us on the rock raise our faces to the sky. The storm clouds evaporate before our eyes.

Holding tight to my new family, I look over my shoulder to the sea.

It's quieting.

Calming.

The waves are receding. And when the water washes away from the sea witch's cove, it's no longer black, but as blue as the coming dawn will allow.

39

Evie

THE SEA KING'S DEATH SHAKES THE VERY FOUNDATION of the ground beneath us. Not from the impact, but from the pure magic inside him. Hoarded, stashed, amassed. Stolen.

He lands with a sick thud, too heavy to bounce and roll, but too magical to sink into the seafloor.

The crowd chokes on its surprise.

Their king, dead on the sand, magic bleeding out of him like a procession of stars. It permeates the waters around us, the azure deep imbued with every particle of magic he was holding for his own. It spreads over the masses like sunlight, blanketing all of us in a shimmering, luscious renewal.

As Alia and her sisters finish their song, the remainder of the royal family draws itself out from the shadows of the castle. The five older girls, their children, their consorts, and their stepmother. Queen Bodil's head is held high, and she looks every inch as regal as anticipated despite being dressed in nightclothes.

I wait for her to address me. She will. I expect her to scream, shout, claw at me.

I'm a murderer now—no one can deny it.

Below, thousands of witnesses look up. They hang together, unsure of what to make of their new magic, of the new balance of power, of the body on the seafloor and the confrontation about to happen above. Some sang along with Alia and her sisters, and now everything is eerily quiet. Above us, the waves calm and the storm clouds clear—as silent above as it is below.

As an entire kingdom watches, the queen approaches. Alia's ghostly hand is wrapped in mine, Eydis on the other side. Ola and Signy bracket us as we come face-to-face with the queen.

If I were the girl I was back on land, this is when I would've begun defending and explaining myself.

I didn't know that spell would kill him.

I couldn't allow him to detonate the mines.

There was no other way.

But now that I'm older, I know there's no way to explain away what you've done. All you can do is stand by your actions and hope others see the good for themselves.

"What may I call you?" Queen Bodil asks, and I'm taken aback. The queen registers the look on my face and clarifies. "I cannot call you the sea witch. Surely you have a name?"

"Evelyn."

Bodil accepts who I once was with a thin breath. "It's true what you said." It's a statement, not a question. She sighs, eyes drifting to the distance below us. "He knew it too."

Alia lets go of my hand and moves to embrace the queen. "It's all true, Mother. Every last word." She looks down at their entwined hands. "I did leave to go above because I was in love with a human. I never thought I'd fail, but I was going to. And Runa went up to save me. She never wanted to stay—she always wanted to be here with you, but she did the best she could."

The queen looks to me. "You can't bring Runa back to us?"

I'm about to answer when I snag on Anna's face as she hovers outside this circle, knowing she could belong but doesn't—and I realize something. "There is a way. But I'm unsure it will work, and it isn't worth the risk to find out." I meet Anna's eyes, and then the queen's. "If Runa were to drown, we might be able to change her back."

Queen Bodil shakes her head. "No, I won't consider drowning my daughter to get her back." She touches Alia's cheek. "I've already lost so much."

"Mother, don't blame Evelyn," Alia says. "I knew what

I was doing, and I'm at peace."

"Then so am I," the queen says. Her eyes rise to mine. "But our monarchy is a different matter."

Here it comes. I hold my head high, hands growing sweaty in the girls' grip. A childhood spent under the disapproving eye of Nik's mother, Queen Charlotte, prepared me for this moment in a way, but it's been nearly a lifetime since I had to submit myself to this.

"We have no king. We have no male heir. And though we have a more-than-capable princess"—here, she gestures to the oldest of Queen Mette's girls, Lida—"by law, the crown is not hers."

Below, the people begin to murmur. I stay stock still. The queen continues.

"It's yours."

"Mine?" I say, or maybe I don't, I'm not quite sure my voice is working. "But—"

"Take it, please." Lida offers the crown that tumbled off the sea king's head. "You've defeated our king, which is enough to place his crown upon your head according to our laws, but you also saved countless lives from the mines, the war, and our discovery. You have more than proved to us that you are our queen."

Queen. They want me to be queen.

I expect the people to complain—violently, loudly. Instead they're silent, waiting. Lida holds her father's crown out farther, waiting for me to take it.

My eyes fall to her offering.

The crown is mangled and imperfect, which makes it ideal for what I am and how the kingdom has changed. Spelling this tattered, twisted crown into something impossibly perfect would wipe clean all that's just happened. We can't ignore what's made us. Its flaws will serve as memories.

I address the people below, willing my voice not to shake. "If you will have me, I will serve you."

For a moment, the people are quiet. They know they're witnessing something no one in their kingdom has ever seen. This is really happening, the truth, out in the open.

And then they begin to applaud.

Lida shifts the crown in her hands from an offering to something to be presented and motions for me to bow. I do, and she places the mangled circlet on my head. It's heavy with the weight of a people escaping from the brink.

I raise myself up and present myself to them.

The former royal family bows first. The people below next. All of them accepting.

I watch, tears that won't fall pushing against my eyes. This isn't the life I had hoped for. I'll never get to go home to my father's cabin. To Nik's ghost. To hiding who I am for a life that's less than mine to live.

Instead, it's more than I ever dared to dream.

Once the applause dies down, I bid them good night.

"Go to sleep, good people, and know that you're safe."

After the crowd disperses, Alia turns to me, her family at her back. The polypi generals float a short distance away. "Queen Evelyn, will you consider a first request?"

"Of course, my little mermaid."

Alia puts on a proud smile. "Will you set me free?"

My heart drops.

The threads of magic were cut from the sea king, but they still tether all of the polypi soldiers to me. Including Alia. And Anna, who hovers apart from us, watching silently.

"Alia, no! We've only just gotten you back to us!" Ola exclaims, eyes already pink at the lashes.

"I'll always be with you, Ola—with all of you. But I can't stay in this body." She looks to me. "None of us can. This isn't where we are meant to rest."

I can't deny her. Nor any of the polypi who've lived so long with me. I nod. "Say your good-byes, Alia."

She does, hugging her sisters tight, her mother. Me.

Then Anna swims forth, her arms out. I wasn't expecting her to come, but I draw her in. "I love you," I say—because I do. Despite all we've been through, and all we've done to each other, I do love her.

The older sisters, the ones she betrayed, circle around us. "Annemette, we'd like to say good-bye . . . we didn't get a chance the first time."

I shift away and give them privacy.

"*Polypi, hjorð*," I command the remaining soldiers.

They gather before me, their faces as beautiful as a cloudless moon, shining and eerie, yet blank.

"*Minn polypi, ráða sjálfraðr.*"

The moment I say the words, there's a rumbling ripple, their bodies shivering under the weight of magic spilling out of them, setting them free. And then they disappear like grains of sand from the beach, drawn up with the tide.

The magic within them leaves us with more balance restored. It won't kill me or even pain me—who I am isn't tied to this magic like the sea king was to his.

When I turn, Anna is there. Her blue eyes meet mine one last time, and she nods.

I take her hands.

"*Minn Anna, ráða sjálfraðr.*"

Like the soldiers, her face shimmers—she is at once solid and then nothing at all. My hands that held hers are empty. I am empty.

Alia gives one final embrace to her mother. Then her hands are in mine. With a nod, she's ready. She looks up to the surface, to the world she hoped to join and watches the first fingers of dawn, lighting the world above.

"*Minn Alia, ráða sjálfraðr.*"

She shimmers, face falling to glitter, and as her figure floats away, a trail of red flowers appears in her wake.

I gather a handful, giving her sisters and mother each

one of their own. Then, with the remaining flowers, I swim to the top of my new kingdom and let them break the surface with a single order.

"*Færa*, Runa."

40

Runa

Dawn comes like a chapter ending—one piece resolved, the rest of the story still going.

The clouds have gone, and the sun rises pink and promising, the sea a shimmering jewel beneath it, waters calm, glistening, at peace.

But beyond the waters' touch, much of Havnestad is a rubbish heap.

The docks are destroyed, ships tangled together. They gape with wounds, their bellies scraped, some taking on water, soon to sink to the bottom of the harbor. The lowest roads have washed away, ancient cobblestones littering the shore while others have been swallowed out to sea. From the top of the rock wall, we can just barely see the vœrtshus and the attached shops—everything is yawning open, windows and doors, the sea cresting the sandbags and claiming them for its own.

But the people are safe, the homes and shops up the hill untouched. Below, my people are safe too. For now—the immediate U-boat threat is gone, but more than that, Father's war is over.

And so is he.

No one needs to deliver the news. I know it as a certainty within my bones, the magic tying us together shifted into something new within me. One day I may learn what happened, but with Alia's voice still ringing in my ears, I feel at peace.

The magical balance is still sorting itself out; the atmosphere here on land is weightier than before. What was dried up and near dead is flush with life again, finding its way into the sunlight.

Behind me, Will places his hand on my shoulder. "Runa, it's time."

We must go. Because dawn also brings something else—the danger of being discovered.

In the new light we're still fugitives.

Witches.

Thieves.

Rebels.

And for me—a murderer.

The guards we dispatched last night will be regrouping, no greater mission for them than to catch us and make us pay. They don't care about our motives, only what we did because of them.

There's a twinge in my heart as I think about Niklas—I placed judgment on him just like it's being placed on my head, motives misunderstood, only the outcome visible. I have to live with that blood on my hands, just like I live with my failure to save Alia. But that won't keep me from doing as much good as possible until the end.

Alone for a moment as Sofie and Agnata scale the rock wall down to the waterlogged sand, I take Will's hand. He turns to me, the toes of our boots touching. The pink light flatters him, erasing the exhaustion in his blue eyes.

"Do you remember what you told me when you recruited me," I whisper, "about what would happen if we failed?"

Will raises his brows, picking through the memories of that morning Alia died and we stood in the countryside, edging around the sharper points of recognizing each other's magic. "Something about how we'd be hunted by angry Germans before the Danes could banish us for witchcraft?"

"Yes. That. Well, what happens now that we've succeeded?"

"We do it all over again."

He grins, and I can't help myself: I have to kiss him—quick and hard enough that he has to take a steadying step, nearly losing his balance on our sliver of rock. I grab hold of him, and once we're both solid again, we laugh.

"Will you two please come on?" Sofie whisper-shouts

from yards away, clearly not wanting to face another round of guards because we're found nuzzling in broad daylight.

It doesn't take much to climb down, and when we set foot on the black sands of the cove's beach, the earth beneath us is soaked but solid. Will takes my hand again, and we slog through the sideways sands to the mouth of the cove, where Sofie is propping up the fallen historical marker as best she can against the boulders bracketing the entrance.

We make a collective decision to leave Freyja and walk back—she's so sodden with seawater that she likely won't start, even with magic. We start up the sea lane, and toward the abandoned cabin in the woods below Ølden-burg Castle.

The little cottage watches us silently, its windows drooping as we pass. The scent of magic haunts this place, and though it's only lived in my periphery, I almost feel at home here. In this place smaller than Katrine's cabin, smaller than the bedroom I shared with my sisters, for sure. I crave the chance to linger and explore, to sit inside and let its walls tell me what they've seen. Hopefully it will still be standing when—if—I get the chance to return to Havnestad without a price on my head.

The stairway carved of stone curves down to the lagoon below, melting hailstones crunching beneath our boots with each step. The switchbacks pile onto each other until we've made it down the side of the cliff and to the rough-hewn sand below, the beach packed and wet, the water still receding.

"Oh, look!" Sofie says, pointing. "Please, God, let it be undamaged."

I glance up to see a little boat that somehow shimmied its way through the narrow mouth made between cliffs and lodged itself into the lagoon. This may be the best way to journey back to Katrine's, the guards chasing us unlikely to be on the water with the condition of Havnestad's docks.

I'm reminded of our promise to remove the floating mines so the fishermen's trade can flourish and Havnestad can survive without the profits from the U-boat sale. With a boat and our magic, we could begin that process on the way to safety.

I take a step to run after them, but then my eyes snag on a gift even more amazing, and I freeze on the spot.

Red flowers.

They're floating a few feet from me in the lagoon, but they are not of this place. They are something only Alia could produce.

Hands shaking, I fish them out of the water. Tendrils of magic bleed off their prickly stems. I can't believe I'm holding these. A piece of my sister, in my hands, her talent a tangible thing.

Oh, Alia.

I press the two fingers on my right hand together, our sign—one, Alia; two, Runa.

There's no me without her.

"You aren't taking flowers from another wizard, are you?" Will asks, his voice a near whisper. He's trying to joke, but I know it's only because he can see my face wavering between grief and joy.

"Never." My voice quivers, my chin wobbles, and then tears—real human tears—stream hot down my face.

The release is both what I need and not entirely enough.

My eyes flash to him as he places his steadying hands on my waist, waiting for what else I may say. He's patient, and it takes me some time to gather the right words. "Alia. She brought these flowers to the sea witch as payment before she knew the cost would be her voice." I draw in a long, shaking breath, the meaning of their appearance suddenly thick in my chest. "I think the sea witch returned these to me as a gift."

Will glances toward the girls, righting the boat and inspecting it for damage. "Why don't you take a moment?"

I nod, grateful I didn't have to ask.

Clutching the flowers to my chest, I strike back into the shadows of the cliff above. Between two boulders is the little cave I saw that first day when I came here to change, its doorway beckoning.

The confines are small, dark. But they swell with magic. Near the entrance, I find a stub of a taper and light it. *"Kveykva."*

A flame erupts and the space reveals itself—a tiny

haven stuffed full of books, bottles, jars, and a crate of oyster shells, toppled by the lagoon waters that visited during the storm. The magic here has the same signature as the little house above.

The same signature as the flowers.

This place was the sea witch's. The house too. Before she became what she is. I don't even know her name, but now I wish I did. Maybe someday I'll learn it.

"Alia, you would've loved this place," I say both to the flowers and to no one at all. Fingertips drifting over the dusty contents.

Flowers pressed against my chest, I bend over to scoop up the oyster shells and their spilled pearls—it doesn't do to leave something of the sea witch's a mess. The sand shifts beneath the crate, and through a crevice in the rock, a book slips out onto the sand.

The candlelight finds the title immediately. *The Spliid Grimoire.*

The binding is different from the one at Katrine's—crumbling with love and use. I lift the book and place it on a small table fashioned from rough wood and rocks. The book yawns open to a passage marked with the triton. Father's symbol. Below it is the passage I'd found at Katrine's, the one that gave me the chance to go home.

The sea is forever defined by its tide, give and
take the measure of its barter. In magic, as in life,

the sea does not give its subjects lightly—payment is
required, the value equivalent, no matter the ask. A
shell, a fish, a pearl of the greatest brilliance—none
can be taken without debt to be paid.

We have paid dearly, Alia most of all. Father and Niklas too, despite their motivations.

I set the candle on the table, the flowers, the book. The past, present, and future fuzzy behind my eyes.

It's then that I realize I can take both Alia and the sea witch with me into this new life. I pluck the petals gently from each flower and lay them along the open page in the grimoire, from spine to edge, Alia's flowers touching every word.

My sister and the sea witch with me. Encased in a reminder of who I am now—an heiress and keeper of magic as it still lives on this earth.

"I'll do you proud," I say, to both of them, pressing the book to my heart as I step out of the cave and into the light—the past at my heels and the future laid out wide as far as the eye can see.

I was a princess. A mermaid. A twin.

I *am* a witch. A human. A rebel.

And I have only just begun.

ACKNOWLEDGMENTS

Sea Witch Rising, at its heart, is about the people *behind* the journey. There's always a support network, and I'm so glad I get a chance to thank mine. Because though it's my name on the cover, there's a whole (fully sentient, non-polypi) army at my back, and I couldn't have done this without them.

First and foremost: This book would not be here without my readers. To everyone who loved *Sea Witch*—bought it, shared it, went to the library to check it out: thank you. Thank you for every Instagram post, Amazon review, and coo of "Ooooh, what a pretty cover!" in public. And thank you to the booksellers and librarians who got it into the hands of anyone who you thought would love it. All of it made a difference.

To everyone who asked me if there would be more, thank you too. It was a privilege and a pleasure to return to Evie's world. I loved coming back to her and exploring the sea witch's point of view during the little mermaid's big journey. I hope you enjoyed meeting the new characters as well—Runa and Will were so fun to write—and savored the flashbacks to Nik as much as I did.

This book would not exist without the vision, guidance, and enthusiasm of my editor, Maria Barbo of Katherine Tegen Books. Maria, thank you so much for believing in me and believing in continuing Evie's story.

Thank you to Rachel Abrams, who totally got where I was trying to go; and Stephanie Guerdan, who worked so hard behind the scenes. To my copy editor, Maya Myers, thank you for your careful eye and thoughtful research on everything from 1914-era rearview mirrors to the origins of the term "face plant." To the production editorial team: Emily Rader, Shona McCarthy, and Mark Rifkin, thank you for your support at the very end. And, of course, thank you to Katherine Tegen and the other wonderful book-lovers at her imprint; EpicReads; and HarperCollins as a whole.

Once again, I was floored by the incredible work of my cover artist, Anna Dittmann. Anna, I don't know how you did it, but you captured my sisters in gorgeous, stunning detail. My books are better simply because of how you see the world in them. Thank you.

To my agent, Whitney Ross of IGLA: you have been the most delightful partner through this process. Thank you for your guidance and thoughtful analysis of all things publishing. If I've made this bonkers year look easy, it's only because I've got you in my corner.

Also in my corner are my wonderful writer friends. Some are far-flung—Joy Callaway, Renée Ahdieh, Sarah Nicole Lemon, Kellye Garrett, Ricki Schultz, Zoraida Córdova, Dhonielle Clayton—but nevertheless wonderful and there when I need them.

But this book in particular is one that was bolstered by those closest to home—my Kansas Writers team. It was they who held me up and made sure I was stocked with chocolate, LaCroix, and heart emojis while working on three books at once. Particularly, huge hugs and thank-yous to Rebecca Coffindaffer, Natalie Parker, Tessa Gratton, Megan Bannen, Adib Khorram (you're in Missouri, but we still love you), and Julie Tollefson. Love to all of you and the rest of our ever-growing group.

To my running buddies, but most especially Nicole Green, Sharah Davis, and Dorian Logan, for logging so many miles with me while I dove back into Evie's world. And for keeping me calm when my plate was overflowing. The same to Randy Shemanski, though digitally.

Thank you to my day job family for your understanding and pride. And to my "Bunco" moms, who coax me out of my writing cave once a month with wine and tales of hilarity (but surprisingly little Bunco).

Also, I want to give a shout-out to the local businesses that support the writing community in #LFK, but especially to Danny Caine and The Raven Book Store for all the love; and to T. Loft, for buoying my creative efforts with green juice, protein balls, and natural light.

And finally, to my family, thank you for, well, *everything*. Thank you to my parents, Craig and Mary Warren, for listening to me babble endlessly about all my projects—I'm sure that's exactly how you expected to spend retirement—and for the pinch-hit babysitting that allowed me to squeeze in a few more minutes of work. To my niece, Emmie, for your bright smile and infectious laugh. To Nate and Amalia, for being proud of what I do and reminding me every so often to "Save your work, Mom!" and go to the park. And to Justin, who is always my answer when people ask me how I manage it all—writing, day job, family, running. You keep me and this whole "big dream" thing afloat. Love you.

Sea Witch

The sea is a fickle witch.

She is just as likely to bestow a kiss as to steal the breath from your lips. Beautiful and cruel, and every glimmering wrinkle in between. Filling our bellies and our coffers when she is generous. Coolly watching as we don black and add tears to her waters when she is wicked.

Only the tide follows her moods—giving and taking at the same salty rate.

Still, she is more than our witch—she's our queen.

In all her spells and tantrums, she is one of us. The crown jewel of Havnestad, nuzzled against our shores—for better or worse.

Tonight, dressed in her best party finery, she appears calm, anger buried well below her brilliant surface. Still, there's a charge in the air as the stars wink with the coming

—1

summer solstice and the close of Nik's sixteenth birthday.

Formally: Crown Prince Asger Niklas Bryniulf Øldenburg III, first in line to the throne of the sovereign kingdom of Havnestad.

Informally: just Nik.

But "just Nik" isn't quite right either. He's not *just* anything to me. He's my best friend. My only friend, really.

And now he's dancing with Malvina across the deck of his father's grand steamship. That is, if you can call her violent tossing and whirling "dancing." My stomach lurches as Nik comes within inches of tipping over the rail after she forces an overenthusiastic spin. I wish she'd just give it up.

Malvina, formally Komtesse Malvina Christensen, is a perpetual royal suitor. She and her father have been vying for King Asger's attention for years, hoping he will make the match. Yet despite Nik's good-natured patience for her dancing, I have my doubts there will be a royal wedding in their future.

I want to look away from the pink silk blur of Malvina, but Nik's eyes are begging me to rescue him. Pleading. Silently calling my name across the distance—*Evvvvv- vieee.*

I am the only one who can save him. Every youth in town is here, but no one else can cut in on a girl like Malvina. For the others, there would be consequences— lost invitations to galas, the oldest horse on the weekend hunt, a seat at the table next to one's senile great-tante instead of the Komtesse. For me, there are none of those things. You can't fall far in society if you're not part of it to begin with.

After another aggressive turn, I finally stride onto the makeshift dance floor, ignoring a chorus of smirks as I go—they've seen this play before. Malvina will be the victim, I'll be the villain, and Nik will let it happen. It can be a messy business, being the crown prince's confidante; enduring small humiliations is only a fraction of the cost. But I won't apologize for helping him. We all make compromises in friendships, and having Nik's loyalty when no one else will even look me in the eye is worth every criticism I face.

I tap the girl on one sturdy shoulder, screw my face into exaggerated panic, and point to the eight-layered, blue-sugar-spackled monstrosity she insisted on crafting.

"Oh, angels, Evie! What is it?" Malvina barks.

"The cake's icing—"

"*Fondant*," she corrects, as if I've spit on her oma's grave.

"The *fondant*—it's bulging."

True panic colors her features as her feet refuse to move. Torn between dancing with Nik and rescuing her masterpiece from a bulbous fate, her eyes skip to my face for a moment, incredulous. She fears I've purposely stolen her turn. It's just the sort of thing the girls of Havnestad think I would do—the ones whispering in the shadows about us now. Except in this case, they're right.

"Do your duty, Malvina. It was lovely dancing with you." Nik bends into a slight bow, royal manners on display, not a hint of displeasure in his features.

When his eyes cut away, Malvina sneaks a glare my way, her disdain for me as clear as her worry that I'm actually telling the truth. She doesn't need to say what she's thinking, and she won't—not if she ever wants to dance with Nik again. So, when Nik completes his bow, she simply plasters on a trained smile and leaves him with the most perfect curtsy before running off in a rush of golden hair and intent.

Now Nik bows deeply to me as if I'm his newest suitor, his mop of black hair briefly obscuring his coal-dark eyes. "May I have the remainder of this dance, my lady?"